Rosebud

Rosebud

By Joan Hemingway
& Paul Bonnecarrère

1974
WILLIAM MORROW & COMPANY, INC.
NEW YORK

Book design by Helen Roberts

Printed in the United States of America.

1 2 3 4 5   78 77 76 75 74

Library of Congress Cataloging in Publication Data

Bonnecarrère, Paul.
    Rosebud.

    In the French ed. P. Bonnecarrère's name appeared first on the t. p.
    I. Hemingway, Joan, joint author. II. Title.
PZ4.B7156Ro [PQ2662.05975] 843′.9′14 74-740
ISBN 0-688-00253-6

PROLOGUE

1

Beirut, Sunday, October 29, 1972, 5 A.M.

Hacam and Kirkbane scrupulously followed the instructions given them the night before by the manager of the boardinghouse. Making their way as quietly as possible down the stairs, they unbolted the double front doors and slipped outside. They did not relock the doors behind them.

Each of the two Palestinians carried a small, well-traveled imitation-leather suitcase of insignificant weight. The early morning light had just begun to fall on the capital of Lebanon and the air was already warm. By noon, it would be stifling. The streets were deserted. At the Rue Emir Bechir they quickened their pace. As they had anticipated, at the Place des Martyrs, Massoud had just opened his dingy little café across the street, just to the left of the Parliament Building. Hacam and Kirkbane entered the little bar and dropped their suitcases on the floor. They were the first customers of the morning. Massoud lit the butane gas ring under the samovar and mumbled a greeting toward the two Palestinians, who nodded in reply.

"Coffee in five minutes," Massoud said.

Not really tall, but broad-shouldered and stocky, Hacam seemed like a giant standing next to his frail companion. His arms were a little longer than normal and so heavily muscled they looked slightly bowed. Since the age of six-teen he had sported a bushy black moustache that was marred only by a thin white scar that ran from the edge of his left eye to the base of his jaw. Women did not like to look at him. Though he was now forty-three, he had never been married.

Kirkbane, by contrast, was twenty-three and beardless. His cheeks bulged slightly with the baby fat his adolescence had not been able to shake off, and he had the hands of a concert pianist. They were not feminine hands, but he never-theless thought so and almost always kept them plunged deep in his pockets. When he spoke, his voice was rarely louder than a whisper and he did not like to look at people straight in the eye.

His skin was the color of a piece of old parchment and his bullet-black eyes resembled inkspots on his pale face.

"Does the airport car stop here?" Hacam asked.

"Across the street, in front of the Parliament Building," Massoud replied. "Are you taking the German plane?"

"Yes, we're going to Turkey."

"That's it. It comes about five after six. You've got plenty of time."

Massoud set two chipped cups of his murky coffee in front of the men and then pushed a bowl of dusty sugar down toward them from the other end of the bar.

At six o'clock, the two Palestinians hailed the Volks-wagen bus as it came out of the Rue El Arz. They clambered in and paid the driver. Less than ten minutes later, the bus pulled up in front of the departure entrance at Khalde airport. Only six passengers climbed out: three Lebanese, one European, Hacam and Kirkbane.

At the Lufthansa counter, the clerk was still half-asleep. Almost mechanically, he checked their luggage, issued their embarkation cards and stamped their tickets. When he finished, he took them over to the office of customs and security control. The passengers then waited patiently for a few minutes until an obese porter arrived pushing a cart filled with their luggage.

The customs officials were laboriously searching the baggage and its owners. After a customs man and three security agents had each subjected the luggage to their meticulous scrutiny, they ushered the passengers behind a shoddy old plywood partition in one corner of the room.

Hacam was ordered to undress completely. Each thread of his clothing was thoroughly scrutinized. Then he was ordered to lift his right leg, place his foot on a stool and bend over. The security agent asked him to cough a few times. Hacam grudgingly complied and then inquired wryly: "Looking for a machine gun?"

"I'm simply acting on the orders of Lufthansa," the agent said. "It's just as unpleasant for me as it is for you."

When they were finished, Hacam and Kirkbane moved off by themselves to sit alone on one of the wooden benches in the departure area. Their false Turkish passports had passed through the security control without incident.

"Did they search you too?" Kirkbane asked.

"What do you think?"

"Perverted bastards."

They fell silent and kept their eyes to the east, watching for the plane where the sun's first rays were falling now on the dirty little village of Mkallés. Before long, they heard the roar of the jet in the distance.

Alone, above the valley of Nahr Beirut, the Boeing 727 began its final descent. Banking over the Tombs of the Pashas, the plane circled over the seacoast until it had completed the downwind leg of its approach. Turning onto its final approach, the landing gear appeared slowly, like big black talons falling out of the belly of the plane, and then it touched down. Having taken off from Damascus less than a quarter of an hour before, it needed no refueling in Beirut and the crew stayed on board.

Unaware of Western superstitions, Hacam and Kirkbane

discovered to their great satisfaction after boarding that there were only thirteen passengers on the plane, nine Arabs and four Europeans. One of the European women had a small child with her.

Their baggage was loaded quickly and there were no delays. Hacam took a seat next to the window and raised the shade.

At the end of the taxiway, Captain Walter Klaussen proceeded with his preflight instrument checks. Rolling up his engines with the plane held at a complete stop, his practiced eyes checked back and forth over the bank of gauges before him until he was satisfied. His plane was the only aircraft moving at Khalde. As soon as he was cleared for takeoff by the tower, Klaussen rolled his engines up to their maximum thrust again and held the brakes for a ten-second pause before letting them go. The plane shuddered for a moment, slowly gathered speed and lifted off.

Above Boabda, the gangly teams of landing gear tucked themselves back up into the belly of the plane. Captain Klaussen dipped his left wing and put the plane into a long, slow ninety-degree turn. Over Damour, he leveled out, picked up his northwest Omnibeacon, locked onto it and continued his climb-out. Ten minutes later he was at cruising altitude and flying on autopilot. While his engineer gave him the latest weather reports from Istanbul, he leaned back in his seat and lit up a cigarette.

In the cabin, Marika, one of the three hostesses, finished her mechanically perfect oxygen-mask and lifejacket demonstration. As usual, nobody paid any attention, even though the tape-recorded instructions had been given in German, English and Turkish. A few minutes later, the voice of the captain sounded over the cabin intercom.

"Ladies and gentlemen, we've reached our cruising altitude of thirty-one thousand feet and are flying at a speed of five hundred and ninety miles per hour. Below us on our right you'll soon be able to see the town of Tripoli. We expect the weather to be just fine all the way to Istanbul and we hope you enjoy your flight."

Hacam checked his watch. It was 7:01. He unbuckled his seat belt and made his way back to the lavatories at the rear of the plane. He entered the door on the left, locked it and calmly urinated. When he finished, he flushed the toilet and then opened the little compartment under the sink. Sliding his hand along the inside of the plastic fascia, he found the screwdriver. A gentle pull was enough to free the little tool, which was held in place only by two small strips of masking tape.

Very carefully, he unfastened the four screws that held the paper towel dispenser in place. When he had the cover loose enough, he slipped his left hand under the pile of paper towels and lifted them up high enough to allow his right hand to reach the plastic sack behind them. Then he refastened the cover precisely into its original position and readjusted the first towel so that its leading edge was hanging out just the way it was supposed to.

When everything was in place, he rinsed his hands in the sink, dried them and began to untie the drawstring of the plastic sack. When the bag was opened, he placed the contents on the counter: two P38 9 mm. pistols with ribbed Bakelite handles and two Czechoslovakian Stasi hand grenades. Checking the clips of both pistols, he made certain they were full. He pumped a bullet from each clip into the chamber of both guns and shoved them behind his belt. Then he dropped the grenades into his coat pocket, unlocked the door and stepped back out into the aisle.

The European woman, holding her young daughter's hand, was waiting in front of the door. The little girl looked as if she was about to reach the limit of her self-control. The girl broke loose from her mother's grasp and rushed into the toilet. Glancing at Hacam with open disgust, the woman snatched her back. With a great flourish, she took a Kleenex from her purse, moistened it with Orsay toilet water (courtesy of Lufthansa) and proceeded to rub the toilet seat furiously. By the time she'd finished, the little girl was turning green. Obviously satisfied that Hacam had witnessed the whole little drama, she let the little girl go again and gave him another very nasty look. Hacam flashed her a tight, wicked little smile that froze her completely.

"In a few minutes, you'll be able to see the coast of Turkey . . ." the captain announced.

It was 7:09. The other two stewardesses were now pushing a cart filled with multicolored fruit juices down the aisle from the front of the plane. Back in his seat, Hacam slipped Kirkbane a pistol and a grenade. Smiling, they both declined the offer of drink. Six empty rows behind them, Ann-Lise served the next passengers. Helga, a dark blonde with a small chignon, was pushing the serving cart. She walked past Kirkbane's seat.

In one move, the little Palestinian jumped up and grabbed her hair, yanking her head back, and brought his revolver up tight against the underside of her chin. She froze, stupefied. With a quick kick, he shoved the cart to the rear of the plane where it struck Ann-Lise square in the stomach. The blow knocked her flat on her back. Hacam was already on his way up to the cockpit with his revolver drawn.

In English, Kirbane shouted: "Group yourselves together in the seats at the rear of the plane and fasten your seat belts. You too," he added, releasing Helga. She obeyed in silence.

Still pointing the P38 at them, he brandished the hand grenade in his left hand and warned them. "All right. Any odd gestures and I blow this bird all to hell. Stay calm, and we'll all land safely."

He repeated the instructions in Arabic to his country-men.

"Don't worry, we'll do anything you say," one of them replied.

From the captain's cabin, Hacam shouted, "Everything okay?"

Kirkbane slipped between two rows of empty seats so he could keep an eye on the passengers huddled in the tail of the plane and shouted back: "Send them out. Everything's under control."

Deathly pale, the crew members came out single file with their hands clasped behind their necks. The copilot, flight engineer and third stewardess moved quickly to the rear of the plane. Hacam, keeping one eye on the pilot, surveyed them for a moment and then disappeared back inside the cockpit.

The passenger section held twenty-two rows of five seats each, three on the left side and two on the right. The five crew members and the thirteen passengers were grouped in the back four rows.

Kirkbane, moving carefully to the front of the plane, ordered, "You. The blond girl. Come here and bring the cart with you."

Terrified, Helga stepped forward. She stopped exactly one yard away from the armed Fedayin.

"All right. Leave the cart here and take the belt of the right seat, the one with the buckle. Good. Now the belt on the left seat. Now fasten the two together across the aisle and pull them tight. That's it. Good. Now do all the rest of them like that and get back in your seat. Good. You're a very bright girl."

Helga, somewhat reassured, complied. She fastened the eighteen barriers one by one as she made her way toward the rear of the plane. When she'd finished, Kirkbane said, "Now come back."

She had to pull her skirt up to midthigh to get over all the seat belts she'd just fastened.

"The cart," Kirkbane continued. "Block it between those two rows of belts—like that. That's it. Right. Tie it tightly. Good—good. Now go back to your seat and don't move."

The little Palestinian took one quick swipe with his revolver at the juice cups covering the top of the cart and knocked them all to the floor. He then plopped himself down on the top shelf facing the rear, reached back and came up with a tiny bottle of Scotch. He eyed each of the captives one by one. Holding the revolver in one hand and the whiskey in the other, he tore the plastic cap off the bottle with his teeth and then downed the contents in two gulps.

In the cockpit, Hacam had settled himself in the engineer's seat. Captain Klaussen could not forget the gun pointed at the back of his head. His first reaction to the hijacking had been very cool and he'd ordered the crew to follow the Fedayeen's instructions without question. The Boeing was still whistling along smoothly, its destination still Istanbul.

"We're now going to change course," Hacam said smoothly. "We're going to Munich."

"We haven't got enough fuel for that," Klaussen said. "We'll have to land somewhere first."

"I'm well aware of that, Captain. We'll refuel in Nicosia. I'll take the radio and you will repeat these instructions precisely: only two men on the fuel truck. Then Nicosia will transmit the following to Bonn: 'We demand the liberation of Ed Denaoui Abdel Kheiz, Samer Mohamed Abdallah and Ibrahim Mahmoud Badran. They are to be driven to the Munich-Reim airport and put on the plane after it's been refueled.' "

"Do you know how to operate the radio?"

Without answering, Hacam quickly switched frequencies on the big Collins radio and said simply: "You're on the line with the Nicosia tower."

At 7:40, Captain Klaussen delivered his message. Half an hour later, the entire world was waiting to see what would come of this attempt to liberate the three surviving Palestinian prisoners of the 1972 Munich Olympic Games massacre.

2

Bonn, Sunday, October 29, 1972, 6 A.M.

In Room 322 of the Steigenberger Hotel, Hans Schloss lay
flat on his back staring at the ceiling through half-open
eyes. His mental alarm clock had told him it was time to
wake up, but getting out of bed was something he never
did easily and he was thinking about it. He'd just about
talked himself into staying under the sheets for another
five minutes when three light raps sounded on the door.
Schloss sat up and rubbed his eyes with the back of his
hands, then swung his feet out of the bed and stood up.
Three more light taps came on the door.

"Ya, kommen Sie herein."

The door opened and a room-service valet appeared
with a breakfast tray. "It's six o'clock, sir," he said. "There's
tea here with lemon and light toast."

"Put it over there," Schloss replied. "Thank you. Now
tell the desk I'm not to be disturbed before eight o'clock.
That includes phone calls."

Hans Schloss was one of the highest men in Haupt-
abteilung I, the most efficient branch of the Bundesnach-
richtendienst—the B.N.D., or German Federal Intelligence
Agency. As befitted his profession, he was rather a small

and inconspicuous man of about fifty. Since his participation in the Battle of Stalingrad, he could not stomach the sight of a gun.

As soon as the valet had left, Schloss slipped on a camel-colored cashmere dressing gown and donned his thick horn-rimmed glasses. He poured a few drops of the tea into a cup, tested it, found it too weak and poured it back into the teapot. He entered the bathroom, flipped on the fluorescent lights and immediately put his hands up over his eyes to shield them from the glare. When they'd adjusted, he brushed his teeth thoroughly and plugged in his electric shaver. Shaved and satisfied, he returned to his bedroom and sat down to breakfast. The tea was now ready.

As he was drawing his bath, he heard the valet at the door once again. This time he appeared with the newspapers Schloss had ordered the night before: *The New York Times,* the *Daily Telegraph,* yesterday's *Le Monde* and the first edition of the *Sontag Zeitung.* As was his daily habit, he scanned the papers in his bath.

It was 7:16 when he knotted his tie and pulled on a gray herringbone sport coat. He turned on the radio, tuned it to the federal station and then listened impatiently to the stammering trivialities of a variety program. Finally, at 7:30, the fourth newscast of the morning was announced by the standard musical chimes.

The national news was devoted to the speech delivered the day before by Vice-Chancellor Walter Scheel in Bremen during his reelection campaign. This was followed by a discussion of the price of wheat fixed by the government on the Duisburg market. Briefly, the international news touched on the upcoming Canadian elections and the possibility of competition for Mr. Trudeau—an American student found dead in Chile, agreements between Rome and Moscow, the resignation of three Uruguayan ministers, a report on five Soviet families who had fled the U.S.S.R., the bombing of a Spanish tourist office in Zurich, and finally the discovery of the seventh female victim in a series of spectacular stranglings and sexual assaults in Stuttgart.

When the newscast was finished, Schloss leaned back in his chair and yawned. The radio began a broadcast of Isaac Stern's performance of Beethoven's *Concerto for Violin and Orchestra in D*. Schloss decided to listen for a while. At 7:53 the program was interrupted by a flash news bulletin on the hijacking over Turkish territory of a Lufthansa 727 with thirteen passengers and six crew members on board.

"It seems," said the announcer, "that the hijackers are demanding the release of the Palestinian Munich commandos in exchange for the passengers and crew. Confirmation and more details in a few minutes on the eight o'clock news."

Schloss pondered, snapped off the radio, sat down on the edge of his bed and picked up the phone. When the operator answered, he gave her a number and told her to connect him immediately.

Three miles away, on the opposite side of the Rhine, the telephone rang in the private residence of General Wilhelm Norddeich, director of Chancellor Brandt's War Cabinet. He answered the call in his bedroom. As soon as he heard Schloss's code name, he hung up. Somewhat annoyed, he put on his robe and descended the back stairs to his personal office. His private security line was already ringing.

"I didn't know you were in Bonn," Norddeich said sardonically. "Though it's true, of course, that such secrecy is in keeping with your profession."

The general deeply despised anyone who had anything to do with the secret service.

"Have you heard this morning's news, sir?"

"No."

Briefly, Schloss related the events of the hijacking, adding, "But I have some information concerning this matter which I must communicate to the Chancellor. Could you get me an appointment immediately? It's of paramount importance."

There was a long silence.

Finally the general said, "Where are you?"

"At the Steigenberger."

"On the Bunderkanzlerplatz! My, what a coincidence. You're only a hundred yards from the Federal Building. Meet me in my office in twenty minutes."

As he hung up, Schloss realized he had underestimated the savvy of his superior officer. He felt sure the general knew what was going on and made a mental note to play it carefully. Picking up the phone again, he asked the desk to prepare his bill.

In the early morning light, the great breadth of the Bunderkanzlerplatz lay empty and gray. With the fall now, the leaves on the trees that lined the square stood faintly crimson against the dark buildings and the pale sky. Schloss crossed the square and then turned down the Avenue Adenauer, following it until he came to the garden of the Schaumburg Palace, the seat of the federal chancellery. General Norddeich's 300 SL gullwing Mercedes pulled up alongside of him just as he reached the first guard post.

"Climb in," Norddeich said.

Schloss popped open the right-hand gullwing door and crawled inside. The two men did not say another word until the door of Norddeich's office was safely closed behim them. The general was openly hostile, but Schloss had decided he didn't give a damn.

"Well, Schloss, what's this hot wind you're bringing from the east?"

"Pardon me, sir. Have you decided to serve as a go-between? I think it would be better if you were merely a witness."

Norddeich pinched the bridge of his nose and eyed the agent coldly. Finally, without answering, he flipped a switch on his intercom.

"Norddeich here," he barked. "Get me an appointment with the Chancellor immediately. I'm with Hans Schloss. Remind the Chancellor that Schloss is one of the top men in the B.N.D. It's about the hijacking."

Four minutes later, the intercom buzzed briefly. Three minutes after that, they were in the private offices of Willy Brandt.

He received them with his hands in his pockets, dressed in dark-brown corduroy slacks, a dusty-yellow pullover sweater and a russet tweed coat. He'd just canceled a hunt arranged for that Sunday morning in the game reserve of the Kottenforst. He gestured to two armchairs, but remained standing himself.

"Mr. Chancellor," Schloss began, "it's my duty to inform you of the results of an investigation we've been conducting for the last two months in conjunction with the French S.D.E.C.E. and the British S.I.S."

"Come to the point."

"We now have firm reasons to believe that today's attempt to blackmail us is only the first of a series. The Palestine Liberation Organization will stop short of nothing to free our three prisoners. If today's attempt fails, a dozen other Black September kamikaze commandos are waiting in different European cities to hijack our planes and kidnap our diplomats."

"Are you sure of your sources, Schloss?"

"Quite certain, sir."

"What's your opinion, Norddeich?"

"I find it strange, if not downright suspicious, that Mr. Schloss has chosen this day of the year to pay a visit to Bonn."

Brandt shrugged his shoulders, either out of annoyance or fatalistic acceptance.

"You military men are always trying to understand and explain things. Schloss just happens to be in Bonn. It doesn't matter how he came to be here. His presence only reinforces the credibility of his information to my mind."

"So we give them the prisoners?" Norddeich said disgustedly.

"There's no alternative," the Chancellor said. "Schloss, I want you to return to Munich immediately and get in touch with Georg Wolfe at police headquarters. He's the vice-commissioner and he'll act on your instructions."

"A B.N.D. agent will be there in fifteen minutes, Mr. Chancellor."

"What beautiful timing," Norddeich retorted.

"You're really becoming rather disagreeable," Brandt said, rebuking him. "Not all truths are necessarily for public consumption. Schloss, you have complete control over the release of the Palestinians. Do whatever you have to, but I obviously do not want a repeat of the bloodbath at Munich."

With a look at Norddeich, Brandt let it be known that the interview was over. He escorted the two men to the door.

"We have no choice," he said as they were leaving. "Napoleon realized a long time ago that 'retreat is a form of courage.' "

"Yes," Norddeich snapped, "as he rode back to Paris in a carriage leaving the troops he'd led into Russia to starve and freeze to death."

Brandt's eyes flared momentarily. Then he said firmly, "I will overlook that remark, General."

And he closed the door.

3

Tel Aviv, Sunday, October 29, 1972, 8 A.M.

At the apex of its arch, the ball settled softly in its flight
for a fraction of a second and then dropped. The lieutenant
stopped short in the middle of his stride, spun and made
a lunge for it.

"Game point," the umpire announced. "David takes the
third set eight-six and leads the match, two sets to one."

On the other side of the net, Colonel David Fulham
stood fit and beaming. After almost a year of daily
trouncings at the hands of this cocksure young paratrooper,
he finally felt sure he was going to win a match. The man
on the opposite side of the net was going to be his son-in-
law quite soon, but he hadn't once shown the old colonel
the courtesy of letting him win anything.

From the terrace of the clubhouse, a second lieutenant
appeared at the railing shouting, *"Bevakkasha!"* Fulham
did not want to be bothered. His aide-de-camp shouted
again, this time holding his right hand up against his ear
and covering his left eye with the palm of his other hand.
Annoyed, Fulham glanced up. The mocking charade was
obvious. He would not finish his match: General Moshe
Dayan wanted him on the phone, immediately.

Fifteen minutes later, Fulham sat at the wheel of his

Ford Torino, bitterly angry at being torn away from his game and firmly enmeshed in the smoggy Sunday morning traffic surrounding Tel Aviv. His car radio was booming out the latest news on the hijacking.

Within thirty-five minutes of receiving the call, he'd passed through the Petah Tigva gate and become stuck behind an armored personnel carrier on an obscure side street. He fired up his siren and the lumbering machine pulled over to the side. Fulham slammed into second and roared on by. When he finally arrived in front of the Sherout Ha Bitachou—the Israeli Secret Service Building more commonly known as the Shin-Beth—Fulham avoided the rickety elevator in the lobby and bounded up the old staircase two steps at a time until he reached the third floor. At the end of the corridor, he rapped on a door and then opened it without waiting for an answer.

Yefet Hamlekh, the number two man in the entire service, was standing at his window looking out over the city when Fulham appeared.

"The Germans must not give in at any costs," Fulham blurted out.

Hamlekh turned around calmly. "What do you want me to do? Pick up the phone and place a personal call to Willy Brandt? 'Please Mr. Chancellor, let the Palestinians play with your Boeing. Let them blow it up and murder all the passengers. You'd be doing all of us here at the Shin-Beth a big favor.' "

The two men had rather an ambiguous professional relationship. Officially, Hamlekh wasn't answerable to Colonel Fulham, the latter being in charge of the Shin-Beth's paramilitary operations. But Hamlekh had, on many occasions, appreciated the support he'd obtained from Dayan thanks to Fulham's intervention in affairs that the political members of the government were trying to overrule.

"Fulham," he said, "there are a few things you just don't understand. We Israelis don't have to suffer under the kind of pressure Mr. Brandt is enjoying right now simply because we have not, do not and will not ever give in to this kind of threat. It's one of the conditions we have to embrace if the nation is going to survive. The citizens of Israel understand this very well. If tomorrow the Fedayeen were to kidnap Golda Meir or General Dayan's daughter and threaten to slice them up unless we reduce the price of dates in the Arab quarter, then, Fulham, we tell them to take their dates and shove them up the appropriate orifice and wait for the return of our distinguished leaders in little pieces. A state funeral would be held and the victims eulogized as national martyrs.

"Unfortunately, things don't work that way in Western Europe. The power of decision in those countries lies in the hands of the public opinion. Years of easy living have dulled and stupefied its ability to react intelligently. Nevertheless, it retains a firm hold on the club hanging above every politician's head."

"And yet Brandt acted firmly, as a true statesman, during the Munich Olympics," Fulham said.

"Yes, and it made him very unpopular. Don't forget, Fulham, that first, Brandt is getting ready for reelection now, and second, this time the threat doesn't involve Israeli athletes."

Dejectedly, Fulham slumped down into an armchair. Since he'd been appointed to the Shin-Beth, Fulham was spitefully rumored to be Moshe Dayan's blind eye. Commander of an armored regiment, hero of the Six-Day War, rewarded with the D.S.O. during the Second World War which he fought in the ranks of the British army, Fulham made a point of showing that he preferred action to the devious methods favored by the secret service. But he had too often admired Hamlekh's subtlety, and was sure that Hamlekh knew more.

"Any other information?"

"Yes, unfortunately. Since hijacking has come into fashion, I've studied all the airport security measures in force throughout the world. And I can promise you that in Beirut, Lufthansa did its job thoroughly. The Germans, I'm sure, would confiscate a water pistol from a three-year-old. And suddenly, today the Palestinians are brandishing, high up in the clouds, a whole arsenal of arms."

"Are you suggesting that Black September had accomplices in the company who were in a strong enough position to hide arms on board?"

Hamlekh made no reply. He moved over in front of an old safe that stood majestically in a corner of his office, drew a flat key out of his waistcoat pocket and twirled the knob. "Read this," he said, handing Fulham a red-sealed telegram. Suspiciously, Fulham took the sheet of paper. He couldn't make up his mind whether to put on his glasses or not, but the agent's sly smile decided him against this. Holding the document at arm's length, he read it through slowly: "Top secret, do not forward, keep origin strictly secret. From legal resident Bonn. Source Sarah B, following search instructions F.33—stop—Signals impending departure exceptional agent Laurent Martin for Beirut after extraordinary consultation on 1st September of representation coded category zero zero, S.D.E.C.E. Paris and B.N.D. Bonn—stop—Seaching more precise information—regarding—Martin—Beirut mission—stop—will watch airports—stop—will transmit flight indications through express channels—stop and over."

Fulham laid the message down on the desk. The exact meaning of the codes used by the secret service often eluded him, but he fully realized the importance of the message and knew that no good could be predicated from a summit conference that brought the French and German secret services together on the eve of the departure of one of their agents for Beirut.

"Who's this Laurent Martin?" he snarled.

Hamlekh hesitated, then answered, "Laurent Martin, born in 1934. Graduated in 1956 from the E.N.A. (École Nationale d'Administration), the renowned French administration school. Very few people have heard of him. One could call him a mediator, a sort of planetary negotiator in dealings that remain under the rug. Physical data: six feet one, solid one hundred ninety-four pounds, green eyes, brown hair, excellent physical condition. Fluent command of English, German, Italian and women."

He paused for a moment and then continued. "Our service started to take an interest in him during the events of May 1958. Martin was then in close contact with the triumvirate Chaban-Delmas, Michel Debré and Georges Pompidou (who are now, as you know, Prime Minister, Defense Secretary and President), who were organizing de Gaulle's return to power. Martin was their man in Algiers. . . ." He paused, then added, "At this time, he was a captain of the First Regiment of the Foreign Legion."

Fulham's reaction was immediate. "The Foreign Legion! Then he must have been at Suez!"

"No, he didn't join the Legion until 1959. He's only thirty-eight years old, Fulham. Anyway, his military performances are of no interest to us."

Fulham was about to reply, but Hamlekh hurried on. "During the Algerian War, Martin remained loyal to de Gaulle, but managed somehow, and this was no small feat, to stay on good terms with the top officers of the French army.

"In 1962, the French government offered him an important although indefinable post, which he accepted. Offically, he doesn't get his orders either from the S.D.E.C.E. or the D.S.T. or even from the Ministry of Foreign Affairs. Yet, he can take advantage of any one of these services, whenever he so desires. Even more curious is the fact that he enjoys the same kind of working relationship with the corresponding secret services of Britain, Germany, the Netherlands, Belgium, Switzerland, Denmark and Italy."

"The Common Market of information?"

"More or less. Martin always seems to be lurking in the background before major political proceedings. He seems to be the man behind all the lengthy and obscure negotiations which precede the most unpredictable and dramatic turn of events. A month before the announcement of the American-North Vietnamese peace talks at the Avenue Kleber, Martin made four trips to Washington, Paris and Hanoi. Then, three weeks before the announcement of the Nixon trip to China, Martin took an eleven-day vacation in Peking. During Biafra, Martin was in Africa. Britain enters the Common Market and Martin has three separate meetings with Heath."

"He seems to be some kind of a blackmailer on a multinational scale."

"Let's just say that he's an astute diplomat who knows how to make requests look like gracious advice."

"A European Kissinger?"

"Much more and much less at the same time. During the Munich Olympics, he disposed of one of our agents in the basement of the Schlosspark Hotel. I must admit that he then called an ambulance service, although anonymously, of course. The man was in the hospital for two weeks. Martin had used no weapons, only his hands. And our man was no lightweight. I can't imagine Kissinger doing that."

Fulham had sunk into a state of gloom since Munich had been mentioned. "Do you know what Martin's mission was in Beirut?"

Hamlekh took a cigarette case from his desk and offered one to Fulham, who waved aside the offer. Hamlekh knew that Fulham didn't smoke, but he wanted to allow himself a moment of reflection before entering on a subject where Fulham might well disagree with him. He took a deep drag before continuing. "This cable from our head agent in Bonn is simply to let us know that some of the top men in the S.D.E.C.E. and the B.N.D. have come together to hold a little meeting before Martin's departure for Lebanon. Therefore, it's likely that the discussions at this meeting were centered on Palestinian terrorism.

"It's obvious, though, that the European intelligence directors don't need a mediator of Martin's status to reinforce security measures in airports and around embassies. What they want to do is to take matters into their own hands, to act instead of giving in. In this light, Laurent Martin's trip to Beirut finally makes sense."

"You don't think you're going a little too far?"

"Certainly not. The presence of those prisoners on German soil constitutes a potential source of trouble for the Brandt government. If they held only one prisoner, you could bet your sweet ass he'd 'commit suicide.' But three suicides—no, no one would ever buy it.

"So, what do they do? They decide to lance the boil before it bursts or before the Palestinians themselves undertake some desperate form of action full of unpredictable consequences. They concoct their own little hijacking plan with a minimal number of risks involved. This will allow them to 'give in' to the hijackers and at the same time explain to the public that they have placed the lives of the passengers above all other considerations. 'We preferred to release the Palestinian "assassins" rather than play with the lives of innocent victims.' And all parties will be satisfied, except for those savage Israelis."

"So you think Laurent Martin went to Beirut to negotiate the hijacking of the German Boeing with Black September?"

"It's a part he plays extremely well."

Fulham stood up abruptly. "It's simple then," he said.

"All we have to do is alert our 'Action' group in Munich. I'll wire them immediately and have them put a sniper in a strategic spot on the airfield. That should screw up their master plan very nicely."

4

Munich, Sunday, October 29, 1972, 11:30 A.M.

In the hallway of the Munich-Riem airport, Hans Schloss had just pushed his way through the exit gates along with the rest of the other passengers on the Bonn flight. Below the departure and arrival timetable stood a tall, broad-shouldered man, his brown hair cropped short, dressed in a well-tailored tweed jacket, a woolen, mustard-colored shirt, a knitted tie and gray flannel slacks that hung neatly over his brown shoes, doubtless from Clark's, Bond Street.

Although he had never met him before, Schloss recognized the man at first sight.

"Laurent Martin, I presume?" he said.

The two men shook hands and proceeded toward the automatic exit doors.

The metallic blue NSU RO .80 was parked in front of a "no parking" sign. Schloss handed the chauffeur the luggage slip stapled to his air ticket.

"I'll drive, Kurt. Fetch my suitcase and take a taxi back to Pullach."

Schloss was a fast and skillful driver. On the Route 12 Autobahn leading to the east-west motorway that bisected the Bavarian capital, he held the NSU comfortably at ninety. The traffic coming the other way was extremely heavy; it seemed as if half the population of Munich was heading for the Ebersberger Forest on a picnic, determined to take advantage of this pleasant autumn Sunday.

Just outside the city, a Lamborghini Miura pulled up behind them and flashed its lights. Schloss pulled over into the right-hand lane and the Miura screamed on by them, quickly accelerating up to one hundred thirty.

Martin laughed. "Terrible soldiers, the Italians, but builders of brilliant automobiles."

"True, true," Schloss said. The Miura was now just a little red speck bobbing in the distance. "Any news about the plane?" he continued.

"Yes, they were forced to land in Zagreb due to bad weather. They refueled there and took off again at eleven-oh-two. They should be over Munich within the hour."

"Any problems?"

"Well, the hijackers wanted to land at Riem, the civilian airport. One of the Fedayeen speaks excellent French and English and knows how to operate the radio perfectly. I spoke with him for a few minutes and convinced him to accept the exchange at the Fürstenfeldbruck military air base."

Martin spoke German without the slightest accent. Had Schloss not known he was French, he would have sworn he was born in Germany. Martin took out a metal box of filterless cigarettes and lit one.

"And your Chancellor?" Martin asked.

"He fell into line. He understood everything, but he didn't let on. The military man showed less acumen. He caught on too. But he was so pleased to have finally understood something in his life he couldn't resist letting Brandt know he knew what was going on. That was where he blundered. Brandt squared him away rather bluntly. So, no problems: we have a free hand."

"And the Palestinian prisoners?" asked Martin.

Schloss glanced at his watch. "They should be arriving at

Fürstenfeldbruck now. A platoon of parachutists is keeping watch over them in the disciplinary quarter at the air base. When the time comes, we'll create a diversion with a helicopter."

On the outskirts of Munich, Schloss turned down the Töginger Strasse. The streets were practically deserted. He held the car at seventy as they whizzed through the Max Weber Platz, crossed the Isar and headed up the Maximilian Strasse in the direction of the central station.

"In an hour, everything should be settled," Schloss said. "The prisoners board the Boeing, then the Fedayeen release the passengers and crew while the pilot and engineer stay on board. We fill up the plane and they depart for whatever destination they prefer."

Martin made no reply. Schloss glanced at him inquiringly. Laurent was smoking, a deep line furrowing his brow. "Let's hope you're right," he sighed. "Obviously, the leaders of Black September haven't informed their commandos that they're mere puppets in this deal. That's why the hijacker is acting so obstinately. They want to show us they mean business. Although they only have blank cartridges and dummy grenades, they'll stop at nothing to show us that we're at their mercy. We'll have to play it cautiously."

The car turned off the Augsburg highway at the Geiselbullach exit. At more than ninety miles an hour, it tore down Route 471, toward the military airport of Fürstenfeldbruck.

They had to present their passes at three different roadblocks guarded by paratroopers before motoring along a narrow road flanked with coils of electrified barbed wire. The airfield was swarming with policemen and soldiers, and there were rows of trucks huddled on the left side of the runway. Many policemen and soldiers were carrying rifles equipped with telescopic sights.

"What's the meaning of all this?" Martin asked. "I thought Brandt said no bloodshed."

"Of course," Schloss grumbled. "This must be Kallenberg's personal doing. He's the assistant vice-commissioner. He'll be expecting us at the control tower."

He pulled up alongside the tower. The two men hurried into the elevator and quickly shot to the fourth floor. There, they entered a vast circular room from which all the air traffic of the military base was controlled. They walked up to the radarscope. At each rotation, a ray quivered gently on the screen. The Boeing would be in sight in less than ten minutes. Kallenberg and Colonel Markt, the commanding officer of the air base, joined Martin and the B.N.D. agent.

"There're some new developments," he explained. "We've received word from reliable sources that the Shin-Beth is going to take some desperate action to obstruct our plans. While waiting for you, I took the responsibility of ordering the police to comb the surrounding area for a radius of two miles."

Martin was frowning. Everybody's eyes were cast in his direction, their looks anxious and questioning. "Are you still in radio contact with the plane?" he asked.

Kallenberg pointed to the radio console. "We've established a permanent contact with them, sir. The Palestinian is still controlling the frequencies. Commander Klaussen is listening in through his headphones."

Tapping lightly on the radio receiver's shoulder, Martin hinted that he wanted to take over. He slipped on the headset and established contact. In German, he said, "Klaussen, do you hear me? I'm the agent in charge. How many hours of fuel do you have left? I repeat—how many fuel hours left? Over."

The sound of the commander's voice came through loud and clear. "Roger. We have three hours fifty minutes' fuel left within the legal security margin. Over."

Hacam's voice broke in. In English, he said, "Speak in English or in French. That's an order."

Martin submissively continued in English. "The instructions that I'm transmitting concern both of you. Do not under any circumstance land the plane. Circle above the airfield. You will be given a holding pattern. Chancellor Brandt has issued strict orders. He will yield to your demands. The delay I'm imposing on you is an extra security measure. On no account must you land."

Hacam answered, this time in French. "No tricks, or we'll blow the plane sky high. We'll accept the delay, but it mustn't exceed an hour."

"Captain Klaussen. How are your passengers reacting?"

"Tower control, this is Commander Klaussen. The Fedayeen have handed out Valium tranquilizers. They were given in massive doses and my passengers are now under their effect. I agreed to and encouraged the idea. Over."

Martin removed the earphones and whistled in admiration. "How refined. We are dealing with gentlemen Fedayeen."

Schloss interrupted him curtly. "Avoid that sort of witticism. I have no desire to see it printed tomorrow on the front page of the *Stern*. What are your plans?"

"We have to route them to another airport. Order an empty plane to land here. We'll put the three prisoners on board and then land the two planes simultaneously at another field."

"Where?"

"That's not important. At Nuremberg, Stuttgart. No, wait a minute: Salzburg. It's on their way."

"I'll transmit your requirements to Bonn. I can't take on the responsibility."

"Hold on, Schloss," Martin interjected. "The ideal place would be Zagreb. If the Chancellor agrees, he could intercede in our favor with Tito. Meanwhile, we'll let the news leak out that the exchange will take place in Salzburg. Zagreb is our safest bet. Their stopover there was only due to atmospheric conditions. The landing wasn't planned, but it worked out fine. Do you have a military plane here that could take off for Zagreb in less than an hour?"

Kallenberg was the one to answer. "We'd have to inform the commander-in-chief of the air force."

Colonel Markt settled the matter abruptly. "The general is on an inspection tour in Oldenburg," he explained. "Today is Sunday, and he'll probably be on a stag hunt. In any case, flying over Yugoslavian territory in one of our military planes on such short notice is out of the question; landing it at Zagreb, even more so."

"Well, then, could you find us a civilian plane?"

"It might be possible," Schloss interjected. "I'll call Schaumburg Palace. Kallenberg, see if you can get hold of the director of a private charter company."

Willy Brandt consented without reservation. His first reaction was to reprimand Schloss for having consulted him and wasted precious time. Schloss raised the objection that only the Chancellor had the necessary power to intercede with Tito. Brandt assured him that he would make the necessary arrangements. He added that in case they couldn't requisition a private plane on such short notice, he'd have the crew of his personal jet standing by. The plane was now at the Baden-Baden military airfield and could reach Fürstenfeldbruck in less than an hour. He added that this expedient should only be used as a last resort, because it could lead to a political incident with Israel.

Schloss came out of the phone booth sweating heavily and summed up his lengthy conversation with the Chancellor in a few words. "Unlimited powers," he said. "The Chancellor will inform the Yugoslavs."

Kallenberg came back looking less pleased. He'd only managed to get hold of an office clerk at the Condor Charter Company. The director's name was Herman Zeisskam, a former Ober-Leutnant in the Luftwaffe. Kallenberg finally got through to Zeisskam at his country estate near Uberlingen, on the Lake of Constance. The ex-pilot promised to ring back in less than fifteen minutes. He called back ten minutes later. He had managed to contact the pilot and the head engineer of one of his planes. The crew, after having flown a group of Scandinavian businessmen to Germany, were about to take off from Zurich without any passengers on board and return the aircraft to its base in Coblenz. Zeisskam had ordered the flight plans modified. The plane would be flying over Fürstenfeldbruck in fifty-five minutes. It was a Hawker-Siddeley 125 and it had a range of eleven hundred miles.

It was now 1:26 P.M. Laurent Martin heaved a sigh and returned to the radio receiver. The 727, holding now above the airfield, began its fifth wide circle, banking first over what had once been the Dachau concentration camp, and then west of Mering.

Hacam and Klaussen signaled that Martin was coming through clearly. The Fedayeen had remained astonishingly cool and collected. Martin decided to deliver his instructions in French. "We have organized an exchange which presents a minimum of risks. You are to return to Zagreb. We are waiting for a private jet which should land here at two twenty P.M. The prisoners will be taken on board during the refueling, which should take less than fifteen minutes. The aircraft will take off between two thirty-five and two forty P.M. It will approach Zagreb between three thirty and three forty-five P.M. You'll be there forty-five minutes ahead of us. Take advantage of this time to refuel the seven twenty-seven. Then taxi down to the end of the takeoff runway. The private jet will join you there as soon as it lands. Your three companions will meet you on board. Transmit this to Klaussen if he doesn't understand French."

"Understand," the pilot answered in French.

"Nothing doing!" Hacam's voice burst out. "You're setting a trap. I've waited an hour too long. We're landing immediately. Have our companions ready to board. Out."

Martin sighed, and once more tried to pick up their frequency. "Are you still receiving? Acknowledge. **Over.**"

"Roger. Acknowledge reception. Go ahead."

"Now, let's start again from the beginning. It's obvious you're no fool. So think it over before giving us your answer. We know that you have two hand grenades on you that could blow up the plane. Should you pull the pins of those grenades while you're airborne or on the airfield in Munich or in Zagreb, the effect of the explosion would be exactly the same. Over."

In less than twenty seconds, the answer came through. "Agreed," the Fedayin said. "We'll change our heading for Zagreb."

"One last point," Martin continued. "I'll see the prisoners onto the aircraft and remain on board for the last part of the flight. Out."

"That's out of the question!" Hacam yelled. "Whoever you are, you aren't needed. I forbid you to come anywhere near the plane."

"My decision is final. Don't argue. I'll be there. You have plenty of time to think this over. You have a gun, I won't have one. Your companions, once they're free, will search me. They can assure you that I won't have any weapons on me. That way you'll be able to calmly shoot me down, while I'm mounting the boarding ramp."

By way of reply, Hacam started swearing in Arabic. Martin snapped the transmit button back up. He was grinning from ear to ear.

"Do you understand Arabic?" Schloss asked.

"A little bit."

"What'd he say?"

"Hard to translate literally, but it concerned sodomy and the female side of my family."

The Hawker-Siddeley landed within the required time. It was an elegant, streamlined plane with a sparkling white fuselage and wings. A narrow red stripe was painted down its whole length and curved up gracefully over the jet engines. Slowly, majestically, the aircraft glided along the network of asphalt taxiways, propelled by the strident blast of its jets. When it finally came to a standstill, a Mercedes fuel tanker painted in the greenish color of the Bundeswehr pulled up behind the wings. Two employees unscrewed the fuel caps and the refueling process began.

Eleven minutes later, the tanker trundled past an Opel touring bus conveying the three Palestinian survivors of the Munich Olympic Games massacre to freedom.

The bus stopped in front of the Hawker's incorporated boarding ramp. The three Fedayeen climbed on board, the guns of four paratroopers standing at the foot of the ramp leveled at them.

At the same time, the RO .80, still driven by Schloss, started off from the base of the control tower. In the front seat, Martin remained as casual and serene as someone off for a two-day vacation.

"Why are you so set on going along?" Schloss asked.

"I have to 'organize' the stories Klaussen and his crew will be releasing. Their explanation of what happened mustn't be too lopsided."

"Do you think you'll manage to convince the Israelis?"

"Of course not, but I couldn't give a damn! They must've come to their own conclusions by now. We just can't let them get hold of any solid evidence. They can make all the noise they want, broadcast their assumptions or get their revenge by striking back across the Lebanese border. I'm not worried about that, but I don't want the front page of their papers announcing that the official report of the events doesn't hold water. And that all depends on Klaussen's report."

"I get you. Well, bon voyage."

The RO .80 now pulled up next to the Hawker. Martin climbed up the narrow gangway. Two paratroopers came

up behind him. The copilot was waiting to fold in the boarding ramp and close the latch.

Thirty seconds later Ed Denaoui Abdel Kheiz, Samer
Mohamed Abdallah and Ibrahim Mahmoud Badran had
turned around and were staring, stupefied, at the man who
had just entered the cabin behind them. Following the copilot's advice, they buckled their seat belts. Their drawn
faces showed how baffled they were by the course of events.

"Does one of you speak English, French or German?"
Martin asked in English.

"I speak French," Abdel Kheiz said hesitantly. "My
brothers only understand Arabic."

Martin sat down near them after the copilot had moved
up to the cockpit. The Hawker picked up speed and then
rapidly gained altitude. It was designed to carry eighteen
passengers, and there were only six on board.

"My brothers and I are prepared to die," Abdel Kheiz
said gravely. "Tell us how long we have left to live. We
knew Germany had abolished the death penalty and that we
would be murdered discreetly, as one murders jackals."

"Forget the heroics," Martin interrupted. "This evening,
you'll be having dinner either in your homeland or in an
allied country. You're already practically free."

He stood up and passed through the curtain to the cockpit. "Everything okay?" he asked the pilot.

"Yes, as far as I am concerned. We'll be approaching
Zagreb in forty minutes."

The little jet was trundling down the deserted runway at
Zagreb when Martin resumed his conversation with Abdel
Kheiz. During the flight, he had given up trying to convince
him and had left the prisoners to their own occupations:
they were piously reading a pocket edition of the Koran,
which they had been allowed in prison.

"I want you to search me," Martin explained, "to make
sure I don't have any weapons on me. You are to inform

your friends that I'm not carrying any weapons before they let me onto the other aircraft. Are you starting to believe what I've been telling you?"

With growing amazement, Kheiz, unconvinced, did as he was told. "You aren't carrying any weapons," he said finally.

"I know, but I'm not the one you are supposed to inform."

The transfer of the prisoners to the Boeing took place exactly as had been planned. Laurent Martin was the first to climb on board the big Lufthansa aircraft. Then came the three prisoners, goaded along by the muzzles of the paratroopers' guns. Once the Palestinians were on the plane, the paratroopers, obviously frustrated, made their way back to the Hawker.

The three Fedayeen finally grasped what was happening. They immediately attempted to rush into Hacam's arms, but he checked them brutally and then ordered the hatch to be shut.

Walter Klaussen rolled up the engines. More than eight hundred yards away, standing on the roof of the terminal building, four reporters had followed the scene through binoculars. They represented the local agencies of UPI, Reuters, AFP and the Soviet agency, Tass. The cables they sent off a few minutes later all mentioned that a fourth person had climbed out of the Hawker-Siddeley and boarded the Boeing. The Yugoslav radio stated the fact. Throughout the rest of the world though, the press took no notice of this detail.

The newspaper *Le Monde* was the only one to note it. In its October 31 edition, which came out in Paris at 3 P.M. on the thirtieth of October, it reported, in an article signed by its Belgrade correspondent, Paul Yankovitch, that a "West German official" whose identity had not been disclosed had boarded the Boeing.

As the 727 cruised steadily, Hacam gave new orders to

the pilot. "Head for Tirana. I'll be giving you instructions progressively."

Klaussen was exhausted. "Listen," he retorted, "you're quite safe now, so don't force me to fly in zigzags. Since our destination is the Near East, we should go beyond Tirana, so I could switch to automatic."

Hacam relented. "All right. First head toward the eastern cape of Crete. From there I'll give you further instructions."

In the cabin, Laurent Martin picked up the interphone and began to reassure the passengers and the crew members.

"You're safe now. We are returning to the Near East. Tomorrow you'll be dispatched on regular flights to your required destinations. Lufthansa offers each passenger a handsome premium to compensate for the unpleasant hours you have endured. Please keep calm and regard this last part of our flight as a pleasant little journey."

His tone was reassuring. The passengers relaxed as Laurent passed through to the cockpit. Hacam stood there, the harmless gun in his hand.

"I must talk to the crew," Martin insisted. "Take them through to the cabin."

"In English. I will supervise," Hacam said firmly.

The crew members crowded into the cabin.

"My name is Laurent Martin. I represent both your government and the Lufthansa Company, who are concerned about what exactly you will relate to the press."

"We will simply tell the whole truth about the matter," Klaussen cut in. "You could have spared yourself the trouble."

"Your attitude does credit to you, Captain Klaussen. Nevertheless, some members of the press might suggest that the German government took precautions to get these prisoners off their hands in order to avoid what might have been a dangerous political trial. Therefore, it would be rational to avoid all mention of the decision to transfer to Zagreb, and let the public believe it was an order from the hijackers themselves."

"There might be some truth to such suggestions, don't you think so?" Klaussen muttered sullenly.

"I wouldn't know," Laurent said in a flat lie. "You know as much as I do. When I was asked to try and convince you, I didn't think it necessary to inquire further."

"You have my consent, then, but only if the other crew members give theirs."

They all nodded.

"And yet," Klaussen added, "what if the two hijackers themselves state what really happened?"

Laurent smiled faintly.

"They won't. It isn't in their interest. The wider their initiative seems, the greater they'll appear in the eyes of their allies. Am I mistaken?"

Hacam turned slowly. His dark eyes pierced them as he nodded.

The indicator showed the approach of the island of Crete. Hacam's words were direct. He ordered sternly, "Now, Tripoli."

Laurent Martin's nerves were tight. He walked over to a window seat and sat down, thinking, *Hell of a mission. Too touchy. If one day some brain ever realizes that blackmailing is the supreme weapon of the twentieth century, we'll be as defenseless as children.*

PART I

5

The Italian liner *Corsican Express*, which ran each year from spring until fall between Genoa and Bastia, sidled up against its landing at Bastia. Many of the ship's passengers stood along the railings of the starboard deck, watching the deckhands skillfully secure the ship to the dock. Other passengers were crowding impatiently into the three exitways waiting to disembark. Hacam stood among them.

The Palestinian was wearing a faded threadbare suit, a cheap shirt covered with patches and a rayon tie, loosely knotted around his narrow collar. He was a portrait of poverty. As he descended the gangway, he was roughly jostled by the other passengers, a group of vacationers dressed in colorful clothes. No one could have associated him with the well-bred, yet intractable October commando. He walked with the gait of people who for countless centuries have struggled to exist. His head was bowed and his back bent—another Arab immigrant on his way to an estate bordering the western coast, where he would join the crowded ranks of farmhands who had settled in Corsica since Algerian independence.

Once on the quay, the Fedayin submissively lined up in a queue that had formed in front of a white wooden table where two French C.R.S. men, members of the tactical police force, were briefly checking passports and identification cards.

By creating a small ruckus, a whole family of vacationers was able to cut in front of him. A few other tourists, noticing that Hacam had remained mute, did likewise.

He finally presented his tattered old Tunisian passport at the control desk. The C.R.S. man examined the false document page by page. "Your employment card?" he asked.

Hacam reached into his back pocket and fished out a worn leather wallet. Opening it, he produced a folded piece of paper and handed it to the C.R.S. agent.

"Unfold it," the policeman snarled. "I'm not your flunky, boy."

" 'Scuse me, sir," Hacam stammered, hurriedly unfolding the sheet of paper.

The policeman grabbed the certificate out of Hacam's hands and examined it carefully. It was flawless. He ungraciously stamped the document, then the passport, and handed them back to the Arab. His eyes were already turned to the next passenger.

At the baggage-inspection area, the customs officials gave him the same treatment. Hacam was ordered to untie the strings that held his battered old suitcase together. Disgustedly, the official then ordered Hacam to unpack his dirty clothes. Finally, he said, "Repack your shit and get the hell out of here."

In the parking lot Hacam spotted Ahmoud, the foreman of the Tardets estate, but waited till the man approached him.

"Are you the fieldhand going to Prunelli?"

Hacam nodded and followed Ahmoud to the Renault 4L. The foreman edged the old Renault into the flow of cars between a Mercedes registered in Zurich and a Parisian DS 21. On the main road, the traffic was heavy, but it thinned out once they passed the airport. After seven miles, at Casamozza, he branched off the road to Corte and swung the little car onto National Route 198, the only straight road in Corsica, which follows the eastern coast down to Porto-Vecchio.

Throughout the whole drive, the two Muslims had only exchanged a few remarks concerning the number of tourists on the island.

"No unexpected events?" Hacam finally asked.

"Nothing here. The old man is a little nervous, but his mind's made up. He won't weaken."

"He doesn't have any choice."

After another thirty minutes, they passed through Ghisonaccia, the heart of a community of Frenchmen who had had to leave Algeria after its independence. It was now the commercial center of an immense plain that former Algerian colonists had transformed, through hard work and willpower, into fertile and prosperous fields.

The Renault 4L turned to the right outside Migliacciar, onto a meandering country road that petered out at the foot of the mountains beyond Prunelli-di-Fiumorbo. But well before the end of the road, Ahmoud had swung the car left, taking a cart track that led to the Tardets estate. A gate cut across the road. It was opened by an Arab, who then closed it behind him.

For the next four miles, the road ran through vineyards. Occasionally, groups of Arab fieldhands would look up from their work and watch the 4L rumbling by. The car crossed the Mohammedan village where more than thirty families had settled and built up an independent community. The Renault had to pass a final gate, surrounded by walls, which were built high enough to hide the low main building and its park. The old Algerian colonist was waiting for them on the front steps.

Adrien Tardets was a tall, stocky bald man. His somber features betrayed a great strength of character. He was not talkative, but his sparse words bore weight. Born sixty-two years earlier on his parents' estate at Vialar, in the heart of the Ouarsenis, in Algeria, and orphaned at nineteen, he carried on his father's business and did well with the estate. He was one of those colonists who were born in Algeria, but to whom the Algerian soil was nothing more than a source of wealth from which they extracted the maximum, a goose who laid golden eggs, needing no love in return. To him, it was a soulless land.

In 1954, when the first waves of the Algerian revolution began to sweep across the country, Tardets realized that the good times would soon be over. As the revolution progressed, Adrien came to understand that if he still wanted to make a living in the country he would have to pay the Algerian National Liberation Front, the F.L.N. He didn't hesitate and gave in to the rebels' ever increasing demands. Because of his compliant attitude, though, the F.L.N. soon asked him for more than a financial commitment to their cause. Old Tardets hid arms, then sheltered men. He seriously believed that because of his commitment to the rebellion from the very beginning, he wouldn't lose his estate after independence. In 1961, however, the F.L.N. presented him with an entirely different proposition.

It came from the headquarters of the G.P.R.A., the acting revolutionary government. One morning, one of the government's major plenipotentiaries arrived from Tunis bearing a long-term plan drawn up by the Arab League that called for the creation of several Arab settlements in Europe, in areas where such settlements would not only seem natural but essential to the economy. They would also serve as ideal hiding places for Arab militants. The League had chosen him to start an immense farm estate in Corsica. Nobody would find this suspicious. He was known to be rich, and no one knew he was far from being rich enough to undertake such a project on his own. In exchange for the land, his fieldhands would be chosen by the Arab League. According to the circumstances, he would either be asked to keep quiet, or else blindly obey the instructions he would receive. Adrien accepted the proposal and founded the Tardets estate, which now covered more than four hundred acres. The Arab League supplied him with enough working capital to fertilize the land in record time. His wealth increased in a spectacular way, but no one found this odd.

Again, in 1968, nobody thought it strange that he should purchase an eighteen-meter Baglietto yacht from the ship-yards of Livorno. Between journeys it was anchored in the port of Bastia. The yacht, though it looked harmless enough, was used several times a year to run arms to the Middle East.

The Tardets residence was a low building, massive and austere. When Tardets acquired it little of the original house remained. He built on the foundation of the old structure, respecting its style, the volume of the stone blocks and the former layout of the rooms. It was a one-story building, containing a lofty living room, a vast study and four bedrooms, but no dining area. Tardets took his meals at a huge wooden table in the kitchen. A Muslim and his wife took care of the housework and cooked. Each evening, they would return to the Arab village on bicycle.

Martha, Adrien's wife, spent all day in her room, appearing only for meals. In 1962, their three sons and only daughter had burned to death in a car accident on the road to Orléansville. Since then, she seldom spoke to anyone. She did no more than keep herself alive now, carried on by the flow of events. At the age of sixty-one, she was a mere shadow. She never left the house and no longer shared her husband's bedroom.

Adrien led the two Arabs into the kitchen. With a sign of the hand, he dismissed the two servants, Lualä and Balir. Before retiring, Lualä put a heavy, steaming soup tureen next to a platter of Corsican sliced meat and cheese, on the big rectangular table she had set for three.

"Now we eat. We'll talk afterward," Tardets said. He served the thick bacon and vegetable soup himself. "Ahmoud told me that you aren't a practicing Muslim," he said. "I hope not, because in Corsica, the basic meat is pork."

Hacam nodded in assent. Adrien held up a bottle of heavy red wine. "Would you like some in your soup?"

They declined the offer.

"You'll never know what's good," Adrien said, shaking his head regretfully. With that he poured a cup of the wine into his bowl.

After the meal, the three men talked for more than four hours. Hacam went over each minute detail of the plan with the meticulousness of a watchmaker and finally concluded that there wasn't a single flaw in it. Nevertheless, before retiring, he asked to see the cellars.

"Of course, if you like," Tardets replied, "but I thought I'd show them to you tomorrow. You're not leaving before ten, are you?"

"I'd like to see them today," Hacam insisted.

The entrance to the stone staircase that led down to the cellars was blocked by a very small Gothic-style door that opened off Tardets' study. Its heavy hinges were deeply embedded in the stone walls, while the door itself was solid oak, two inches thick. It was locked by a modern system of perpendicular steel bars that slid horizontally into the rock walls.

"We haven't touched the foundations," Tardets explained. "All this has been kept as it originally was, hewn out of the rock, way before the invention of dynamite."

Hacam counted off forty-six steps, the height of two good floors. Then they came to a halt in front of a second door, as thick and even lower than the first one, and locked in the same manner. Adrien and the Arabs had to bend over to pass through it.

"It's in perfect condition, no sign of dampness."

"And the ventilation?" Hacam inquired.

"There're four shafts drilled through the rock. There's one right above you. Each one of them is about three inches in diameter, although it varies. These cellars were carved out of the rock more than two hundred years ago, originally as a place to cure *bruccio,* a goat's cheese as old as Corsica itself. That explains the ventilation shafts. While they were in use, these cellars produced up to five thousand cheeses. Believe me, if the air here was sufficient to cure five thousand *bruccios,* a hundred men could spend their entire lifetime down here without fear of suffocation."

Hacam nodded in agreement. They continued their inspection. Five army cots had been placed in the largest cellar. Each of them was covered with a down-filled sleeping bag. There were also three chairs and two wood tables. Two of the corners contained elementary washbasins. "I installed the water and electricity myself," the old man added. "But you will have to attend to the disposal of the feces." Adrien Tardets never used crude words. Instead, he would look in his father's old *Larousse* dictionary for equivalent terms that were often technical and uncommon. This added a touch of quaintness to his French, which he spoke with the thick and melodious accent of the Algerian colonists.

"Don't worry about that," Hacam replied. "My men will take care of it. Only a bucket is needed. The ventilation shafts are what I am worried about. What would happen if one shouted into the opening of a shaft?"

Adrien smiled. "Nothing. You wouldn't hear a sound. The shafts wind through the rock. I had a shot fired with a thirty point oh six down here, and I couldn't hear anything up above. In any case, nobody is allowed on the grounds without my permission."

"That sounds perfect," Hacam concluded.

"It is perfect. If anything goes wrong, it won't happen here."

"It won't happen anywhere," Hacam snapped. "Nothing will go wrong."

6

The Paris-Vintimille express pulled into the station at Cannes. Patrice Thibaud was the first to step down from the second-class car. His only luggage bulged in the left hip pocket of his blue-jeans: a two-franc twenty-centime Gillette hand razor, a packet of razor blades and a toothbrush wrapped in Kleenex. Wherever he went, he could always find a piece of soap that he used both for shaving and as toothpaste. His only clothes were the jeans and a navy-blue T-shirt with gray stripes around the neck. It was clean and new, but the model was ten years old. Patrice had bought it the day before at the Aix-en-Provence flea market. He wore simple canvas shoes, French espadrilles. He had the thick long hair and lean slender look of his young hip contemporaries. His eyes flashed a kind of passion that revealed the intellectual fanaticism that consumed him.

At the end of the platform, he handed his brown cardboard ticket to the gate man and sauntered out onto the Place de la Gare, the railroad public square. He had the impression of entering a Turkish bath. The sky was pale and cloudless, and a damp mist shimmered above the asphalt roadway. It was a hot ninety degrees as he strode over to the Rue d'Antibes, turned to the Croissette and continued along a sidewalk overlooking the beach.

He arrived at the entrance of the Port Canto before eight. The guard was not yet on duty. He sauntered unheeded into the manmade port, where the most magnificent floating palaces of the Côte d'Azur were anchored. The docks were deserted. The only person about was a young boy listlessly sweeping the pavement in front of the Moby Dick, a private bar and restaurant for the yacht owners. Patrice walked up to the restaurant.

"Could you tell me where the *Rosebud* is moored?" Obviously delighted at the opportunity to give up his sweeping, the young boy answered gaily in a melodic southern French accent, "I can easily tell you that! It's the biggest, the most beautiful and most luxurious ship in the harbor. It's moored at gate B Twelve. But look, you can see it from here. It's the big white one, sparkling white as the veil of our Holy Virgin! If ten men like me slaved for more than five hundred years without spending a single centime, they still wouldn't be able to afford such a ship."

He could not know how pleased Thibaud was by this little speech hinting of class distinctions. "Do you know where I might shave and clean up a bit?" Thibaud asked.

"There are four bathrooms on the *Rosebud*."

"They're not for me."

"Well, that suits me better, to tell you the truth. I thought you might be a relation of the Fargeau family. It's hard to tell, these days. Millionaires are dressed like beggars and beggars are dressed like pimps. The crew members' showers are behind the Moby Dick."

Patrice thanked him and made his way to the low gray cement building where the showers were located. A leaky washbasin stood in the entrance with a cracked mirror hanging above it. The young man found a piece of soap in one of the showers under the rotten slats of a duck board. Ten minutes later, he was thoroughly refreshed. As he strode by the bay window of the bar, the boy, still holding his broom, spotted him.

"If you're still looking for the *Rosebud,* here's her captain." Patrice's eyes met the watchful gaze of a stocky little red-haired man who introduced himself cautiously. "Brian Joshman. Can I do something for you?"

"Thibaud," Patrice replied. "I'm looking for Sabine Fargeau, but I would imagine she's still asleep."

"I expect so too," Joshman retorted. "But she isn't on board. Mlle. Sabine and her girlfriends announced last night that they were bored. They've driven down to Saint-Tropez. I'm to meet them there later on this morning."

The young man's eyes clouded over. "Are you still leaving for the islands tomorrow morning?"

Joshman nodded.

"And tonight in Saint-Tropez, is Mlle. Fargeau still planning to have dinner with her grandfather?"

"You're very well informed, M. Thibaud. Yes, those are their plans. The only change was the sudden departure of Mademoiselle and her girlfriends last night. Earlier, they'd planned to leave for Saint-Tropez this morning on the *Rosebud.* But you can contact M. Charles-André Fargeau at the Hotel de Paris in Monte Carlo. He isn't leaving for Saint-Tropez until about four o'clock after his nap."

"Do you know where the girls are staying in Saint-Tropez?"

"I would guess at the Byblos."

"Is there a phone I can use?"

"There's a line behind the bar. The number is nine seven two one two one."

When the operator at the palatial hotel in Saint-Tropez answered, Patrice asked for Sabine Fargeau. Helène Nikolaos answered the phone.

"Patrice! Where are you?"

"Where's Sabine? I'm in Cannes like a fool."

"Hold on a second, I'll wake her up. We were up most of the night."

On one of the twin beds, Sabine, entirely naked, was

fast asleep, lying on her stomach. Helène stood up and carried the phone across the room. Her long, thick honey-blond hair tumbled in total disarray down around her shoulders and swung heavily as she walked. She was also naked. Her body was round and firm, although her limbs were long and slender. Long hours of nude sunbathing had left her skin deeply tanned, yet it was still soft and smooth. Even when she was stern, her face seemed to be smiling. Her deep dark eyes always had a sparkle of mischievousness about them. Now she held the receiver up against her friend's ear and shook her to wake her. Sabine, by way of reply, simply grunted reproachfully.

"Wake up, Sabine. The love of your life is crying his eyes out in Cannes."

She sat up like a bolt. "Patrice?"

"Ha! You mean there's someone else?" rather sarcastically. Patrice had been trailing Sabine around for years.

Sabine finally became aware of the sound of a voice crackling at her ear.

"Chéri. How wonderful to hear your voice. What are you doing in Cannes?"

"You were supposed to be here. I came down to say good-bye. I was going to take the first train to Aix-en-Provence after you left."

"Listen, come to Saint-Tropez. Do hurry, Patrice, my grandfather won't be here until this evening. We'll have the whole day to ourselves. Patrice, I'm so thrilled. I'll wait for you. Jump in a cab, quickly." As she talked, Helène paraded around in search of a T-shirt, then nodded and yawned at the familiar course of events.

"Must I remind you, once again, that I'm not as well off as you are?"

"Come on. Don't be ridiculous. I'll tell the hotel to pay the driver. You can pay me back later."

"I can't afford to borrow money from you, Sabine."

Sabine bit her lips in confusion, then suddenly the obvious solution came to her. "Listen, go to the Port Canto. My grandfather's ship is anchored there. Ask for the captain. His name is Brian Joshman. Tell him to call me up. All you have to do is step on board. The *Rosebud* is coming to pick us up at Saint-Tropez."

"Wake up, will you, Sabine? I am at the Port Canto. Brian Joshman is standing by close enough to hear our conversation. He's the one who told me you were staying at the Byblos."

"Oh, yes! Of course. Well, let me speak to him."

Joshman's side of the conversation was rather scanty. "Yes, mademoiselle, certainly, mademoiselle. Yes, of course, mademoiselle. No, no, catering and fuel have been taken care of. We're ready to get under way. We'll be at the quay in Saint-Tropez in less than two hours. Good-bye, mademoiselle."

Sabine got out of bed to comb her long auburn hair. She wrapped it instantly into a little bun and turned toward Helène. "Well, my God, Helène, quit looking at me that way—it's never been all *that* serious, you know that. . . ."

Helène climbed back into bed and turned over, ignoring her.

Off the rocky coastline of the Estérel, the *Rosebud* slipped through the clear blue sea at an even, quiet speed of eighteen knots. Brian Joshman, upon leaving the Bay of Cannes, had taken the ship out into the open sea for a distance of four miles and then altered his course to a heading of eighty-five degrees west. Joshman had sailed the *Rosebud* so often between the two ports that he knew the headings going both ways by heart. When the yacht was firmly lined up pointing toward Cape Camarat, he fed the heading into the autopilot and flicked it on.

Patrice knew little about the sea or navigation.

"As we near port, I'll take over," Joshman explained to him. "A device that would steer corks into the harbor and line them up along the quay hasn't been invented yet, but it'll come!"

Patrice was interested and Joshman was delighted to teach him. He spoke about the *Rosebud* with as much pride as if he had designed her himself. "She's the most fantastic pleasure cruiser. M. Fargeau had the work started on her in 1967. She was designed by the research agency Navigation in Monaco. The four best marine architects in the world spent over a year just getting her down on paper. The actual building process was entrusted to the Van Lent and Zonen shipyards at Kaag, in the Netherlands. From fore to aft she's a hundred and ten feet long, and her upper works are made entirely of aluminum. She's propelled by two Caterpillar two-thousand-six-hundred-horsepower diesel engines. The autopilot is steered by both the gyro compass and by one of the magnetic compasses."

With Joshman leading the way, they saw everything from the flying bridge to the engine rooms. The captain showed him the depth sounder, the radiotelephone (B.L.U. and Very High Frequency), the Maxi-Fin Wosper stabilizers. By the time they had finished their tour, the *Rosebud* was off the coast of San Rafael. Patrice was wondering what other questions he could put to the captain. Finding nothing else, he asked, "Why was she christened the *Rosebud?*"

Joshman smiled. "Oh, don't you know? Well, M. Fargeau was fascinated by the Welles film on Hearst's life, *Citizen Kane*. He's seen it at least a dozen times—"

"Oh, yes, of course. 'Rosebud,' the magnetic and mysterious word that Kane pronounced just before his death. And so, to our millionaire, the two syllables of that one word stand for all the wealth on earth. . . . Funny to choose a rosebud as the symbol of opulence. What's a rosebud? In old English it's the nipple of a girl's breast for one thing. . . . Strange."

Shrugging his shoulders, Patrice sauntered over to the

quarterdeck and flung himself onto the crescent-shaped davenport, where he sat, his gaze sweeping along the foaming trail of the ship's wake while his thoughts turned to Sabine.

Patrice Thibaud had met Sabine five years earlier during the stormy events that took place in France in the month of May, 1968. He had been captivated by this girl not quite sixteen years old, who had awakened to life on discovering violence. He would never forget the first time he saw her, at the corner of the Boulevard Saint-Michel and the Boulevard Saint-Germain. Two young girls standing behind a flimsy-looking barricade were violently throwing, or trying to throw, cobblestones that missed their mark by a good twenty yards.

Although the girls were stimulated by exhilaration and hatred, their movements were supple and graceful. The picture they offered was not one of violence but of a fascinating ballet. They had both tied thin silk scarves across their faces. Their eyes were glistening with tears from the gas canisters set off by the police.

A squadron of C.R.S., the French tactical police force, stood menacingly facing them, in no way moved by the girls' beauty. An officer shouted out an order. In a herd, the solid body of riot police rushed the intersection, causing people to flee in hasty and inglorious retreat.

Patrice, his eyes riveted on the flawless curves of the girls' silhouettes, stood ten yards behind them, bemused by the way they were facing up to the police. Dressed in faded blue-jeans, they held their ground. They stood there, quite alone, feet apart, brandishing their cobblestones and firmly waiting for the black horde to come within range. Then he had rushed down to the girls, seized them by the arms and spun them around. His brutal gesture snapped them back into reality. The girls darted down the Boulevard Saint-Michel ahead of him, with tear gas grenades exploding now everywhere.

They turned into the Rue Serpente. Patrice overtook them, yelling: "Follow me!"

That evening Patrice became Sabine's lover.

For the next weeks the girls followed him everywhere, from the Sorbonne to the Odéon Theater, listening to speeches, planning revolutionary action over coffee and ruthlessly attacking the Establishment. It was later in June when Paris was recovering that Patrice learned that his mistress was the grandchild of the "richest man in the world." Sabine lived at Helène Nikolaos' home, where they both attended the lycée Fenlons, one of the best schools in Paris. Georges Nikolaos, a Greek exile, supported his family as a bilingual translator for a large European publishing house. They were not wealthy but Fredericque, Helène's mother, retained a distinguished grace and style in an unconventional, free manner. Her beauty and elegance were well known throughout Paris.

Two years ago Sabine had pleaded with her grandfather to move in with the Nikolaoses. The old multimillionaire was a man of insight and was quick to realize that to spend a few years in the home of these "gypsies"—whose morals were irreproachable—would be excellent for Sabine's upbringing. In any case he was prepared to do anything to get Sabine away from her parents' wild and empty social life. After making the necessary inquiries, Sabine's grandfather visited the Nikolaos home and insisted on giving a check of $250,000 to Helène's parents. He asked them to please forgive him for having run the risk of injuring their pride by offering them such a magnificent gift.

Georges Nikolaos interrupted him. "You're not being honest with yourself, M. Fargeau. You couldn't really give a damn about our pride. But I can assure you that we will accept your offer with pleasure and won't say another word about it. Why try to fool each other? For totally opposite reasons, money means no more to me than it does to you."

Fargeau decided that he really liked this man and his family. "I'll send along my interior decorator."

"I'd rather my wife did the decorating."

"Just send me all the bills then."

"Don't worry, I will."

It was the first time in his life that Charles-André Fargeau had remained cheerful for such a long time. Still smiling, he said, "Thank you, Nikolaos. If you're ever looking for a job, don't come to see me. I'd never entrust any sort of responsibility to a man as intelligent as you are."

"I'll take note of that."

They had never seen each other again. Nor had they phoned or even exchanged Christmas cards.

Several years later, Patrice received his doctorate in philosophy and was given a position as an assistant professor at the University of Aix-en-Provence. The relationship between the two young people then fell into a familiar, friendly routine, even though they were separated by a distance of five hundred miles. He had not seen her in three months, as her busy schedule seemed to include him less and less. Now, he was looking forward to the yacht's arrival in the Saint-Tropez harbor.

7

The *Rosebud* arrived off Saint-Tropez at 11:45. The harbor office instructed Joshman where to anchor. Near the port exit, the yacht lined up parallel to the quay, facing the village. Two deckhands lowered the gangway, and Thibaud bounded down the steps onto the shore. Sabine was waiting with open arms.

From his room on the second floor of the Sube Hotel, Hacam watched the landing through a small pair of binoculars.

At two in the afternoon, the Café des Arts was practically deserted. Kirkbane stood by the bar and ordered an orangeade. His hands were plunged in his pockets. Although he was wearing light summer clothing, his frail body was sweating heavily. With the back of his hand he pushed the moisture from his brow into his black greasy hair. With a small, red rosebud patch sewn on his T-shirt over his heart, a sailor sat at one of the tables, carefully sipping a cup of hot coffee and apparently paying no attention to the little Palestinian.

Kirkbane leaned over the bar and asked the cashier where the men's room was.

"Through the kitchen. Stairs on the right in the back."

At the top of the steep, narrow staircase, Kirkbane checked both the men's and the ladies' lavatories to be sure they were empty. He turned on the cold-water tap above the sink and washed his hands with slow deliberation. His fingernails were chewed to the quick.

Frank Woods, the boatswain's mate on the *Rosebud*, slipped through the door. Kirkbane signaled that they were alone.

"Everything's ready," Woods said. "We're lucky, I'm on watch tonight."

"Any idea when the girls'll be getting back on board?"

"There's no way to tell for sure. All five of them are dining with old Fargeau at the Byblos. But they went to bed late last night, so I expect they'll be back before midnight this evening."

"And the crew?"

"No change in plans. We still weigh anchor at five tomorrow morning. Captain Joshman's eating in town with his wife. She came down from Toulon to see him off. I'm fixing dinner for the first mate and the three deckhands. They'll all be in their cabins when I go on watch at eleven."

"Who's the kid who got off the boat, the one the Fargeau girl threw her arms around?"

"That was unexpected, but it doesn't make any difference. He came on board at Cannes. Joshman didn't enter his name in the ship's log. He won't be going along on the cruise."

"Are you sure?"

"Yes."

"Fine. The signal's still the same: you light a cigarette. Remember, your only one tonight. You won't see me, but don't worry about that. An hour later on the dot, I'll climb on board."

"I get it. . . . But I . . ." Woods faltered.

"What's wrong? Hurry up, somebody might come."

"You're the one who's going to knock me out, aren't you?"

"Listen, I've told you time and again. You won't even lose consciousness. Just a little bump on your head to prove that you're innocent. You can't complain with all the money you've already raked in. And there's still more to come."

"Sure, sure, but do it gently, will you?"

"It's my profession," Kirkbane whispered. "I know what I'm doing."

Charles-André Fargeau had ordered an elaborate table set up at the Byblos Hotel in the garden near the pool. Dinner was to be served at nine o'clock. All five girls arrived together. In deference to M. Fargeau they had slipped on light summer dresses, relinquishing their customary blue-jeans and T-shirts.

Sabine and Helène went up and kissed the wealthy, white-haired old man. The other girls gaily shook hands with him. Charles-André Fargeau, forever haunted by numbers, wondered whether the combined wealth of the four girls' families would equal his own personal fortune. He concluded that it wouldn't.

Yet indeed!

Joyce Donovan, a charming and vivacious redhead, was the only daughter of United States Senator Erskine S. Donovan, himself the sole heir to a steel fortune amassed by his grandfather before the turn of the century. It was often said that Senator Erskine S. Donovan could possibly be a strong Republican candidate for the presidency in the next election.

Gertrud Fryer was the daughter of Gunter Fryer, head of a Hamburg-based banking empire, founded by his great-grandfather, that was considered by most European financial experts to be one of the strongest lending institutions in the Common Market. Gertrud's mother was French. She had divorced Gunter four years earlier.

Marian Carter was the youngest of the six children of Lord and Lady Anthony Carter. Lord Carter, related to the royal family, was one of the largest shipbuilders in the United Kingdom.

Among the five, only Helène Nikolaos came from a family of modest income, but her keen wit and her disquieting charm always delighted the elder Fargeau. He sat patiently through the meal, listening vaguely to the girls' carefree chatter about their plans for the one-month cruise to the Greek islands on the *Rosebud*. As soon as he had finished his tea, he saw them back to the yacht. It was 11:21 P.M.

As the girls climbed on board, Frank Woods greeted them, rising from the stool where he was keeping watch.

"Good night, Frank," Sabine said as she passed by.

"Good night, mesdemoiselles. Do you want me to wake you tomorrow morning?"

"God, no, Frank. We're dead tired!"

"Then I'll see to it that we set off without making any noise."

"Thank you, Frank."

The girls went below to their cabins.

Brian Joshman climbed on board at half-past two in the morning. He had dined with his wife Rachel at the Da Lolo Restaurant on the Place de la Mairie. Then, taking her by the hand, he had led her into the pine grove behind the citadel, where he made love to her on a bed of pine needles.

Joshman, with Frank's help, raised the gangway and then slipped it below the trapdoor on deck where it was stored. Joshman reminded the boatswain to wake him at 4:30, then disappeared along the fore gangway, down into the crew's quarters, which were separate from the passengers' cabins. The crew was asleep.

Brian Joshman prepared for bed. Two things had been bothering him on his way back, but he had easily dismissed them from his thoughts. First of all, he was angry with himself for having told his wife all about Sabine Fargeau's lover. He had gone on and on about him, describing him in detail. But it didn't really matter. His wife was discreet, she would keep it to herself. No, what really annoyed him was that he might have made her pregnant. And they already had three children. He sighed and soon fell asleep.

At 2:47, Frank Woods pulled out his Zippo lighter and lit a Gitane with the long, flickering flame.

Huddled like a cat in the doorway of the port lighthouse, Kirkbane stood watching the *Rosebud*. He had seen the girls coming back and then, late in the night, he had seen Joshman returning. As soon as he spotted a flame on the *Rosebud,* he checked his phosphorescent watch, made a mental note of the exact time and looked toward the second floor of the Sube Hotel across the harbor. A flashlight blinked momentarily. Hacam, through his binoculars, had also seen the signal.

In spite of his small size, Kirkbane in fact was a perfect killer. And yet, he was in no way sadistic. He had simply become the ruthless and deliberate instrument of a cause that he served with controlled fanaticism.

Calmly, he removed his weapon from the pigskin sheath strapped flat on his chest underneath his cotton T-shirt. Now, in the open, its shiny steel surface reflected the green light of the beacon flashing off and on in the tower fifteen feet above his head. At first glance, the weapon looked exactly like an ordinary leather worker's awl, or perhaps a foreshortened ice pick. What differentiated Kirkbane's awl from one normally found on a cobbler's bench was the quality of steel he had used in its fabrication. It was his own little invention, and he considered it to be the ideal weapon: it allowed him to kill quickly and silently while at the same time inflicting a minimum amount of pain on his victims. Kirkbane was morbidly conscientious. He had studied the human brain and spinal cord and memorized the exact points at the base of the neck he had to strike in order to kill his victims quickly. With these facts in mind, Kirkbane had encountered only one problem in fabricating his killing tool: the metal to be used. He had to have a high-quality steel alloy that would not bend even when the tip of the shank was sharpened to a needle-fine point. It was a problem without a solution. When steel is sharpened, the alloys within it are decarbonized. Unfortunately, the amount of carbon in any steel is directly proportional to its strength.

For a long time, he used a weapon that he considered imperfect because the shank of the awl was too thick. To be sure, the weapon was efficient, but he felt that it inflicted an unnecessary amount of pain. The twitching facial muscles of his victims and the prolonged duration of their final spasms as he lowered them to the floor were more than he could bear. This distaste was more the product of his search for perfection, however, than an inappropriate sense of squeamishness.

The solution was placed before his eyes some months earlier. While waiting for the hour he was scheduled to execute an Israeli agent, out of boredom he switched on the color television in his posh room at the Europaisher-Hof in Baden-Baden. A sports broadcast of almost inconsequential importance flashed onto the screen. It was devoted to the highly specialized work of a Milanese engineer who had built a bicycle on which the Belgian champion, Eddy Merckx, was going to attempt to break the world's sixty-minute distance record next week in Mexico. Kirkbane was listening to the reportage rather absentmindedly when suddenly he heard something that interested him.

"The carbon content of the steel used in the spokes of this bicycle is point seven four percent." A steel with a carbon content of .74 percent then existed!

One month later, at the bus station in the village of Ateibe, Kirkbane received a package sent by the Sunn-Dalsora Steel Works in Göteborg, Sweden. The package contained enough unfinished bicycle spokes to spring four wheels. For the next five days, the little Palestinian worked with loving care perfecting his new weapon.

Now, the only thing left to be done was to test it.

At 3:35, Kirkbane moved out of the shelter of the lighthouse doorway. The quay was completely deserted except for a few drunks who were too far away to see him. Every thirty feet, small cold pools of fluorescent light fell on the stones of the dock. Kirkbane moved only in the shadows between the lights. Approaching the prow of the *Rosebud*, he saw that the mooring line on the port side was as taut as a bowstring. He swung lightly out over the water, hanging onto it, and with three swift moves he had his hand on the steel railing running around the quarterdeck. Seconds later, he landed softly on the deck of the yacht. Frank Woods was waiting for him.

"Everyone's asleep," he whispered nervously.

"Turn around, you won't feel a thing."

Woods was so panic-stricken, he was almost welcoming the blow that was to come. He turned around with his back to Kirkbane and sat down on a rope locker. Kirkbane placed his left hand on the sailor's shoulder and said, "Relax."

He felt a bit of the tension leave the man's shoulder muscles briefly and then quickly plunged his slender weapon deep into the nape of Woods's neck. In one swift move, the inflexible shaft slid upward past the occipital bone, piercing the brain stem and driving on into the bulb of his brain. For Kirkbane, it was a typically precise execution. What particularly fascinated him this time was his victim's reactions. Still holding onto Woods's shoulder, he noticed that the man had died without the slightest shudder. A feeling of pride surged through him momentarily. Gently removing the shaft from the sailor's brain, he let the lifeless body slip down to the deck and then used the dead man's shirt to wipe the blood off the weapon before replacing it in its sheath.

Kirkbane leaned over the railing and spotted Hacam standing in the shadows on the quay below him. Hacam was already slipping off the straps of the bulky rucksack he was carrying. Though the flank of the yacht was only as far away from Hacam as the width of the several old truck tires used to keep it from chafing against the quay, the deck was nearly ten feet higher than the edge of the dock. Because of the absence of the gangplank, he felt it would be easier to climb on board the way Kirkbane had than attempt to clamber up the side. Before starting for the prow of the yacht, he removed a small nylon cord from the rucksack, tied one end of it to the pack's back straps and then tossed the remaining length of the cord up to Kirkbane. With some considerable effort, the little Palestinian heaved the heavy pack up onto the deck while Hacam swung hand over hand on the forward mooring line to board the yacht.

Five minutes later, Kateb, another Palestinian, boarded in the same acrobatic way, and five minutes after that, Cheikh, a fourth Fedayin, joined them on deck as well. As their accomplice Frank Woods had promised, none of the cabin doors were locked. Before long, the four Fedayeen had made their way to the wheelhouse.

It was 3:56; it would soon be dawn. The Palestinians removed the weapons that Hacam had packed on top of the other equipment in the rucksack. Modeled after the old German Schnell-Pistole Mauser, the guns were actually nine-millimeter Soviet Stechkin machine pistols. Fully automatic, they could fire off all twenty-two rounds in their cartridge clip in three seconds.

With their pistols in hand, Hacam, Kateb and Cheikh followed Kirkbane out of the wheelhouse onto the deck. Outside, he moved quickly and quietly. When they reached the hatch leading to the hallway in the crew's quarters, Kirkbane once again removed his slender awl from its sheath. Seven steps, Woods had said. Kirkbane counted them off. Moving his hand along the wall, he came to the first door on the left, found the knob and turned it. The portlights filtering through the cabin curtains in the room enabled him to distinguish a human form. Brian Joshman was sleeping on his left side with his back to the door. His top sheet had slipped off him and now lay in a crumpled pile on the floor. Kirkbane struck. The captain's regular snoring suddenly ceased.

Moving to the next cabin, the young Palestinian executed the other three sailors in exactly the same way. Unfortunately, the first mate was sleeping on his back. He was an extremely thin man and the bony outline of his rib cage looked quite frail in the light. Kirkbane shoved his little weapon directly between the man's fifth and sixth ribs, deep into his heart. Leaving it in up to the hilt, he grabbed the pillow at the head of the bunk, pushed it down over the sailor's face and then leaned on it with all his might. Beneath him, the dying man went into convulsions that lasted for nearly twenty-five seconds. Finally the body seemed to stiffen into motionlessness. But the first mate had a final convulsion when Kirkbane, having stood up, pulled the pillow off his face. For one brief instant the mate's blood came frothing up out of his nose and mouth, and then he lay still.

The four Fedayeen carried Frank Woods's body down into the forward cabin and heaved it up onto his bunk. They closed the doors to the crew's quarters and then locked the deck hatch. Hacam checked his watch. It was 4:21. In silence, the four men returned to the wheelhouse.

The weather was beautiful. The air was dry, windless and hot, and the sea was flat. To the east, the first faint glimmerings of dawn were beginning to appear behind the town. Soft outlines of the buildings were taking shape against the sky.

The interior of the wheelhouse had the discreet charm of an English drawing room. Taking a quick look around, Hacam satisfied himself that the layout Woods had given him was both precise and complete. In any case, he wouldn't have been worried. He had spent most of his childhood and adolescence first as a cabin boy and later as a quartermaster on a pilot boat in the Suez Canal.

At 4:40 Hacam turned over the portside engine after giving the cylinders two minutes of electric preheating. The 2,600-horsepower diesel came to life quickly and quietly without producing the slightest trace of hull vibration. He repeated the procedure on the starboard side, and the sound of the two great engines rose up to him in the wheelhouse in a harmonious murmur. Checking his tachometers, he reduced the diesels' idling speed from 400 to 250 revolutions per minute.

Hacam leaned back and lit a cigarette. Occasionally, he glanced down at the engine thermostats while he waited for the needles to rise up into the green area on the dials. Twenty minutes later, everything was "go," and yet he waited another five minutes before casting off, because he was determined to follow his prearranged timetable exactly.

At 5:06, he signaled to Kirkbane to cast off the bowlines. Cheikh, in the stern, did the same. Without altering the rpm's of either engine, Hacam slipped the starboard transmission into reverse for a moment and then put it back into neutral. The bow of the *Rosebud* swung slowly away from the quay. When it was sufficiently clear of its anchorage, Hacam slipped the portside engine into forward and pulled the starboardside engine into reverse, whereupon the yacht began to pivot in place. When the bow was pointing almost directly toward the harbor entrance, Hacam slipped the starboard engine into forward again. The yacht began to move forward slowly. Taking hold of the helm, he headed out of the pleasure port at a speed of five knots, according to harbor regulations. After passing the farthest point of the port jetty, he slowly increased the speed of the diesels until they were both finally turning over smoothly at 1,400 rpm's. Once the *Rosebud* had reached its medium cruising speed, he put the yacht into a wide, twenty-degree turn.

Outside the port, in the Bay of Sainte-Maxime, the sea remained calm and the sky cloudless. Three peasant fishing boats were drifting slowly out to sea off the port side of the yacht in the Bay of Canebiers. Hacam increased the rpm's of the engines up to 1,600 and then checked the ship's speedometer to be sure that it was cruising at an even twenty-two knots—1,600 rpm's, twenty-two knots. Woods had not erred.

Hacam checked the digital log on the autopilot. Joshman had set it at zero the night before. He then fixed his eye on a point on the horizon at the end of an imaginary line that passed through the approximate center of the four-mile distance between the black beacon of the Basse Rabiou and the rocky endlands called the Sardinaux. The needle on the compass came around slowly and then settled at a heading of exactly southeast.

Hacam called Kirkbane. "Take the helm and keep the compass at one thirty-five. Don't touch anything else. If anything goes wrong, call me."

Searching quickly through the chart rack, Hacam had no problem finding the yacht's navigational map for the Tyrrhenian Sea. Spreading it out on the chart table, he noticed with a certain smile that Joshman had traced off two possible routes for the *Rosebud* to follow along the coastline between Marseille and Messina. To head south from Saint-Tropez to the straits of Sicily one could hug either the eastern or the western coasts of Corsica and Sardinia. Hacam, though, had no choice. He found his heading at a point between the Basse Rabiou and the lighthouse of Camarat and plotted his course accordingly. The point he had chosen was situated fifteen miles north of the island of Capraia and twenty-seven miles off Cape Corse. Moving back to the helm where Kirkbane was standing, he switched on the automatic pilot.

"It's all right," he said. "You've been replaced by a machine. Why don't you go below and make us some coffee."

There was nothing left to do then but wait. The three Fedayeen installed themselves comfortably in the main salon. Kirkbane appeared shortly with the coffee. At eight o'clock, Hacam climbed up the ladder that led to the flying bridge. There was neither another ship nor a coastline in sight. When he descended, he told Cheikh and Kateb that it was time to get ready.

The two Palestinians made their way forward to the wheelhouse and carefully unpacked their equipment from Hacam's rucksack—a heavy telescopic tripod, a sixteen-millimeter Coutan movie camera and a Stella Vox tape recorder equipped with a sensitive microphone and a soundman's headset. All the equipment was new and professional.

After setting up the tripod near the rear of the fantail so that he'd be shooting with the sun to his back, Cheikh mounted the camera in place. Then, with his eye riveted to the viewfinder, he checked the rotation of the tripod head and the self-adjusting focus on the zoom lens. Satisfied, he slipped a magazine containing five hundred feet of Ektachrome color film into place on top of the camera. He had enough film for twelve minutes' shooting. He then quickly checked the camera motor to be sure it was functioning properly and took a light reading with the latest Japanese meter on the market.

Hacam watched his companion's precise and efficient movements with serene satisfaction. Kateb had gone to install his microphone in the main salon. They didn't intend to use their sound equipment until the second phase of their filming.

Kirkbane and Kateb joined them on the fantail. It was 8:30. The three Fedayeen glanced at Hacam inquiringly. "Let's go," he said.

Kirkbane and Kateb, their pistols drawn, headed down into the hallway leading to the passengers' cabins. They opened the first door.

Sabine Fargeau was sleeping nude on a bed at the far side of the cabin. Kateb tapped on the open door with the barrel of his pistol. The girl opened her eyes, rolled over and then froze at the sight of the two Arabs and their guns. Stunned, she made no attempt to cover her nudity.

"Get up," Kateb snapped, "you and your friends are now prisoners of the Palestine Liberation Organization. Just do what we tell you to and nothing will go wrong. Go and wake the others. We'll follow you."

"My grandfather will pay the ransom," Sabine stammered.

"Shut up."

Waiting on the fantail, Hacam was getting impatient. He shouted down the hall, "What the fuck's going on down there? All you have to do is yank their asses out of bed and tie their hands together."

"They're awake," Kirkbane squealed back. "But two of them are naked."

Hacam smiled. He heaved his weight over to the ramp and shouted down to his partner.

"Then send them up naked!"

8

Hacam returned to the fantail and told Cheikh, "Did you hear that? The girls are all coming out naked. Don't let it distract you, and be sure to shoot them full on. We want that on the film."

"I wouldn't have it any other way."

"It can only increase its impact."

The girls appeared shortly on the fantail, their hands tied behind their backs, their faces terror-stricken. All their modesty overshadowed by the intensity of their fear, they moved slowly out into the sunlight in a daze. Nevertheless, they looked superb. Mechanically, following Kirkbane's instructions, they lined themselves up facing the camera, approximately ten feet in front of the lens. Cheikh started shooting, then stopped momentarily.

"Have them move back a little," he said.

The girls immediately stepped back three feet. Bending over his viewfinder again, Cheikh checked to be sure he had all five of them, full length, in the camera's field of vision. The camera started with a soft, electric whirr as he panned first over the whole line of them and then came back slowly to zoom in close on each one of the girls' frightened faces. When Helène appeared in his viewfinder, he let the camera linger for a while on her breasts. A large drop of perspiration had formed at her left underarm. As it started to run down the side of her breast it left a slender glistening trail of moisture on her skin.

Joyce Donovan's eyes had clouded over, her heartbeat had weakened and her nerves were cracking. She slumped back limply against Helène who, although her hands were tied behind her, managed to break her friend's fall by catching her against her thigh. Cheikh had filmed the sequence in its entirety before stopping the camera once more. He checked the film counter. He'd used up a hundred twenty feet; three minutes, twenty seconds' worth.

"I've got everything I need," he said.

"Untie their hands," Hacam ordered Kirkbane, "and take the little one who fainted inside."

Turning, he said to Sabine, "Try to revive her, then go back to your cabins. Get dressed and rejoin us in the main salon. Kirkbane, you go with them."

The girls were gone for only a few minutes and returned wearing jeans and T-shirts. The American girl had regained consciousness, but Sabine had to help her along. Hacam was lounging very nonchalantly in the corner of one of the salon's plush sofas, smoking a cigarette, with his feet propped up on the low English coffee table in front of him. Six comfortable club chairs were arranged in a semicircle around the other side of the table.

"Sit down, mesdemoiselles," Hacam said courteously.

They complied. With the exception of Joyce, they had now all regained some composure and some of the color came back to their cheeks. Hacam spoke calmly. "I assume that you have a rough understanding of the situation you're in. You are our prisoners and will be used as the merchandise we have to barter with. You will be released one after the other as each of our demands is successively satisfied."

"I've already told you my grandfather will give you all the money you want," Sabine exclaimed.

"It's not a question of money, mademoiselle. The only importance your family fortunes have in our eyes is the corresponding worldwide prestige they lend to our names. Our motives are purely political."

"You're members of the Black September?" Helène interjected.

"I see no reason to hide it from you."

"What have you done with the crew?" Sabine interrupted.

Hacam had already decided how to answer this question. "Don't count on them," he said. "They were knocked out last night and taken off the yacht while it was still in port, so forget about them. You've all got some hard times in front of you now. For some of you, it could last for weeks, for others, it might go on for months. But if you behave calmly and with some intelligence, you'll have nothing to fear from us and it will make all of our lives a lot easier."

"Considering the position you have us in, I don't see how we could behave in any other way," Helène said contemptuously.

"All I want to do is avoid scenes of hysterics or panic on your part, mademoiselle, which for instance might inspire you to jump overboard in an attempt to escape. By the way, do you all speak French?"

They nodded.

"For the time being," Hacam continued, "you will all remain on board the *Rosebud*. Tomorrow morning, however, you will be transferred to another boat. For obvious reasons, you will have to be blindfolded. It is for your own future security. If one of you should see even the smallest detail of anything we're trying to hide from you, it would make it impossible for us ever to release you."

He leaned forward and stubbed his cigarette out in an ashtray on the table and then continued. "Are you the Greek?" he asked, pointing at Helène.

"I'm French by birth, but Greek by my father. My family has neither money nor power."

"We know all that, Mlle. Nikolaos. And we also know that you've been studying drama for two years at the Conservatoire de Paris."

"How did you know that?" Helène asked with surprise.

Hacam ignored the question and continued. "Well, now you're going to have a chance to put your talent to work on worldwide television. Here's your script. Study it. In one hour, we're going to put you on film. You're going to be a star, mademoiselle, a great international star."

It was nearly ten o'clock when Cheikh and Kateb finished setting up their equipment to film with synchronized sound. Cheikh had removed the polarized sun filter from the camera lens in order to shoot inside. Kateb had placed the microphone on the coffee table so that it could pick up Helène's voice from the couch where she was seated.

"Wait a minute," Kateb said. "I want to run a sound test." Putting on the earphones, he pointed to Helène and said, "Count."

Methodically, she started counting out loud.

"All right," he interrupted, "that's fine. Kirkbane, tell the girls to come inside now."

When they appeared, Kateb placed them on the sofa near Helène, but outside the camera's field of view. Marian, who came last, was shoved up beside the others.

"Stay where you are and keep your mouths shut while we're shooting," he ordered.

"Are you ready?" Hacam asked.

"Anytime," Kateb replied.

"And you?" he asked Helène.

"Yes, I guess so."

"Okay, let's go."

Kateb hunched over his viewfinder, focused briefly once

again on Helène, raised his hand and said, "Go." Calmly, and staring straight ahead, Helène launched into her monologue.

"My name is Helène Nikolaos. My friends Sabine Fargeau, Joyce Donovan, Gertrud Fryer and Marian Carter and I are prisoners of the Palestine Liberation Organization. We do not know where we're going to be taken, but we have been assured that our whereabouts cannot be discovered by any of the world's intelligence services. Each time you comply with the Palestinians' demands, one of us will be released. The first of these demands is insignificant and yet it will allow one of us to be freed. Today, the Palestine Liberation Organization demands only that this film be shown on every major television network in the Western world during prime time, that is, at eight P.M. Whatever commentaries newscasters may wish to make following the projection of the film will be the responsibility of the network directors. However, the opinions reflected in these commentaries will in no way alter the agreement. The liberation of one of my friends is solely dependent on the film being shown on time and in its entirety.

"The Palestine Liberation Organization has insisted that this film be shown in its entirety because, as you will soon see, we have been filmed in the nude. This insignificant violation of the public's sense of decency, they feel, will expedite the governments' compliance to their demands. This in turn will permit the Organization to demonstrate to the world that it will stand by its word, by freeing the first hostage. If, however, you should refuse to comply with its demands, the Organization will be forced to show that it is dead serious and it will then be one of our bodies which will be found.

"It's hardly necessary to tell you of our fear. Help us. You represent the strongest force in the world: public opinion. Collectively, you can do anything. Don't for a moment doubt it. We appeal to you. In the event of a happy outcome to all this, the girl who's released will have another film with her, which will contain further instructions. However, a fixed condition will be attached to each further liberation, which is that every new film must be projected in its entirety.

"Now you will see what happened on our yacht following its hijacking at sea. Good-bye." She then folded up the typed monologue and quickly handed it back to Hacam, who was staring at her impassively.

For the next nineteen hours, the *Rosebud* continued on her course of south-southeast. Hacam had changed his original heading once he had passed Cape Corse and then later had verified his calculations by taking sightings off the islands of Elba and Monte Cristo.

Nearing Sicily, the yacht avoided the Strait of Messina and instead swung around the western side of the island past Marsala. Luck remained on their side; the following day at dawn there were no other ships in sight and the sea was glassy. Tardets' eighteen-meter Baglietto was waiting for them.

The girls were blindfolded, and then Kirkbane, Cheikh and Kateb transported them from the *Rosebud* to Tardets' yacht. They were locked below in a cabin that had been outfitted with five bunks. The portholes in the cabin had been blacked out, and the girls weren't able to see anything outside.

Hacam remained on board the *Rosebud* alone. Rechecking his exact position on a chart of the eastern Mediterranean, he programmed a new heading into the autopilot, set the throttles at 1,400 rpm's and slipped both hydraulic transmissions back into forward. As the *Rosebud* started to move slowly ahead, the Baglietto pulled up alongside her again and Hacam jumped on board. For a while, the two yachts moved through the sea parallel to one another. Then the Baglietto turned north, leaving the abandoned *Rosebud* cruising at a speed of twenty knots, heading almost due east.

For the next forty-eight hours, the Baglietto moved at a reduced speed in a large circle around the islands of Sardinia and Corsica. On the third night, at two in the morning, the girls, blindfolded once again, were put ashore on the eastern coast of Corsica. A small, canvas-backed truck drove them to the residence of Adrien Tardets. At 3:18 the same morning, they were locked in the cellar beneath his house.

9

In spite of the pain caused by the effort, Nahoum Zabra refused to slow down. Sweating heavily, he was rowing as hard as he could. Having left from one point on the beach, he was returning to another spot a hundred yards farther down after feeding out a long line of fishnet in a large semicircle. Six fishermen stood together in a small group on the beach delightedly watching Zabra sweating through his self-imposed ordeal. They thought he was highly eccentric to be rowing so hard simply for exercise. They performed the same tasks every day, but for them it was a livelihood.

Nahoum Zabra was the chief curator of the historical sites of Caesarea, considered by the nation's archeologists to be the richest excavations in the entire state of Israel. Three miles away, the little fishing village of Sdot Yam perched on the edge of an immense gray strand of sand. It was just off this beach that the curator was attending to his excess fat.

While the fishermen were sorting through their morning's catch, many of which were still flopping around on the sand, Zabra's eye was caught by a small white dot that had appeared on the horizon. Boats were not unusual in this area; nevertheless, this one intrigued him. It wasn't following the normal course for ships coming from Greece or Cyprus to Haifa. It hadn't come from Tel Aviv either; it was sailing too far from the coast. Zabra thought that it might be a ship conducting some kind of underwater archeological survey, or perhaps a private yacht heading toward Caesarea to visit the ruins on the isthmus there. After a while there was no doubt about it. The boat was cruising directly toward the imposing Citadel of Croises constructed in 1251 by Saint Louis at the tip of the natural breakwater that protected the port of Caesarea.

Zabra reached the shore. Now the fishermen as well were contemplating the white dot growing larger on the horizon. Zabra hurried on. He had to walk ten minutes before reaching the dirt road above the beach where he'd parked his old Chevrolet. Once at the car, he turned to look at the boat again. He opened the trunk and took out a large beach towel to protect the upholstery on his front seat. His clothes were wringing wet with sweat. Looking back out to sea, he noticed that the boat had drawn considerably closer, but its course seemed very strange. Perhaps it was an optical illusion, but it now appeared to be heading straight for the fishermen standing on the beach. By now, he could also see quite clearly that it was a yacht. It was magnificent. He decided to wait and see if he could figure out what it was doing. Its course seemed totally incomprehensible. Ten more minutes passed and the captain still hadn't corrected his heading. After another minute, still seated behind the wheel of his car and transfixed by the oncoming yacht, Zabra muttered, "My God! What in the hell are they doing?"

On the beach, the fishermen were in a minor uproar, shouting among themselves and flailing the air with their arms. Their agitation confirmed his apprehensions. Zabra knew the offshore seabed well. In addition, he had a fairly good idea of how much water the hull of the yacht would draw. If it continued along on the same course, within a minute or two it would run aground. It was now no more than five hundred yards from the beach and still hadn't slowed down in the least. Bolting from his car, he sprinted back down off the road and onto the beach, yelling toward the yacht and waving his arms above his head. It was a futile gesture. Twenty yards from the fishermen, he stopped, stupefied. The sand beneath his feet shivered sickeningly with a dull, slow, grinding sound. Offshore, the yacht's stern seemed to rise momentarily up all the way out of the water, and then the whole ship settled slowly over on its side into a huge roiling boil of sandy yellow water.

Seconds later, the concussive wave generated by the grounded yacht surged up onto the beach almost as high as the fishermen's knees, refloating the bulk of their morning's catch. Its energy spent, the swell throbbed back down off the beach toward the yacht again, its crest littered with the dead and bloated fish swept from the shore, until it pushed past the stern. There its surface took on the oily, iridescent gleam of the diesel fuel now spreading out in an oval around the rear of the yacht.

It was just past six o'clock in the morning. Along the whole, empty gray strand of the beach, Zabra and the six fishermen were the only witnesses to the event. The strangest part of the whole thing was that there still appeared to be no sign of life on the decks. Nahoum thought it would be better to climb on board before calling for help. It could be done easily. He would simply have to swim out a few yards and then crawl up onto the exposed port side of the hull. The starboard deck railing by now was lying just beneath the surface of the water. He turned to the fishermen. "Three of you come with me," he said. "The rest of you stay here on the beach in case anything goes wrong."

He handed the contents of his pockets to one of the fishermen and then waded out into the water. When it reached his chest, he started to swim. In a few minutes, he'd come to the prow of the yacht and clambered up onto

the deck. Hanging onto the portside railing, he made his
way to the stern. When he reached the grand salon, he tried
the door and found it unlocked. After opening it and crawl-
ing inside, he paused for a minute to look around. The
three fishermen behind him were astounded by the opulence
of the deserted room.

"Anybody here?" Zabra shouted.

Hearing no reply, he inched his way forward, hanging
on to the furniture bolted to the floor, toward the hallway
that led to the main cabins below. After checking each of
these and finding them all empty as well, he was really
perplexed. Intelligent as he was, he could not come up with
an explanation.

At the end of the hallway there was a staircase leading
up to the crew's wardroom. After crossing the wardroom
and the adjoining chart area he finally reached the wheelhouse. The silence was unnerving. The air had a faintly
nauseous smell. Holding on to the helm and looking out
through the windows before him, he noticed another part
of the superstructure a few feet above the deck just behind
the bow.

Turning to the fisherman standing beside him, he said,
"Check down there. There must be more cabins."

There were two sliding doors on either side of the wheelhouse that opened out onto the bridge. The fisherman
opened the one on the left, climbed outside and then side-
stepped toward the stairs that led to the main deck below,
with his back up flat against the side of the wheelhouse.

Searching through the materials scattered around the
chartroom, Zabra came across all the yacht's navigational
and legal documents—the charts, photobooks of coastal
profiles, channel maps of the major tourist ports in the
Mediterranean, the fat log of international maritime laws
and the log of the *Rosebud*. Finally, he found what he was
looking for in a cabinet by the radar screen, the yacht's
official French registration. On the second page of the

document there was a photograph of the man who owned the yacht. Zabra recognized the face immediately. Glancing just below the picture, he saw the man's name printed in large, block letters. Just as he had expected, it said, CHARLES-ANDRÉ FARGEAU. Nationality: FRENCH. Occupation: INDUSTRIALIST. Domicile: DOMAINE FARGEAU, 78120. RAMBOUILLET, FRANCE. He took a deep breath and then let out a long, low whistle.

Zabra followed the fisherman down the stairs. The stench permeating the air gave them some glimmering of what they would soon find. The door had been bolted. It took them ten minutes to find a screwdriver, but it was impossible to force it.

A quarter of an hour later, his clothes soaked with saltwater and sweat, Nahoum Zabra was sitting behind the wheel of his Chevrolet hurtling down the road toward Caesarea.

Zabra drove to the nearest hotel, ran past the cleaning woman and the night receptionist in the lobby, who both looked up in surprise, toward the telephone booths at the end of the hall.

Commissioner Golam answered the phone.

Commissioner Golam joined Zabra back on the beach forty minutes later. After having swum out to the grounded yacht to verify the unbelievable information the archeologist had given him over the phone, Golam returned to the beach and gave instructions to the technicians he had brought with him. When he had finished, Zabra spoke up.

"Well, what do you think?"

"Incredibly messy business."

"Have you contacted anybody else?"

Golam's reply was cut short by the sudden appearance behind him of a light observation helicopter moving toward the beach at very high speed. Passing directly over their heads with a scream, the jet-powered chopper wheeled up on its side into a tight, skidding turn out over the water around the stern of the *Rosebud*. In the middle of the turn, the rotors slapping against the sky resounded across the sea like heavy machine-gun fire. Coming around from behind the grounded yacht, the little chopper flared up on its tail for an instant and then settled down and headed back toward the beach at a slow, screaming hover. Shortly after it landed, Colonel David Fulham and Yefet Hamlekh stepped out onto the sand, accompanied by a captain and an ensign who had been contacted at their naval base thirty-seven miles away.

Zabra and the commissioner reported what they had discovered inside the second cabin of the enormous yacht—the five bodies of the murdered ship's crew, tied up in blood-soaked gunnysacks. At 10:45 A.M. in the central Hadera police headquarters, the naval officers dictated their findings to a secretary. In his own office, Golam typed out his brief personally. At 11:30, the combined findings of all the agencies involved in the investigation were handed over to the Shin-Beth officials, in triplicate, in the dining room of the old Achdar pension.

Hamlekh and Fulham read the briefs simultaneously. The naval officers had included a general map of the Mediterranean in their file. Fulham's military background enabled him to decipher all the technical navigational terms the two officers had used in their brief. He explained their findings to Hamlekh.

"Do you see this penciled line here starting from where the yacht ran aground? It was figured from readings taken off the last headings fed into the automatic pilot."

"How accurate is this particular model? Have you allowed for any margin of error?"

"It's accurate to within one second of one degree. Like every other piece of equipment on that yacht, it's the finest money can buy. The key to the whole system is a small computer that can accommodate for wind drift, currents, bad weather, you name it. So the navy boys feel the hijackers must have had this spot in mind when they fed their headings into the autopilot. On the other hand, the computer's timing mechanism wasn't turned on. To quote the navy's brief, 'In all probability, the timer was deliberately left off.' "

"I'm having trouble following you, Fulham. I don't have a very thorough understanding of the mechanics of navigation."

"It's very simple. A sailor is calculating his route on a map. He traces a straight line from the point where he is to the point where he wants to go. A compass card, which you could learn to use in less than half an hour, when placed over the line, will give you the exact heading you have to follow. At random, let's say the heading you've taken off your compass card is two hundred eighty degrees. If you're going to follow this route by manning the helm yourself, you have to keep the needle on your compass at two hundred eighty as long as the boat is under way. But if you want to navigate with the assistance of an autopilot, all you have to do is feed your heading directly into the system's computer. Simultaneously, you set the autopilot's timer for the number of hours you want to cruise in that direction. The computer takes care of the rest. The deductions of the captain then are very logical.

"The hijackers didn't want us to be able to determine the exact point at which they abandoned the yacht. With the data we've been able to gather in the wheelhouse and our estimate of the yacht's range, we've only been able to establish one thing for sure: the *Rosebud* was abandoned at some point along this line—that is, somewhere between here and Ibiza. It would have been impossible for the yacht to have been abandoned near the Spanish mainland, because it would have run into Ibiza. At other spots along this line, however, it nearly touches Bizerte, passes directly between Sicily and Malta and then comes close to Crete before running aground here. But we've checked with the ship's log and we know she was in Saint-Tropez three days ago. It makes much more sense to think that she came down through the Strait of Messina and was abandoned only a few hours ago. This would mean they boarded another boat somewhere at sea. The second boat could then have taken the passengers either to Egypt or Lebanon. Do you follow me?"

"Only too well."

At 12:45 the two men were back in Tel Aviv. At 12:53 a coded cable was transmitted to S.D.E.C.E. headquarters on the Boulevard Mortier in Paris. It was addressed to a Colonel de Savigny, and marked "Highly urgent." Shortly after one, Hamlekh walked over to the Herbert Samuel Esplanade to meet with the French ambassador to Israel.

At the Quai D'Orsay, the French Minister of Foreign Affairs received the news half an hour later. Picking up the old interministerial phone built into the front of his desk, he dialed the personal number of the Minister of the Interior, Raymond Marcellin.

"De Savigny just called here about it," Marcellin said. "He wants me to try and keep the French National Police out of the whole affair until his men at the S.D.E.C.E. have something solid to go on."

"I think that'd be a good idea."

"So do I, but I didn't want to give him anything until I'd spoken with you first."

"Well, give de Savigny all the help you can."

"Yes, sir."

After Marcellin hung up, he had himself reconnected with the colonel.

"I've just spoken with the Minister of Foreign Affairs," he said. "The National Police will stay out of it until they can be of some real assistance to you. For now, Colonel, the top priority case of the special services has one name: Charles-André Fargeau."

10

At 3:15, Laurent Martin stepped out of a taxi on the Avenue Kleber in front of the Fargeau Building. Savigny had had no problems contacting him at the Dolmen Restaurant in the new Montparnasse station. Martin was not looking forward to the potential messiness of the mission he had just been assigned.

The Fargeau Building, seven stories high, was new, simple and elegant. The central administrative offices of each of Fargeau's largest firms were located on the first five floors. In addition to Fargeau Steel, the building also housed the Maritime Petroleum Transport Corporation, the C. A. Fargeau Construction Corporation, Fargeau Rocket Propulsion Laboratories (a division of which specialized in the development of surface-to-air and surface-to-surface missiles) and Fargeau Militaire, an offshoot of the research laboratories that fabricated lightweight amphibious missile launchers. Fargeau Militaire had recently acquired some notoriety by selling an undisclosed number of the vehicles to the U.S.S.R.

The editorial and administrative offices of the weekly magazine *Femmes de France* were installed on the sixth floor. Catering to the tastes of the nation's fashion- and status-conscious leisure class, the magazine was devoured at the rate of a million copies a week. Its glossy, full-color pages were filled with the latest news on Parisian fashions, the international jet set and the surviving European aristocracy. Fargeau's curious attachment to the magazine had long been looked upon as something of an enigma by the other professional members of the publishing trade. He had started it as a hobby and had sunk a small fortune into the magazine getting it on its feet. However, in the last five years the situation had reversed to the point where it was now not only holding its own but showing a fine year-end profit as well.

Five uniformed ushers were stationed in a tinted-glass control booth in the lobby. Upon seeing the agent enter the building, one of them stepped forward smartly.

"Good day, sir. May I help you?"

"Yes. I have an appointment with M. Fargeau."

"You are M. Martin?"

"Yes."

"We've been expecting you, sir. Take the seventh-floor elevator there, the one on the far left."

"Each floor has its own elevator?"

"Yes, sir."

"Thank you very much."

Once inside the elevator, Martin was whisked silently to the top floor in a matter of seconds. When the doors opened, he found himself in a massive reception room staffed with no fewer than six secretaries. The office was completely quiet, and none of the women even so much as glanced up at him. One of the secretaries was on the phone. *"Oui, monsieur. Merci. Au revoir."* Looking up, she saw Martin and said, "Just a moment, please."

She pushed a button on the intercom. "M. Fargeau, M. Martin is here."

Immediately, a gruff yet polished voice replied, "Send him in."

"This way, please," she said to Martin.

At the end of the reception room she opened one of two heavy leather-padded doors. Fargeau's office could have accommodated a tennis court. At one end of the room there was a conference table surrounded by thirty high-backed leather chairs. Each place at the table had a small microphone and an earphone headset built into a console in front of it. Charles-André Fargeau's desk stood majestically in the opposite corner of the room, facing a semicircle of six deep club chairs upholstered in dark green leather. Between each of the chairs there was a small table with a lamp and another integrated console. Martin suddenly realized that the four glass booths he'd seen in the outer office were intended for simultaneous translators during international business conferences. With the exception of the partition behind Fargeau's desk, the walls of the room were composed entirely of sliding brown-tinted glass panels.

Charles-André Fargeau stood up and stepped around from behind his desk to greet Martin. The agent was pleasantly surprised by the friendliness of the gesture. The room had such an air of power about it that Martin had felt momentarily as if he were in the presence of a monarch.

At the age of seventy-six, Fargeau stood as straight and solid as a young soldier, though his overall bearing was distinctly aristocratic. His hands, long-fingered and fine, had never known manual labor. His skin was sun bronzed and taut, his nose straight and his hair, though still thick, was now silver. His clear, sharp eyes moved over Martin with a kind of quick, liquid curiosity before he extended his hand and invited him to sit down.

Dressed simply but elegantly, the old millionaire was wearing a light beige linen suit, a pale blue sea-island cotton shirt and a solid navy-blue knit tie. He spoke slowly, clearly enunciating each syllable. "I'm pleased to meet you, Martin. Your name has been mentioned in this room on several occasions."

"Favorably, I hope."

Fargeau laughed. "No, not always. But respectfully."

Martin leaned back in his chair and took one of his cigarettes from their little red metal box. He lit it without offering one to Fargeau, whom he knew neither smoked nor drank. He inhaled deeply, then came straight to the point. "This morning we were notified by the Israeli secret service that your yacht, the *Rosebud*, had run aground on the coast between Tel Aviv and Haifa. The bodies of five crewmen were discovered in one of the forward cabins. There was no trace of your granddaughter or her four friends, though according to the ship's log, they were on board when it left Saint-Tropez. It was under the guidance of the autopilot when it ran aground. The Israeli navy was able to determine the angle of the course it had followed, but not the point where it was abandoned."

Fargeau froze momentarily. His eyes caught Martin's head-on and his hands, which moments before had rested lightly on the surface of his desk, now whitened at the knuckles. The agent did not avert his gaze. Quickly regaining his self-composure, the old man spoke up softly. "Are you aware of the fact that I'm Jewish?"

"Yes. You don't think they were abducted by anyone other than the Palestinians then?" Martin asked.

"M. Martin, I'm not in the habit of fooling myself about anything in order to make reality easier to bear. You said the *Rosebud* was deliberately directed toward the coast of Israel. I think this is a significant message in and of itself."

"I agree, but I wouldn't completely rule out the possibility that the girls were kidnapped for purely mercenary reasons. Whatever the kidnappers' motives may be, though, I think we can reasonably assume that the girls are still alive."

"Hopefully," Fargeau said. "At least it seems to me that if they had been murdered, their bodies would have been left behind on the *Rosebud* as well. Who knows about this?"

"Six Israeli fishermen and an archeologist from Caesarea. They were witnesses to the grounding of the yacht. The

Hadera police, two top agents in the Shin-Beth, the French ambassador in Tel Aviv, the French Foreign Minister and the Minister of the Interior, and the two top men in the S.D.E.C.E."

"Can you exercise any pressure on the Israelis to remain silent until they receive notice from us?"

"That's been taken care of. As a matter of fact, they suggested it themselves."

"And here in France?"

"It's a little more delicate, but I think we can keep it hushed for a bit. If we inform the police, the press'll get wind of it immediately, but if we don't, they're going to scream like hell. The autopsies proved almost for certain that the crew was murdered three days before in French territorial waters at the beginning of the hijacking. Either way, when it all comes out into the open, the police will surely blame any blunders they may make on us—probably using the excuse that we gave them the facts in the case too late for them to act."

"I don't give a damn about the police. I can make the necessary arrangements with the minister. If I have to, I'll contact the Élysée."

Fargeau jabbed a button on his intercom. A secretary appeared in the doorway almost instantly. "Nicole, reserve four suites at the Hotel Raphael. I want them all on the same floor. I'll move in there myself this evening. Cable Donovan, Carter and Fryer and tell them to catch the first plane to Paris they can. Then call Nikolaos and tell him to get over here immediately. If he's not home, let me speak to his wife. Cancel all my appointments. I'm to be available to no one but the four men whose names I just gave you, plus M. Martin here and the Minister of the Interior. I might as well tell you right now that I'm expecting someone to attempt to blackmail me soon. . . . So if an unusual call should come through for me, I'll take it. That's all."

Martin admired the coolness of Fargeau's executive

secretary. Before turning smartly around and walking out of the office, she said simply, *"Oui, monsieur."*

"How can I get hold of you, Martin?"

Laurent jotted a number down on a card and handed it to the old man across the desk, explaining, "This is my security line. If I'm not there a tape recording will give you the number where I can be reached."

"Thank you."

As Martin rose to leave, Fargeau added, "Oh, Martin."

"Yes."

"I think there's one more thing you should know before you go."

"What's that?"

"Sabine is really the only thing I truly hold precious in my life."

11

Jean-Pierre Badinot worked in the basement clipping room of the Paris newspaper *France-Soir*. For the last three years he'd been sorting out the letters to the editor that arrived by the sackful each morning in the paper's mailroom. On the average, at least a third of the letters he opened were immediately thrown away. The rest were classified according to their topics and then filed. Particularly brilliant pieces of correspondence he summarized briefly on a small form which he then attached to the top of the letter.

He opened the next letter in his pile, scanned over all of its ten typewritten lines and then tossed it into the file marked "Nuts." He opened two more and was in the process of unsealing a third when some kind of gnawing suspicion in the back of his mind made him return to the letter he'd just thrown in the Nuts file. He read it through very carefully two more times and then examined the outside of the envelope. It had been postmarked in Nice the night before. It was signed "Black September." Paradoxically, that was the reason he had originally thrown it in the Nuts file—each week no fewer than a dozen crank letters passed over his desk with the signature "Black September."

This one, however, was particularly disconcerting. In simple, typewritten capital letters it said: "The yacht of Charles-André Fargeau, the *Rosebud,* has been commandeered with his granddaughter Sabine and four of her friends, Helène Nikolaos, Marian Carter, Joyce Donovan and Gertrud Fryer, on board. Simultaneously with the mailing of this letter we have posted a twelve-minute film reel and an accompanying sound track to the main office of the O.R.T.F. (Office de Radiodiffusion Télévision Française) on the Rue Cognacq-Jay. We demand that this film be shown immediately on nationwide television."

Jean-Pierre Badinot hated being laughed at by his superiors. He slipped the letter into his coat pocket, hurried out of the clipping room and bolted up the stairs to the fourth floor. There he pushed through the double doors opening onto the newsroom and set out down the long central corridor that bisected it. Just past the photo department he came to the steel staircase that spiraled upward around the freight-elevator shaft. The air was filled with the smell of fresh ink and the sound of the presses running two stories below. He sprinted up one more flight of stairs and then entered the offices of the F.E.P., a clipping service at the disposal of the paper as well as *Vogue* magazine and *France-Dimanche.* Each of the organizations had its own filing section, but they all had access to the central files.

At one side of the room, on ten large drafting tables, a group of news analysts were busy marking out and classifying, according to their special categories, the most important news, business, sports and social items in all the major European papers and magazines of the day.

"Do you have the dossier on Charles-André Fargeau?" Badinot asked the man on the filing counter.

"Which one? There must be about twenty of them."

"The most recent, everything from this year."

Three minutes later, sitting at a green felt table well scarred with cigarette burns, Badinot began thumbing through Fargeau's file, starting with the last entry. It didn't take him long to find a clipping from the paper *Nice-Matin* showing the old man surrounded by five exquisite young girls in the garden of the Byblos Hotel in Saint-Tropez. The photo had been taken from the social page of the Parisian edition of the paper. Below it, there was a caption giving the girls' names and saying that they were leaving the next day for a four-week cruise on Fargeau's yacht, the *Rosebud*, through the Greek islands.

The clipping was four days old. It didn't mean much, but he'd gone through the files expecting to find an open contradiction to the letter from "Black September" and had instead found an article confirming it.

He checked his watch. It was 11:05. The second edition was already going to press. Laury would give him three minutes. He made a quick photocopy of the clipping and then dashed upstairs to the news editor's office.

As usual, Laury was on the phone, staring vacantly at the ceiling with his feet propped up on his desk and his head resting on the back of his chair, listening to the impassioned sales pitch of a stringer in one of the provinces who was trying to get him to buy a feature on grape pickers. Every now and then he would yawn and issue an unconvinced grunt into the phone. Three other receivers were lying on his desk waiting to be answered. Occasionally a secretary would pick up one of the receivers and say, "Don't hang up. M. Laury will be with you in a moment."

"All right, I'll give you thirty lines," Laury said finally. "Hang on."

Badinot stepped up to the desk and thrust the note and clipping under his editor's nose. Immediately, Laury's eyes widened. He set down the phone and stabbed a button on his intercom.

"Get Guillaumin in here."

"He's on the fag murder in the *Bois*," a nameless voice responded.

"Then get Dobert, quickly."

"Right."

Dobert was the oldest staff writer on the paper. He took the papers Laury handed him without the slightest bit of interest and left the office without looking back. Once in the hallway, he started reading them. His pace quickened. Back in the city room, he picked up his private-line phone and started to dial the Fargeau Building. Halfway through dialing, he hung up. He paused for a second and reflected on the whole situation, and then picked up the phone again and dialed the number of the Office de Radiodiffusion Télévision Française, the O.R.T.F.

"Give me the courier's pool, please. Hello, is Marcel there? No? Well, this is Fernand Dobert calling from *France-Soir.*"

"Ah, Dobert. How are you? We met in fifty-five covering the Tour de France, do you remember? That was the year that outsider appeared out of nowhere and took the race."

"Walkowiak. Yes, I remember, but it was in fifty-six."

"Perhaps you're right. At any rate, what do you need? Is there anything I can do for you?"

"Well, yes, maybe you can. Did you receive anything that looks like a sixteen-millimeter film can from Nice this morning?"

"Yes, we were just talking about it. It came in by mail instead of with our usual courier. Normally any of the films that come in here are snatched up immediately by the guys in the photo lab. This one's been sitting here for two hours."

"Listen, this could be serious. Get everyone out of that office and don't touch that box."

"Are you kidding? What is it, a bomb?"

"I don't know. I don't think so, but you never know. How big a package is it?"

"It looks just like a sixteen-millimeter film reel in an

aluminum can. There's a bump on top of it that's probably a sound track."

"Okay. Well, switch me back to the operator then. Hello, hello . . . Shit!"

He hung up and redialed the number. "André Bordenave, please."

The secretary answered.

"M. Bordenave, please. This is Dobert at *France-Soir.*"

"I'm sorry, sir, M. Bordenave is in conference. Would you care to leave a message?"

Dobert knew he was in trouble. The girl had been hired for one purpose and one purpose only: to protect her employer from unwanted calls. Her voice told the whole story.

"No, go get him. It's a question of life or death."

"I'm sorry, sir, I have strict orders not to disturb him. You can reach him if you call back in an hour or an hour and a half." She was delighted, the bitch.

"Listen to me, *ma petite,*" Dobert snapped back. "In an hour and a half you're going to be job hunting in the 'Hire the Handicapped' column. Now get Bordenave!"

Dobert knew that would thrill her. There was an indignant huff on the other end of the line and then it went dead. Dobert slammed the phone down on his desk, grabbed the letter and clipping and headed for the door, swearing as he went. "Typical. Typical, stupid, thick-skulled dimwitted bitch. Stupid, stupid, stupid."

He raced across the city room and down the stairs. Outside, there were three taxis parked on the Rue Reaumur. Two of them were driverless. In the third, the cabbie was eating a sandwich and listening to the radio. Dobert opened the back door, jumped inside and prepared himself for the eternal midday argument with the cabbie, which he knew was soon to come. With his mouth full of food, the cabbie said, "Where do you think you're going?"

"O.R.T.F., Rue Cognacq-Jay."

"Not in this cab, you're not. I'm eating lunch."

"You are now going to drive me to the Rue Cognacq-Jay."

"Get out. I'm not going to ruin my lunch for a lousy three francs."

"Listen to me. Now listen," Dobert said slowly. "I've worked in that building there for twenty years and I know the words to your song. Tomorrow you can find someone else to buy your booze, but today, right now, you're going to drive me to the Rue Cognacq-Jay. It's either that or I get the cop on the corner and you pay the fine. What's it going to be?"

The cabbie glowered like a martyr in the rear-view mirror. Reluctantly, he started the car and then pulled away from the curb with a lurch. He grumbled all the way to the Rue Cognacq-Jay. "Even the pimps, thieves, assassins and junkies are eating at this hour, and I'm getting an ulcer for a lousy three francs. And do you think anybody gives a damn? Hell no. Jesus Christ himself is probably sitting down to a good lunch right now and me, I'm pushing a hack. I'll tell you, it's a sad, goddam world it is. . . ."

"Sounds like a personal problem to me," Dobert said. "If you shut up, I'll give you fifty centimes and you can call your priest and tell him all about it."

At the O.R.T.F. Building, Dobert jumped out and tossed the cabbie ten francs.

"I've thought it over," he said. "You're beyond any help the Church could provide. Get yourself a psychiatrist with the change. Oh yes, and I need a receipt for the fare too, please."

In the lobby, the elevator lights indicated the sixth and eighth floors. He took the stairs. On the third floor, he burst past a bewildered-looking security guard and strode on down the corridor toward the conference room with a great air of authority.

Without knocking, he pushed open the door to the Channel 1 newsroom. A news briefing was under way. Everyone looked up at the sudden intrusion. Almost all of them knew Dobert.

"Pardon me for interrupting you all," he said, "but I have some rather important news for you."

Though his friendship with Dobert was well known, André Bordenave looked a little annoyed. "Later, Fernand. We'll be done here shortly."

Jacqueline Boudrier, senior news editor, cut in. "What is it, Dobert?"

The old journalist stepped up to the conference table and set the letter and the clipping down in front of Bordenave and Jacqueline. Bordenave perused the documents, then handed them to his secretary to toss away. Jacqueline intervened.

"André, you haven't even looked at the clipping."

Bordenave lifted the letter and reread the clipping. "It doesn't mean a thing, Jacqueline. Look, the letter was mailed from Nice and the clipping is from *Nice-Matin*. The whole thing is obviously just the creation of some mad Niçois who saw the picture in the paper and felt inspired. I should think that after twenty years in this business you'd be aware of the fact that we get sacksful of this kind of stuff every day." As he spoke, Bordenave smiled condescendingly toward Dobert.

The newsman's patronizing attitude was too much. Dobert snapped back, "This clipping is from an edition of *Nice-Matin* that isn't even sold in Nice. It's from the Parisian social page."

"Well, what in the hell are you getting at?" Bordenave replied angrily. "I don't doubt your professional capacities but I know the business pretty well myself. Your letter says that a film and sound track would be sent to us the same day."

"André, there's an unclaimed film can downstairs in the courier's pool right now that's been sitting there for more than three hours."

Bordenave's eyes widened. Jacqueline checked her watch and then settled the matter. "This meeting is adjourned for thirty minutes."

They followed her out to the receiving room and hesitated before the box. "Stop this comedy. So you think it's a bomb? Well, I'll open it myself," she announced, ripping off the brown paper wrapping and removing the film can and sound track inside. She was not surprised. There was a small, stenciled note taped onto the outside of the film can.

"Operation Rosebud," it said. "Ektachrome film. To be developed normally. Exposure: 125 ASA."

"Take this film to the lab," she said curtly to Bordenave. "Then come back to my office. We'll wait for you before listening to the sound track. Tell them we want the film ready for projection in less than an hour. I presume you'll be attending the projection too, M. Dobert?"

A half hour later in the projection room, the lights dimmed off, and then the still blackness of the room was broken by the brilliant blue panorama of the Mediterranean projected on the screen. In a slow pan, the camera angle swung around to reveal the deserted port deck of the *Rosebud* before stopping finally on the door to the main salon, where shortly afterward, Sabine and her four companions appeared.

There was a hushed gasp from Jacqueline. In spite of the girls' beauty, the scene had something both sad and obscene about it. The fear on their faces, their total nudity, their frightened and awkward gestures; all this combined to make the whole exhibition unbearable. A hushed murmur rose up in the room, even though as newsmen almost all three of them were brought into direct contact with one atrocity or another nearly every day.

After the scene on the fantail, the film went blank for twenty seconds. Then suddenly, a closeup of Helène Nikolaos' face appeared on the screen. Her lips started moving, but the only sound in the room was the mechanical whirring of the projector. Jacqueline Baudrier jabbed a button on the intercom next to her. "That's enough, thank you. Rewind it now, please."

Bordenave leaned over toward Jacqueline. "If this is released, we've had it. Nothing could stop it from snowballing then."

"Don't be stupid, Bordenave. We're already in it up to our knees and there's nothing we can do about it."

As the lights came back on, an intercom voice announced the replay of the sound track. "We've already heard it," Jacqueline said into the intercom. "But as soon as it's synchronized with the film, make thirty copies. I want ten copies in English, ten in French and ten in German. And above all, keep your mouth shut about anything you've just seen."

A few minutes before four o'clock that afternoon, another screening was held in the same room. This time the sound track was in perfect synchronization with the film.

Few premieres ever attracted such a distinguished audience. In addition to the Prime Minister of France, the Ministers of the Interior, Foreign Affairs, Defense and Information, the general director of the National Police and the director of the O.R.T.F., Charles-André Fargeau, Georges Nikolaos, Laurent Martin, Colonel de Savigny of the S.D.E.C.E. and the Parisian representatives of all the major European television networks—B.B.C. (Britain), A.R.D. and Z.D.F. (West Germany), R.A.I. (Italy) and C.B.S.-Europe (U.S.A.)—were also in attendance. An extraordinary conference followed the projection.

At 6:45 P.M., in the south wing of the Élysée Palace, President Georges Pompidou and his closest advisors were shown the film. At 7:32, a decision was reached. The three major television networks in France would broadcast the film simultaneously at 8 P.M. that night. The decision by the French left the other Western governments no alternative, and at 8:01, the curtain rose on an international drama without precedent in history.

PART II

12

For the past forty-eight hours, the pulse of the whole world had been beating to the agonized rhythm of the progression of events in the kidnapping.

The divisional police commissioner Eugène Le Breton had been assigned to head the investigation into the murders of the crewmen on the *Rosebud*. He had immediately dispatched two of his own detectives to Tel Aviv. Another twenty of his investigators were given orders to compile a complete dossier on Sabine Fargeau's circle of friends as well as on all the friends and relatives of the murdered crewmen. But the man who remained responsible for all the major decisions in the case, and who served as the chief mediator between the families, the government representatives and the press corps, was Laurent Martin.

Within hours after he started working on the case, the French agent discovered that he had a very powerful friend in Charles-André Fargeau. The understanding, the clear, sound reasoning and the incredible influence of the old millionaire had been invaluable in counteracting the irrational ideas of all those involved who wanted Martin to leave immediately on a clandestine "fact-finding" tour of the Arab nations in the Middle East. Fargeau and Martin had finally managed to convince the authorities that only the release of the first hostage would really permit them to act on some truly valuable clues.

With the exception of the Nikolaoses, the families of the kidnapped girls had taken up residence on the fifth floor of the Hotel Raphael, where the government could keep them posted on the latest developments in the case. Day and night the hotel's lobbies swarmed with journalists, photographers and television crews sent on special assignment from all over the world to get anything they could on the families. In front of the hotel on the Avenue Kleber, no fewer than thirty policemen were on duty twenty-four hours a day to keep the crowds of curious onlookers from blocking traffic.

Coverage of the kidnapping had grown to the point where it dominated the news. Everyone was talking about the promised liberation of one of the girls. The slightest rumor was reason enough for another special edition of all the big papers. The number of "flash bulletins" on Western radio stations had quadrupled, and each quarter hour the announcers struggled to invent new phrases.

None of the major newspapers wanted to assume the responsibility for its own stories so each ascribed its dispatches to other foreign papers. "According to the London *Daily Mirror* . . ." their stories began, or "According to an editorial in the Hamburg *Morning Post* . . ."

Two days after the worldwide projection of the film, at eight o'clock in the morning, a little yellow Deux Chevaux mini mail truck rolled along through the vineyards of the Tardets estate. Coming up to the main gate, the mailman stopped the truck, climbed out and slipped Tardets' mail through a small slit cut into one side of the stone gateway.

From the house, the main gates could not be seen, but Tardets' practiced ear had caught the sound it was waiting for, the truck backing up, turning and then driving back on down the road.

With Hacam at the wheel, the old man climbed into the back seat of his Renault 4L. The two men motored slowly down the gravel drive that meandered along for nearly half a mile before reaching the main gates. While Hacam was turning the car around, Tardets unlocked his stainless steel Yale mailbox and retrieved the morning edition of the Corsican *Provençal* and the day's mail, four letters.

Tardets got back into the car and closed the door as Hacam slipped it into first gear. The old man went through the letters very carefully. The third one was postmarked *"Postampt in Hauptbahnof,"* the central post office in Hamburg. The address was typewritten: "Adrien Tardets, Prunelli-di-Fiumorbo par Ghisonaccia, 20, France."

"It's here," he said.

"Open it," Hacam replied.

Tardets pulled a small pocketknife out of his coat and slit open the letter along the top crease. Inside, there was a single piece of onionskin paper on which two words had been typewritten in lower-case letters: *"la grecque."*

Tardets read the laconic message out loud. Hacam nodded in agreement as they pulled up in front of the main house. After climbing out of the 4L, he took the letter from the old man's hand, checked it with a quick glance and then set both the letter and the envelope on fire with his lighter. When they had burned completely, he ground them into the gravel with his boot.

"Breakfast," Tardets said.

In the kitchen, Kirkbane, Cheikh and Kateb were all seated around the big wooden table watching Lualä, the cook, as she poured steaming hot coffee into their cups. The smell of the bacon she had simmering on the stove permeated the entire room. Hacam addressed her in Arabic. "You can go now. Neither you nor your husband are to return today. Do you understand?"

The woman bowed her head slightly and left the kitchen without asking for any explanations. Like Balir, her husband, she knew the value of her silence.

Hacam picked up the coffee, filled Tardets' cup and then his own. The two men sat down. Hacam took a sip. "It's the Greek," he announced. "Let's eat and then get on with it."

The three Arabs remained silent. Finally Tardets spoke up. "The choice seems debatable to me."

"To me, too," Hacam admitted. "But that's none of our business. I will repeat: we are soldiers and we do what our superiors tell us to do. I have received only one order—follow the instructions mailed from various German cities. The first one is Hamburg, the second one is Berlin. When I receive my next orders from Berlin, I will obey them without question. Those are my orders, my only orders, our only orders. I have complete confidence in them, and my chief in Beirut, who knows who is in charge, obviously wouldn't put himself in their hands if he didn't have complete faith in them as well. But that's enough on that. Let's go to work."

Leaving the old man in the kitchen, the four Fedayeen crossed the hallway and the office and unbolted the two massive doors leading to the cellar. Kirkbane was carrying a tray laden with coffee, milk and slices of buttered toast.

The five girls were lying on their cots. Helène Nikolaos was smoking, and Marian Carter was staring vacantly at the ceiling. The other three were asleep.

Kirkbane set the tray of toast and milk down on one of the wooden tables, picked up a water jug and filled a glass. He fished a tube of ten-milligram Valium tablets out of his shirt pocket, gently woke up the girls who were sleeping and then gave them each a pill.

Without complaining, they washed down the tablets with the water Kirkbane offered them. Helène set her half-smoked cigarette on the chipped saucer she used as an ashtray and held out her hand. Kirkbane, smiling, put the cap back on the tube of tranquilizers and replaced it in his pocket.

"No peace pills for you today, mademoiselle."

The other girls sat up instantly. This was the first time since they'd been locked up that their jailers had made the slightest variation in their daily routine. For the last three days the anguished solitude of their captivity had been broken only by their meals, the sound of one of the Arabs changing the buckets in their "bathroom" every four hours and the regular appearances of the little Arab with their Valium.

Hacam offered the explanation. "The conditions of our first demands have been satisfied. The first to leave us will be Mlle. Nikolaos."

Helène's pulse doubled. Instinctively, she struggled not to show the excitement and relief she felt, but those two emotions vanished quite suddenly. Looking around the room at the faces of her companions changed all her relief to guilt, as if by leaving, she were betraying them. Marian Carter burst into tears. Helène rose to comfort her, but a glance from Sabine told her it was better to leave her alone.

Hacam continued. "Calm down, girls. You'll all be free soon. Your parents and the governments of your respective countries have chosen to act intelligently in this matter. Greek, we're going to put your talents to use again now, on another film and sound track. Do it right and it will lead to the liberation of the next one of your friends. You'll be taking this new film with you when you're released. I trust you will use all the influence you can command to have it broadcast in exactly the same way as the first one was. Apart from that, we will also allow you to give interviews to members of the press, whether it be the papers, radio, television, whatever. You can be sure that you'll be in high demand. Consider yourself free to describe your stay here, the appearance of these rooms, your treatment, your food and all the events of the hijacking of the *Rosebud* that you can recall. Briefly, we are putting no restrictions on you. Even if you choose to criticize us publicly, it will have no effect on the fate of your companions. Our future actions will be totally dependent on the response to the film by the governments involved. Do you understand?"

"Oui, je comprends."

For the next seven minutes and forty seconds Helène read aloud the text Hacam had handed her for filming. When she finished Kateb removed the film magazine from the camera, placed it in a black canvas bag, and then checked the tape to be sure Helène's voice had registered. The film case and the sound track were sealed into separate containers and slipped into a belted pouch. Hacam took the pouch and handed it to the girl. "Strap this around your waist," he said. "And don't take it off until you're sure it's in the proper hands."

Lifting her shirt, she fitted the pouch around the small of her back and clasped it just over her navel. Four extra holes had to be punched in the belt to compensate for her slender waistline.

"That's fine," Hacam continued. "Now, you're going to have to wear a hood during the long hours of your trip to freedom. You are not to utter another word once you've got the hood on. You will neither be given anything to eat or drink. If you're thirsty, say so now. If you have any personal biological necessities to attend to, you'd better do that now as well."

"I'm all right," she said.

Hacam slipped the black cotton hood over her head himself. Two holes had been cut in the cloth just at the height of her nostrils and another one around her mouth. An elastic band around her neck held the material in place. Hacam took the girl's right hand and placed it on his shoulder.

"Follow me," he said. "I'll let you know where to watch your step."

She climbed the staircase, heard the two heavy doors locking behind her, crossed the office and then the hallway before stepping outside into the fresh air. She felt the heat of the sun on her shoulders immediately.

"You're going to get into a car," Hacam warned her. "I'll help you. There you are. Kirkbane," he ordered, "take the wheel. And now, Mlle. Nikolaos, move over. I'm going to sit next to you."

They started off. For an hour they drove in a giant figure eight through a part of Tardets' estate that had not yet been cultivated. Kirkbane shifted gears and varied the speed on the car constantly. Seventy-five minutes after Helène had climbed into the car, the little Arab pulled up and stopped in front of the house once again. Hacam climbed out and walked around to the other side of the car to help Helène as she stepped onto the gravel drive.

For the second time in less than an hour and a half, they crossed the hallway and made their way to the office. Cheikh switched on a tape recorder. Four quadrophonic JBL speakers were installed in each corner of the room. The tape deck could run without interruption for fourteen hours. Driven by a MacIntosh amp and preamp, the system's level of sound reproduction was the highest professionally available. The Fedayeen had even installed a Honda generator on the driveway outside in case of a power failure. All these subtle points of the plan had been drawn up by the organization in West Germany. When Helène entered the office, still with her hand on Hacam's shoulder, the room was filled with the distant sounds of orders being given in Arabic.

In the middle of the office they had built a small platform that stood three feet above the floor. An aircraft seat taken from a Cessna 172 was bolted to the center of the platform and surrounded on three sides by heavy wooden panels. Four long handles had been bolted to the outside of the front and rear panels, and the whole top of the platform itself rested on two huge truck tires so that to a certain extent, the seat was unstable. A small stepladder had been placed next to the platform to provide access to the seat. Hacam climbed the first two steps, then stopped and turned around to help Helène.

"Okay, be careful. There're five steps here. Bend down when you get to the top so you don't hit your head." Once the girl had reached the platform, Hacam helped her into the seat. "That's right," he said. "Put your arms on the arm rests. I'm going to strap you in now."

Helène felt the familiar tug of a seat belt being tightened around her waist, and then Hacam carefully bound her wrists to the arm rests and her ankles to the supports of the seat with four leather straps.

"You aren't too uncomfortable, are you?"

"I'll be all right," Helène muttered nervously. "Will it be long?"

"More than a few hours. Just remain calm. I won't be going along with you and the pilot can't hear you, so relax. I didn't give you any drug because I want you clearheaded when you're released. *Au revoir.*"

"Au revoir," the young girl mechanically replied.

Hacam climbed back down from the platform and checked his watch. The tape had been running for four minutes and ten seconds. He had secured Helène within the allotted time. Finally, the speakers broadcast the sound of the door on a lightplane being closed and then locked. This was followed shortly by the groan of an aircraft engine turning over slowly a few times before popping to life. The tape had been made during the flight of a Cessna 182. The little plane had landed four times to refuel and the tape had recorded all the sounds of these operations as well.

The wooden partition around Helène's seat, with its long handles protruding from both the front and the rear, gave the whole platform the appearance of a sedan chair. Cheikh and Kirkbane were each standing between these handles, one in front of the girl's seat and the other behind her. The room filled with the deafening sound of the plane's engine winding up to its takeoff rpm's, and the pitch changed as it started rolling. Taking hold of their handles, the two Fedayeen started shaking the platform. After about twenty seconds, Cheikh lifted the front of the platform while Kirkbane pushed down on the rear. The sound of the plane changed distinctly as it left the ground. The two Arabs maintained the platform in this position for some time before tilting it to one side to simulate a turn. Smiling, Hacam watched the young girl's hands clinging to the arm rests. The two Fedayeen shook the platform a few more times and then gently brought it back to its original horizontal position. The speakers now broadcast the regular drone of the engine running at its cruising speed. They left the room after having checked their watches. Each of them had taken the "flight" during rehearsals and found it flawless in the effect it produced.

Approximately twice an hour, the Arabs returned to the office to shake the platform, whenever the even cadence of the plane's engine changed because of "turbulence." Hacam came with them to watch Helène's reactions. Every time her seat was shaken her hands would tighten their grip on the arm rests.

At 2:15, 5:15 and 8:15 Helène felt sure the plane was landing. The chair was shaken so abruptly on these occasions that she had the impression they were landing in a country field somewhere. At 11:30, they landed for the last time.

Adrien Tardets unstrapped Helène's wrists and ankles and then helped her down off the platform. Again, she was told to watch her head though there was nothing she could have hit it on. In front of the house the old man lifted her up onto a mattress in the back of his little canvas-covered truck. He closed the tailgate, climbed inside with the girl, and then lowered the canvas flap over the back. Hacam was sitting up front behind the wheel.

Cheikh was waiting at the main gates. He closed them carefully after the little truck with its hooded cargo had passed through.

13

The old Corsican, Antoine, saw her first through the dusty soot on his windshield walking along the edge of the forest almost a hundred yards in front of him. Mashing the brake pedal to the floorboards, he was able to produce nothing more than a sickening, grinding sound of metal against metal. The little car slowed imperceptibly. Undaunted, he revved his engine up almost to its explosion point and then double-clutched from second down into first gear. The maneuver created a huge, oily black cloud of smoke behind the car, but twenty yards past Helène, the Deux Chevaux mini-truck finally came to a full stop. Craning his weathered old neck out the window, he called back to her in a thick, French-Corsican dialect. "Aye. And what are you doing way out here all by yourself at this hour, little one?"

Helène had first thought she was in either Italy or Spain, but hearing the coarse, yet friendly voice of the old man and seeing his license plate made her realize she was wrong.

"Can you take me to the nearest police station, please?"

"At Calenzana, if you want. But not at Calvi. Get in."

"That's fine. Thanks."

The old man had to let the car roll a bit and then pop the clutch in order to get it started again. He shifted into second gear, and then, taking his feet off all the pedals, concentrated on holding the car on the road. Helène thought the turns came as quickly as on the driving machines in penny arcades, but she remained silent.

Antoine had just returned from checking the bird snares he had set out in the forest. He could neither read nor write, and really did nothing in his life other than sing to himself and conjure up all kinds of improbable schemes for making money, most of which were against the law.

"I'll leave you in front of the stationhouse," he explained once they were off the mountain. "I'd go inside with you, but them and me, we don't get along too good, if you know what I mean. What happened to you? No one tried to attack you or anything?"

"Oh no. No. I'm okay. Thank you."

Just before they reached the Calvi airport, Antoine turned right onto a winding country road that ended in Calenzana after passing through Moncale. The old peasant was not a criminal, but he had lived outside the law for the better part of his life. The brevity of Helène's reply was all he needed to know she really didn't want to talk. He didn't say another word until they were forty yards away from the police station. It was a sterile, modern and ugly building that looked totally out of place among the other warm and time-worn structures in the town.

As Helène was climbing out of the car, the bells in the campanile across the plaza tolled out five o'clock. She rang the night buzzer on the door of the police station. Nothing happened. She rang it three more times before she finally heard doors slamming inside and then the double click of the lock on the door in front of her. The young gendarme who stood in the doorway was buckling his belt. He was wearing his pajama top and his rheumy eyes betrayed the fact that he was still half-asleep. Seeing Helène, his first reaction was to run his fingers through the tousled mop that kept falling down over his eyes. Something in her face seemed familiar to him. He rubbed his eyes with the back of his hands and then looked at her a little more attentively. Suddenly, he realized who she was.

"Jesus Christ! . . . Come in."

Helène, somewhat surprised, followed him inside to the lieutenant's office. He pulled up a chair for her and asked her to sit down. "God, I can't believe my eyes," he stammered. "You're the last person I ever expected to see here. Where have you come from? This just isn't possible. You are Helène Nikolaos, aren't you? I mean I'm not dreaming?"

Helène looked at him curiously. How in the hell did this man know who she was?

He caught the look of surprise in her eyes. "Everyone has seen you on television! All of France. God, the whole world. Nobody's been talking about anything else for the last four days."

"Really? I never thought it was for real. . . . I guess of course it's obviously true. But the old man . . . The old man who brought me here. He didn't know who I was. I'm sure of it."

"Which old man?"

"I don't know his name. He didn't say much. He was very small, with a heavy accent."

"Did he have an old Deux Chevaux mini-truck?"

"*Ancient* would be a better word."

"That's Antoine. He sleeps here occasionally." The young man jerked his thumb over his shoulder toward the barred door behind him.

Helène laughed. "Yes, he said he wasn't too fond of this place."

"He's harmless, really, but half the island could sink and he wouldn't know it was gone."

"I know what you mean. Could I call my parents?"

"I'll have to call the lieutenant first. I can't take the responsibility myself. I hope you understand. It'll only take a minute."

He picked up the phone and dialed a number. "Clara? Pierre here. Listen, Clara, wake up Dominique and tell him to come quickly. No. . . . Nothing. An accident, but tell him to hurry."

"Why didn't you tell her the truth?" Helène asked when he'd hung up the phone.

"Clara is my sister. The lieutenant is my brother-in-law. If I'd told my sister the truth, the entire population of Corsica would be outside that door in less than an hour, and there're only three roads leading into Calenzana. Would you like some coffee? . . . Christ, I haven't even asked you—are you all right?"

Helène barely heard what he was saying. She let the thought of Corsica sink in a moment. Then she smiled vaguely. "Yes, I'm fine, and yes, a cup of coffee would be awfully nice."

The lieutenant arrived ten minutes later. After recovering from his initial surprise, he refused to let the girl call her parents, explaining quite energetically that he could do it much faster. He picked up the phone and asked for the chief of police in Ajaccio, who in turn called Central Intelligence on the Rue Saint-Didier in Paris. Less than two minutes after that, the phone rang at the residence of Jean-Pierre Cochard, director of the National Police. Cochard then contacted the Minister of Defense, Robert Galley. Before long, Galley had Raymond Marcellin, the Minister of the Interior, on the phone. After a brief conversation, Galley hung up and Marcellin then phoned Laurent Martin, according to their prearranged plan.

The agent immediately called Georges Nikolaos and Charles-André Fargeau and told them to meet him at the office of the Minister of the Interior as soon as possible. The governmental response to Helène's release then moved back down the line through the same channels. Half an hour after he'd placed his original call, the phone rang again in the lieutenant's office in Calenzana. He answered it immediately, engaged in a quick series of Corsican affirmatives, and then hung up with a great flourish.

"Your parents have been contacted, mademoiselle. For now, I'll have to ask you not to leave the station under any circumstances until I receive some new instructions."

"There's no way I can talk with my parents now?"

"I'm sorry, there isn't."

"That's absurd."

"Please don't complicate things, mademoiselle. I'm only doing my job and you won't have to wait long."

"I've been waiting in a cellar for five days. I want to call my parents, take a bath and rest."

"Your friends will be waiting longer than that, mademoiselle. Think of them and be patient. You're free, and you're safe. Think about it."

Helène fell silent.

At 7:20, Charles-André Fargeau phoned his personal pilot from the office of the Minister of the Interior and told him to have his Mystere 20 jet ready for an eight o'clock departure from Le Bourget. He paused in his instructions for a moment and turned to Martin. "My pilot says the field at Calvi's too short for the Mystere."

Laurent understood. "Tell your man to file his flight plan for Bastia." Turning to Marcellin, he continued. "I'll call Lieutenant Colonel Huguenain. He's second in command of the Second Foreign Legion Paratroop Regiment and their base is only five miles from Calenzana. I think it'd be better if he picked up the girl personally. Then the Legion can get us a prop plane, a Nord 2500 or a Transall, pick us up at Bastia and fly us to Calvi. It'll save us a good hour."

"That would involve the defense department," Marcellin said. "I'd have to contact them."

"And that would involve the air force, who would have to contact the air base at Istres, who might or might not be able to meet us, etcetera, etcetera. Instead of going through all that it'd be faster if we took a regularly scheduled flight on an airline. I think it would be simpler my way. Besides, Huguenain is an old friend of mine and he'll take all the responsibility."

"All right, go ahead," Marcellin said with a smile. "But I don't know anything about it."

Martin reached the young colonel without much difficulty and explained the situation briefly. The response he received didn't surprise him in the least.

"You're on, Laurent," Huguenain said. "But tell the police at Calenzana. When I arrive, I don't want them to think she's being abducted again. As for the Transall, there're no problems. We've got one in the air right now unloading a few jumpers. I'll have it land in Bastia. Cover me with the air minister. My colonel is jumping with the First Battalion, so I'm in charge here until tomorrow."

"I'll cover you completely, Jean. Oh . . . and, Jean?"

"Yes, Laurent," replied the colonel.

"Behave yourself with this girl."

"Slanderer. I'll see you soon."

Within hours, Lieutenant Colonel Huguenain, the officer in charge of the now exhausted Helène, was informed that the Transall would soon be landing at Calvi. The big, twin-engined jump plane was circling over Pointe de la Revellata when a black Peugeot pulled up on the taxi strip reserved for military traffic. The plane landed awkwardly, like a pelican coming into water, and then taxied up to the colonel's car. Fargeau climbed into the back seat of the car next to the lieutenant colonel, while Martin sat up front with the driver. The millionaire started questioning Huguenain as soon as the doors were closed.

"How is she, Colonel? How did she get to Corsica? What did she say about her treatment?"

"She's sleeping, sir. When she first arrived she was suffering from complete nervous exhaustion, but the doctor said there's nothing to worry about. She's been sleeping for the last two and a half hours and it should be all right to wake her. Her clothes have all been washed and ironed. After a cold shower, she'll be in good shape.

"Judging from the statements she gave the police, it seems that all of them were well treated. Mlle. Nikolaos returned blindfolded. From where, she doesn't know, but she said she thought she was transported in a light, single-engine plane. She estimated the flight time to have been somewhere between eight and fifteen hours. The plane landed and refueled three times before its final landing here in Corsica. Last night, still blindfolded, she was moved around in a car for several hours. Consequently, it's impossible to determine exactly where she landed."

"Didn't your radar pick up anything last night?" Laurent interrupted.

"Nothing. I checked with our controllers immediately. But that doesn't mean much. They could have made their last stop on the east coast of Algeria or in Tunisia and then come in just above the water. Any altitude they could maintain under a hundred fifty feet is undetectable with our equipment. The Italians didn't pick up anything either. If we presume that the plane took off from somewhere in the Middle East, and if the girl isn't mistaken in her reckoning, we can guess-timate their cruising speed to have been about a hundred twenty miles per hour. We also think it must have been a small plane, because Helène said it was able to land quickly on very short and bumpy strips. That means they could have set her down near anywhere around here. The only thing we know for certain is that the kidnappers had accomplices here in Corsica last night. That's it, Laurent. I'm sorry, but it's not much to go on."

"It's something, but it sure as hell isn't going to do us much good now."

14

Charles-André Fargeau's Mystere 20 took off from Bastia at noon. In the noisy interior of the Transall, doorless and still outfitted with canvas-sling seats for the paratroopers, there had been little conversation. Helène had merely tried to appease the old millionaire's fears concerning Sabine's treatment by giving him a thumbnail sketch of their time in captivity. The camp doctor's prediction had proven correct —the young girl woke up from her nap feeling quite rejuvenated. Only the dark circles under her eyes belied the ordeal she had just been through.

The Mystere was completely soundproof in sharp contrast to the jump plane. Its cabin had been designed to permit the old man to continue working while the plane was in flight and was as comfortable as a small den. Helène sat facing Martin, her right leg resting casually on her left knee. After the plane had made a wide, circling climb-out over the sea and leveled off, she lit a cigarette and gave Martin a cool but not disinterested looking-over. The French agent caught her eye and immediately transferred his gaze to the line of firm thigh outlined by her jeans.

"You have retained your tan, I see," he said.

Helène smiled, but did not reply. She took a drag of her cigarette instead.

"Do you know what's on that film they gave you?"

"Of course. I narrated this one as well."

"Can you remember exactly what's on it?"

"We could listen to the tape now," Fargeau suggested. "There's a tape deck on board."

"I prefer to hear her version first," Martin said.

"Go ahead then, Helène," Fargeau said. "And try not to forget anything."

"It's quite delicate, sir. They've made entirely unrelated demands. The first one concerns you personally." She hesitated and looked from Fargeau to Martin confusedly.

"I'll hear the tape eventually anyway," Fargeau insisted. "Even if you find it a little embarrassing, go ahead."

"Well," she said, "the Fedayeen had me read a text stating that their intelligence network had confirmed the fact that in early August, 1970, M. Fargeau had arranged for a large arms shipment to the Middle East, the most important pieces of which were twenty-one small tanklike machines."

"Armored personnel carriers?" Martin interrupted.

"Yes. That's what they called them."

"Go on."

"Anyway, the rest of this shipment was mostly American automatic rifles. The rifles were all loaded onto one of M. Fargeau's freighters, the *Aquitaine*, in Brazil. The ship's regular crew was changed in Brazil, too, and the crew from the *Rosebud* was brought on board. Then it sailed to Sète, France, where the armored personnel carriers were loaded on. The carriers were disassembled, though."

She paused, trying to order her thoughts, then continued. "I must tell you, until I read this text I didn't know the *Rosebud* crew had been murdered. The other girls still don't know. Anyway, the Fedayeen said the crewmen were killed because of their participation in this whole shipment, that they were really little more than genocidal mercenaries whom they held directly responsible for the deaths of hundreds of innocent Palestinians."

"Did they tell you anything about where these weapons were delivered?" Martin asked.

"Yes, but I didn't understand it completely. They said after the carriers were loaded in Sète, the ship then sailed all the way around Africa and up through the Red Sea to Aqaba, Jordan. All the weapons were supposedly for King Hussein. One of M. Fargeau's engineers, I can't remember his name, then came to Amman for three weeks to help the Jordanians reassemble the carriers. The Fedayeen believe that these machines were the determining factor in Hussein's suppression of the Palestinians in September, 1970—the Black September."

She blushed and looked up at Martin, obviously avoiding Fargeau. Nevertheless, it was the old millionaire who urged her to continue. She went on. "They want . . . they demand that M. Fargeau and that engineer appear on television and tell the whole story, verifying everything in the text I had to read. They also want the story published in all the newspapers. I remember a bit of it exactly."

She paused and then turned to look directly at Fargeau. "To quote them . . . 'we demand that this heartless, money-hungry industrialist and his mercenary subordinate publicly and truthfully admit to the Western world that their hands are covered with the blood of the aged, the infirm, women and children. They must also insist that the media immediately cease referring to the execution of the "innocent *Rosebud* crewmen" as "cold-blooded murders." This campaign by the media to paint these men as innocent victims is a moral outrage.' "

"Anything else?" Martin asked.

"Yes. They said they would not hesitate to take the lives of others if, by these actions, they could further the survival of the Palestinian people."

Fargeau was staring blankly at Martin. His face was colorless, his eyes empty and glazed like those of a boxer just saved by the bell. The agent pressed him. "Is this true?"

The old man pulled himself together and quickly took up the question with his usual combative spirit. "From A to Z, I can recite all the facts, figures and names that have escaped Helène's memory. The conclusions to be drawn are extremely complex. On the one hand, they're reassuring because they demonstrate the Fedayeen's desire to win over public opinion, and they can't do that if they kill any of the girls. On the other hand these demands are quite frightening for two reasons: A) they're clearly indicative of the prowess of the Palestinian intelligence network and B), the subtleness of their thinking promises us a lot of trouble in the future. At any rate, their plan for the present seems to insure the girls' survival for a while. They've put so much effort into wooing public opinion up to this point, I think it highly improbable that they might risk turning it against themselves soon."

"I'm sorry, M. Fargeau," Martin interjected, "but I think your reasoning concerning their intelligence network could quite possibly be built on a false foundation. Their precise knowledge of your involvement in the events of 1970 could have come through nothing more than the simple complicity of one of your crewmen. And the same man could have assisted them in hijacking the *Rosebud*."

"That's impossible. Those men were all highly trusted."

"How did you manage to get them to deliver those armored personnel carriers? It was in flagrant violation of international law."

"With money, of course. All tax-free and deposited in their own numbered accounts in Switzerland."

"Your five trusted men were all capable of selling their principles then. You should know that loyalty wanes when gold glitters, M. Fargeau. But I don't wholly condemn your crew. The amounts of money you're capable of dangling in front of them would be quite hard to resist; however, to buy the loyalty of a man is one thing, to buy his silence is another. Your purchase remains valid only until that time when another party raises the bidding. Don't you agree?"

"In principle, yes," Fargeau admitted. "But how can anyone buy the complicity of a man in an action that will result in his death?"

"Obviously he didn't know that."

"I'm sorry, Martin. I'm awfully tired, but continue."

"Well, now we have to face the essentials, M. Fargeau. I think it would be fair to say that we're dealing with a very subtle, very demonic organization. These people mean business. The murder of your crew has shown the public that the Fedayeen are more than capable of killing their hostages just as cold-bloodedly as they did the diplomats in Khartoum. What makes them even more dangerous is the fact that they will be able to get the public to support them in these actions now. Instead of psychotic assassins, they'll become champions of justice, heroic martyrs and proponents of the 'truth' in the eyes of the public. And by such a brilliant process! Soon the voice of their most hated enemy, Charle-André Fargeau, the man who risks nothing and controls everything from the shadows, shall announce to the world that he, simply for money, brought about the massacre of hundreds of innocent people. The truly ironic thing about it, though, is that now the Fedayeen are risking nothing. Their ultimatum concerns you and you alone. And they're holding your dearest possession. Yes. It's brilliant, truly brilliant. And you're going to give in, M. Fargeau, they know that. I know it too, because there's no one on earth who could stop you. But let me tell you this, sir. Your surrender to these demands is just going to up the pace of their game and at the same time drag the four governments involved along with you into a situation from which, at the end, they will have only one way of extracting themselves. And that way will be the way chosen by the Fedayeen.

Pardon the brutality of my words, sir, but I think the time for being diplomatic about all this has passed."

"Yes, Martin, I will give in and what's more, I'm afraid you're right all the way down the line. It's obvious the organizers of this nightmare are not going to play their aces until the last hand in the game. Little by little, they're drawing us into their system so that eventually we'll have to go along with their final, true demand, something we probably wouldn't have done if they'd presented it right at the beginning."

"There's a second demand," Helène interrupted. "They said they'll free the next girl only after both of them have been met. They want the French Supreme Court to order the immediate release of a man named Rachid Ben Aloush who's been in Fresnes prison for nine months."

"Do you know this man?" Fargeau asked Martin.

"I've never heard of him, but that doesn't mean much. The French have jailed a lot of Palestinian militants and sympathizers. I can't place his name because the secret service has probably underestimated his true position in the Fedayeen hierarchy. Did they tell you anything else about this man, Mlle. Nikolaos?"

"Yes. You interrupted me. They said this man was arrested for exhibitionism. He's Algerian and had a regular working permit in France as a laborer on construction sites. The court sentenced him to two years last May. The Palestinians insisted that he had never been arrested for political activities."

"It's quite possible he might even be one of their top agents, clever enough to have avoided detection by our counterespionage service," Fargeau interjected.

"I certainly doubt that a top man in any intelligence organization would show such a lack of intelligence as to expose himself in public," Martin said sarcastically.

"M. Martin, couldn't one fairly assume that he had himself jailed on purpose, in order to contact someone already inside the prison? If I'm not mistaken, all French convicts are first sent either to Fresnes or la Santé, depending on the first letter of their last name. He would obviously have known where he was going then, wouldn't you think?"

"That's true," Martin admitted.

"They also said," Helène continued, "that M. Fargeau has one week in which to appear on television. They're giving the justice department two weeks to free Aloush. Once he's freed, he must then be given a one-way plane ticket from Paris to Algiers. The Fedayeen said they expect him to be questioned before he's released, but if he's physically abused in any way, the deal's off. If everything goes smoothly, one of my friends will be released in about two weeks."

"Perhaps you're right, M. Fargeau," Martin said. "In fact, there's no doubt about it. This Rachid was trying to reach someone at Fresnes and now his superiors want him back."

All the assumptions Martin had been turning over in his mind since the hijacking of the *Rosebud* had just begun to crystallize, but he thought it wiser if he played his own guessing game alone for a while.

The cabin bell rang twice. Fargeau pushed a flashing green light on his arm rest and the door between the cabin and the cockpit slid open. Paul Sheridan, the plane's captain, appeared. "We're fifteen minutes out of Le Bourget, sir, but I've just been informed that our plane was spotted before our departure this morning. United Press International released a small bulletin on it, and now half the Parisian press corps is waiting for us to land."

"Get us a clearing for the military flight center at Brétigny. Radio Fargeau Militaire to have a car there to meet us. No, wait, they might be followed. We'll land, then wait and see what happens there."

A test pilot working for Marcel Dassault Aeronautique Corporation lent them his car, a Citroen-Maserati. Laurent drove. After about five miles, he felt quite sure no one was following them. Their conversation remained inconsequential until they reached the access tunnel to the periphery boulevards of Paris.

Since the beginning of the whole affair, Martin had remained hidden from the eyes of both the press and the public. He had no illusions about the precariousness of his present position, but so far, at least, his personal residence had not been besieged by the press corps as had the Hotel Raphael, the Fargeau Building and the Nikolaos apartment on the Rue Guynemer.

Martin avoided the Porte d'Orléans and drove instead along Montsouris Park. At the Avenue Reille, he turned toward the Lion de Belfort. "I think it would be best if we stopped at my place," he said. "I want to postpone the announcement of Helène's release as long as possible. She can phone her parents from there."

Fargeau agreed.

Martin's apartment was on the fourth floor of a building on the Quai Voltaire between the Rue des Saints-Pères and the Rue de Beaune. At one time, it had served as an officers' quarters for the gray musketeers of Louis XIII. It consisted of six spacious rooms, three of which overlooked the Seine. In one of the rooms Martin had constructed an immense two-story library with a ceiling that was open to the beams in the eaves. It also contained a tight little corkscrew staircase to provide access to the balcony that ran around the second level of the bookshelves. The apartment was furnished with a harmonious collection of Victorian and neo-antique English pieces, a few of which bore the signatures of the houses of George Hepplewhite and Thomas Sheraton.

Helène was led to the guest room by an elderly Hungarian butler, where she made a long phone call to her mother and father. She finally hung up after promising them she would call back as soon as possible. When she rejoined the two men in the library, Laurent asked her to sit down and then started speaking unhurriedly. "I'm sorry," he said, "but you will stay here until further notice. I must have you available to me at all times, because I'm going to have a lot of questions to ask you during the next few days. Some of them might seem surprising, some superficial, others stupid and others still just downright insulting. But I want you to understand, right now, that any and all conversations I may have with you will be inspired by one motive, and one motive only, and that's the safe liberation of your friends."

Outwardly, Helène seemed annoyed. In fact, she had no objections whatsoever.

"When I accepted this assignment," Martin went on, "I insisted that I must be free to do whatever I deemed necessary. So understand this, mademoiselle: the security of your friends is my only concern. It's becoming clear now, as this whole case is unfolding, that my line of reasoning is going to be running into stiffer and stiffer opposition from the four governments involved. I am prepared for that. Whatever happens, though, I shall remain a staunch advocate for the safety of your friends. Is that clear?"

"Quite."

"Well then?"

"I'll do whatever you want."

"Good. Now call your parents again. Tell them to pack some traveling clothes for you. I'll send my butler over this afternoon to pick them up. When you finish your call, we'll take the film over to the O.R.T.F. to have it developed. Once it's been processed, we'll take a look at it. Then there's going to be a press conference. You'll have top billing. Whatever happens following that doesn't depend on me, but I'll be up on all the latest governmental decisions, and consequently so will you. Until something new pops up, that's all we can do. At any rate, we have one week to decide whether or not the film will be broadcast internationally."

"How could you possibly think of not showing it?" Fargeau asked incredulously.

"I know I used 'we' a little hastily, sir. The ultimate decision of course lies in the hands of the government. But now that we know the Fedayeen's exact demands, I think we can expect Nixon, Heath, Brandt and Pompidou to gather together their respective ministers of defense, interior and foreign affairs, along with the top men in their intelligence services, to decide what each nation is going to do. I will personally be present at the French conference, along with my superior, Colonel de Savigny. An international summit conference could then quite possibly be called. Most of the delegates will be from the secret services. Where we would be meeting remains to be seen. When we do meet, though, I'm sure our main concern will be to come up with a modus operandi that's agreeable to all the parties involved."

"What will be your exact status at this conference, Martin?"

"Well, I hope that the credits I've earned while working with the different European intelligence services will allow me to act as more than just the French delegate, perhaps as a . . . spiritual advisor of sorts. My colleagues in this business can be a little abrupt with human lives, if you know what I mean."

Turning to Helène, he continued. "Mlle. Nikolaos, I want you to feel as if this apartment were your own. My butler will do anything you ask. You can move into the guest room where you made your phone call."

"Thank you," Helène answered. "But in that case, I'd like you to do me a favor."

"Yes, of course."

"Stop calling me Mlle. Nikolaos."

Laurent couldn't help but smile. "As you wish," he said.

15

Hamlekh had turned fifty just a few months earlier. The most striking feature of his swarthy, gaunt face was a rather distinguished long bony nose. Otherwise his clothes, his physique, and his walk were all almost painfully ordinary.

He slipped through the curtain at the rear of the first-class compartment like a young sailor ducking into a strip show. Spotting Martin sitting alone in the middle row next to the window, he flopped down into the seat beside him. "Well, how are you, *mon ami?*" he said. "I see that you too have taken an interest in exotic flights."

"Cut the bullshit, Hamlekh. My congratulations, though. The Shin-Beth is on its toes."

"Israel is on its toes, Martin. If it weren't, it wouldn't exist. Now, where would you like to begin?"

Martin stood up and retrieved his jacket from the seat in front of him. He removed three mimeographed sheets of paper from the inside pocket and handed them to the Israeli. They contained the entire text of the Black September declaration Helène had read on the film.

"This will save you some time in New York," he said.

Hamlekh glanced at the documents and handed them back. "I've already seen this text," he said cheerily.

"Who?" Martin asked with resignation. "The Germans or the Americans?"

"Really, Martin, you know better than to ask such a foolish question as that."

Laurent shoved the papers back inside his jacket.

The Shin-Beth agent continued. "Listen, Martin, are we going to lay down our cards or engage in mental gymnastics? Between the two of us, it could go on forever."

"Go ahead," Martin said. "You're the one who wanted to attend the conference in New York. I assume you have something to say."

"Forget about the conference. You know as well as I do what goes on at those sessions."

"That's true, and I must admit I'm not looking forward to it."

"Good, then that's settled. Now let's talk about Black September."

Martin shifted uneasily in his seat. "What about them?"

"Come on, Martin, do you want to talk or don't you?"

Martin looked at the Israeli coolly. So he wasn't the only one to have suspected the truth. He was a little disappointed. "Okay. So we've both arrived at the same conclusions and we're both asking ourselves the same question. If it's not them, who is it? Personally, I have nothing more to offer than a lot of weak guesses, none of which are even remotely strong enough to take any positive action on."

"Then let me see if perhaps I can't make some small addition to what you already have. It's not impossible that you may be holding some key piece to the puzzle without being fully aware of it yourself. What I'd like to do is explore the whole subject from A to Z, hoping that, at one point, the confrontation of our guesses might forge some certainty that would be useful to both of us."

"We have five hours. Go ahead, I'm listening."

Hamlekh opened his attaché case and pulled out a large sheaf of notes. He thumbed through them briefly before finding the one he wanted. He started speaking without looking up from his notes. "Question One. Is Operation Rosebud directed against Israel? Corollary—against Israel alone?"

"The answer is no to the corollary."

"All right. Second question. Is Operation Rosebud an action of Black September? Corollary—of Black September alone?"

"The answer's still no to the corollary."

"Good. Then the third question. Does Black September have anything to do with this at all, or has another organization taken on their name just to confuse us?"

"This is just a guess, Hamlekh, but I do think Black September has participated in this. We know for sure that the commandos were Arabs. If your organization 'X' exists though, I think they're probably using these Black Septemberists as little more than cannon fodder."

"And how do they get the Palestinians to go along with that?"

"Yefet, I think the Palestinians have a lot of legitimate complaints to lodge against the state of Israel. I don't think they need much encouragement to behave as they do; nevertheless, I still believe they're being used as a tool by another group with ulterior motives."

"Do you think this organization 'X' is getting that man Rachid Ben whatever his name is back for the Fedayeen as a form of payment for their services?"

Martin smiled. "You're terrible, Hamlekh. Terrible and clumsy. Your services have been picking their brains on this guy for the last twenty-four hours, this Rachid Ben you-know-perfectly-well-who. And like our services, yours have found nothing on him. I think you and I have both reached the same conclusions about him, though, and that is that he's no one. I haven't submitted this idea to any of my superiors simply because I don't think they'd buy it. I'm quite sure that Rachid Ben Aloush is nothing more than the simple, sexually frustrated Algerian worker he appears to be. One day he dropped his fly and coolly displayed his sex at a bunch of schoolgirls in the Twentieth Arrondissement. The act enjoyed a great success until one of the girls told her parents. Then end of show and end of Rachid Ben Aloush."

The Israeli had been nodding his head in agreement. "But do you really think it'd be useless to put this thesis before your superiors?" he asked.

"Yes, for a number of reasons. On the one hand, the big boys consider themselves too important to believe me and on the other hand, if they did believe me, it would create too powerful an atmosphere of skepticism in the agency for me to work effectively. I'm not saying our top advisors are fools, but at least their thinking isn't as demonic as the subtle bastards pulling the strings on this affair."

"For someone who's so anti-aggressive, you've certainly done a good job of sniffing out the intricacies of all this, Martin."

"My role in these complicated affairs is never clean and sweet. You know that yourself, Hamlekh. At any rate, we've touched upon the same conclusions."

"Yes, but I blundered in thinking my superiors would believe this thesis, and consequently received the cold dunking you managed to avoid. Golda Meir is convinced that I'm insisting on Aloush's innocence because the Shin-Beth hasn't been doing his job. It hasn't been easy."

"Well, we must move slowly. To recapitulate, first of all our enemies have attacked old man Fargeau directly because they know he'll make the confession they've demanded. Even if the government tries to stop him, he controls enough of the media to make it anyway. The government knows that too. Consequently, the first thing that was decided at the meeting last night was that the film would be shown, and Fargeau will have all the television air time he wants.

"Secondly, the liberation of Ben Aloush. They know the government can't justify keeping him in jail except under common law. Plus that, he only has a few more months of his sentence to serve anyway. So, if we refuse to give in we'd be forced to admit to the French public that we're prepared to sacrifice the life of a young girl in defense of our moral indignation over the behavior of a simple Arab exhibitionist. Do you remember what happened in Khartoum? The situation was exactly the opposite. The hostages weren't gentle young virgins, but old, international diplomats. And the world public couldn't have given a damn about what happened to them. On top of that, the man to be freed wasn't just some sad son-of-a-bitch arrested for giving some little girls a few cheap thrills, but the man who assassinated Robert Kennedy. Nixon could do nothing but refuse and the commandos were forced to kill. Especially after their fiasco in Bangkok. Now that their image of strength and seriousness has been reestablished they can afford to call the shots. Marian Carter for Ben Aloush? No way. He's going to be freed."

"So you want to give in to everything they demand."

"Precisely. And for the second time they'll have attained their true goals—to expose the vulnerability of the system and place the governments involved in a position from which they cannot retreat without disgracing themselves, both now and in the future. The way things are heading, though, one could easily imagine who they're reserving their last demand for: you, Hamlekh. For you and the state of Israel. If that's true, the last hostage is already condemned."

"For us, Martin, it's a question of survival. We can't give in."

"I know it and they know it too. With one girl, they're going to turn the whole tide of world public opinion against

Israel. That's how they're paying the Fedayeen for their complicity."

"They're paying them well. If that comes off there won't be one organ of information in the Western world who'll stand behind us. The masses, the governments, and the press who, one after the other, have gone along with this debasing rape, will all try to cleanse their consciences by turning against Israel. We must find the organizers, Martin, it's as simple as that. We must find them and then slit their fucking throats."

"I've told you everything I know, Hamlekh. It's your turn now."

"For starters: Do you remember when the Baader gang crossed the Berlin wall going from west to east in 1970?"

"You mean that extreme-left German group, the Fraction of the Red Army?"

"Yes, but unfortunately it's more complicated than that. When the group passed over the wall, Andreas Baader had already been in Beirut for nearly a month. I'll remind you here of his escape from the Berlin authorities—one guard van ambushed, two guards injured and one killed."

"Yes, I remember. Rather bold commando thing."

"Right. So, from there the group went to Lebanon, where they joined up with Baader. Our services were able to get a positive identification on five of the thirty who left Europe— Hans Jurgen Backer, Manfred Grashof, Holger Klaus-Meins, and two girls, Gundrun Ensslin and Marianne Herzog. We're not sure, but we think Horst Mahler, the attorney, went with them."

"We have exactly the same information," Martin said. "I went over the dossier this morning. It seems that we've been thinking along the same lines."

"Yes, but we've taken it a little further. All the people I've just mentioned have police records. They're all known by the press and all have blood on their hands. None of them has a good rapport with the Palestinians on either doctrine or action. We think they're still hanging around Syria or Lebanon somewhere. Now, however, they've plunged into intellectualism, writing tirelessly and badly, producing reams of raving shit nobody reads, a hundred fifty pages at a time of absolute garbage with four, five words thrown in now and then from Engels, Lenin, Marx or Mao. They've traded their pistols for pamphlets, so to speak. End of Baader story."

"Come to the point, Hamlekh. We're only going as far as New York."

"I will. I just don't want to leave any gaps in your information. Besides Baader, though, there's always been a strong nucleus at the heart of the group. Strong in ideology and strong in revolutionary actions, invariably they chose the most ruthless options open to them. From everything we've been able to gather, we think this group was behind the massacre at Lod airport—an operation that was disapproved of by Baader, Mahler and cohorts according to their writings. Do you follow me?"

"Perfectly."

"This group has remained strong because it stays in the shadows while Baader and Company, unwittingly, have been maneuvered into the limelight. The nucleus has convinced these poor fools that their spectacular actions in Germany were effective, but that they had to be explained afterward, hence the plethora of pamphlets being published. Are you still with me?"

"What you're saying then is that the nucleus has complete freedom to do as they please while the Western governments can do little more than chase after those who write the manifestos."

"Exactly. The Lod airport massacre is a classic example."

"So you *did* get your prisoner to talk?"

"Oh yes, he sang like a bird, starting at the rate of about two or three words a week."

"You must have suffered terribly."

"No vulgar allusions, Martin. You mustn't get the Shin-Beth and the Gestapo confused."

"Well, what did the little Japanese boy say after you treated him so gently for eight months?"

"Number One in the 'nucleus' and his brain trust were with the group that came to Beirut from East Berlin. They spent practically a year in Lebanon. Since 1970 we've known for sure that they're the ones who call all the shots on any actions signed Black September."

"Can you be more precise about them?"

"Yes, providing I can expect a frank exchange of information from you. It's nothing, really."

"I felt that coming. . . . Go on."

"When I say all actions signed Black September, I mean all of them but one: the liberation of the Munich Olympic massacre terrorists. On the Boeing hijacking, we have other ideas. It's at the same time a quality and a fault with the Jews; we try to be ready for the bad side of everything. It's a little pessimistic, because often we even have to go so far as to doubt the sincerity of our allies. . . . That's not always sporting, but it's our nature."

Laurent remained impassive and mute. He slipped a cigarette out of its red box, lit it calmly and inhaled the first drag deeply. He seemed indifferent to the change of course the conversation was taking, but in fact he was weighing two possible replies to Hamlekh's probings. The first one was something along the lines of, "You son-of-a-bitch, you're overreaching. . . ." The second required a decision on whether or not to tell him the truth. Finally, he spoke up. "All right, Hamlekh, but spare me the sermons. I haven't got time to listen to your phony lily-white pronouncements."

"Whom did you work with on the Boeing hijacking?"

"That wouldn't get you anywhere. . . . Oh, sorry. I see what you're driving at. I only had contact with some flunky intermediary for the Black Septemberists. It took him forty-eight hours to answer my offer. This in itself doesn't give any solid backing to your theory, but it does reinforce its credibility a little. So, you've got what you wanted—now I'm waiting."

"I'll give you what I have, but first let me open a parenthesis in this conversation. Do you know that our computers consider the intelligence services of the Western powers to be at least five years behind the Shin-Beth in analyzing information? Whereas the Soviet KGB is only three years behind us. The Soviets, however, are starting to realize what the ultimate weapon of the future will be, and that is the ability to exercise total manipulation of the masses simply by controlling every aspect of public opinion. What do you think of some of the funnier stories in our Jewish folklore?"

"They bore the shit out of me, and you're starting to as well."

"I rarely say anything without a reason, Martin. Don't forget that, even if I speak in metaphors."

"Continue with your stories and your folklore then, my friend. You're dangling the carrot."

"In 1967, not long before the Six-Day War, a story spread purely by word of mouth from Tel Aviv to Haifa, from Haifa to Jerusalem. Let me relate it to you briefly."

"God save me."

"A cuckold came home one night and found his wife in bed with her lover. After yanking her out of the bed and giving her a few good belts, he turned angrily to face the lover. 'Even though the nation needs you,' he said, 'if I catch you around here again, I'll blind your other eye.' You couldn't walk into a public place for two months prior to the war without somebody grabbing your arm and asking you, 'Have you heard the story of the cuckold?' "

"Dayan does have a way with women."

"True, but that's beside the point. The important thing about this story is that it was created and then disseminated entirely by the Shin-Beth's office of rumor control. And it achieved its purpose. Within five weeks, Dayan's popularity was at its zenith. Let me remind you, Martin—1967, Israel and the manipulation of the masses, and you, six years later, still so oblivious to the dangers of this weapon that you've placed it in the hands of our common enemy. And now they're holding it to your head while they play with the public opinion of the world as if it were nothing more than a puppet on a string."

"I am aware of the dangers of global control of public opinion, Hamlekh, but I would like to remind you, as you gloat on the glories of the Shin-Beth's accomplishments in this area, that Goebbels, in 1945, managed to prolong the war for another six months simply by using the same tactics. All he had to do was change the approach of his propaganda from the 'invincibility of the panzer divisions' to the 'imminent invasion of the Asiatic hordes,' thereby reversing the psychological climate of the German people. He was so good at his work he brought about the death of another million people, for nothing."

"You know, with the exception of a few major ideological differences, I admire Goebbels. He was the forefather of a frighteningly powerful new psychological school."

"A school civilization would be better off without. But you're beating around the bush. I want some names."

16

Hamlekh pulled a manila folder out of his attaché case. Without any enthusiasm, he continued. "We have four names. They might be good for something."

Laurent pulled out a small leather-bound notebook and a pen.

"All right," Hamlekh continued. "Number One in the nucleus was born in February, 1939, in Potsdam. That makes him thirty-four today. His name is Wilhelm Schrantz. He's a mystic trying to persuade the Jews outside of the Zionist movement that the creation of the Israeli nation has in fact sounded the death knell of Judaism. To strengthen his argument, he uses our sacred texts as the foundation for all his arguments—the Old Testament, the Torah, even the Dead Sea Scrolls. According to his interpretation, the 'spirit of God' saves and delivers, not the 'force of man.' True patriotism doesn't lie in the love of the land, but in the love of the past and the veneration of those generations that have preceded us.

"Finding an ample number of citations in the Scriptures is not difficult if you know them well enough. For example, Chapter Three, Verse Ten of the prophet Micah says, 'They build up Zion with blood, and Jerusalem with iniquity.' Here, Martin, read this. It's imperative that you understand these texts if you're going to know anything about the strength of the anti-Zionists. But before you start, let me point one thing out. These texts don't come from Wilhelm Schrantz's clique. Their source is much more threatening. All these proclamations have been written, published and translated into various languages by Jews living outside Israel. The authors are intellectuals, often some of the best minds in the Diaspora, men of renowned wisdom. At least half of them are highly esteemed rabbis."

For a quarter of an hour, Martin pored over the texts. They were astounding. Every one of them was fully annotated and indeed, each of the authors seemed to possess impeccable credentials. It was unbelievable. "The violence of the Palestinians is a direct measure of the violence of the Israeli nation. If Sirhan Sirhan had not been traumatized by the Zionist aggressions that brought about the creation and expansion on Palestine territory of the state of Israel, the idea of killing Robert Kennedy would never have entered his head.

"Those who destroy the Zionist state shall accomplish the will of God. The terrorists of Al Fatah are the servants of Yahweh. Even the most criminal of their actions is not without cause, because GOD IS A MAN OF WAR.

"I don't believe that Jesus was the Messiah, but I do think God is embodied in every poor man, as Jewish theology teaches us. Jesus was a poor man and a victim of the rich. Rich Jews assassinated Christ with the Romans. Since then, they've paid their intellectuals and historians to prove the contrary, but their endeavors are useless because the state of Israel, by the crimes it commits daily, has shown, and will continue to show, that the rich are guilty. The state of Israel, in declaring itself a sovereign state, dethroned the King of Kings from his rightful place as it has driven the Arabs from their homeland. Injustice to the Arabs is injustice to God. This is why I cannot say yes to God and to the Jewish faith without saying no to Israel. . . ."

Laurent handed the dossier back to the Israeli agent, who carefully replaced it. On the outside of the folder, Hamlekh had written, *"Christ Is a Palestinian Refugee."* Glancing up at Martin, he was visibly pleased with the effect the documents had produced.

"Does it surprise you?" Hamlekh asked. "You know, this kind of shit has been settling out of the atmosphere since 1950. We Israelis thought at first that it was only an unbalanced intellectual's game. For all practical purposes it was relatively harmless. But with the advent of Schrantz's little group, the number of believers in this trash has swollen to the size of a small Mafia."

"What else do you know about Schrantz?"

"Schrantz is the son of a doctor. His parents emigrated from Germany to the U.S. the year after he was born. The elder Schrantz, until he died in 1948, was a secondary staff physician at New York Hospital. They lived in a cheap apartment on Ninety-ninth Street. At the time, it was on the fringes of Harlem. Today, it's the center of Manhattan's Puerto Rican district. It was in this neighborhood that our man took his first hard looks at life. His intelligence showed itself early in his education, and by the time he was fourteen, he'd entered Columbia University. His professors claimed he was a genius, but his studies were impaired by his frenzied desires to sow disorder. He studied medicine for three years. But then, without any apparent reason, he abandoned that in order to get doctorates in both language and philosophy. By this time, the Puerto Ricans in his neighborhood had started to organize themselves politically. Schrantz dropped his studies altogether then and joined one of the more militant wings of one of these new groups. That was his first taste of power and it was more than enough to whet his appetite. Before long he started writing and publishing pamphlets defending several politically oppressed minorities.

"In 1960, he moved to Frankfurt, where he served as a secretary to a prominent anarchist attorney. During a journey to Hamburg, he met Horst Mahler, the attorney for Andreas Baader and cohorts. You can imagine what followed that match. . . . Oh, one other thing. He's addicted to amphetamines. Intravenously. He rarely sleeps more than two or three hours a day. In short, he's brilliant. He's mad. He's hooked on speed and he's very dangerous. Being the fanatical anarchist that he is, he has little use for order or logic except when it can assist him in creating chaos. His current defense of the Palestinian cause is nothing more than his first big step toward achieving his aims on a worldwide scale."

"I can well understand that he could easily have rallied a crowd of fanatics to his cause, but you seem to be implying that his pedantic efforts have made an impact among some of the non-Zionist Jews as well. . . ."

"Impact is not the right word. The rabbinical texts you've just learned about are no more than an intellectual game and have never had the least bit of influence on the real masses of world Jewry. The virulent and nearly epidemic hatred which emanates from Schrantz's meetings has been able to convince a few of my fellow Jews here and there, those with weak minds, and really, it's upset them more than convincing them . . . No, that's not the real danger. What he's managed to do is convince the Palestinians whom he controls that the great majority of non-Zionist Jews is with him . . ."

"Still using the texts to support his arguments?" Martin asked.

"Obviously. And it's not very difficult. The Palestinians want to believe him in the worst way. They see in it a tangible means to the dissolution of the state of Israel. Can you imagine those poor bastards thinking of themselves as desperados admired by the whole Western world and supported by the international Jewish community?"

"Hasn't he ever tried to recruit any Jews as militants?

That would seem to me to lend considerable weight to his thesis."

Hamlekh continued with a satisfied grin.

"I see you understand me perfectly. From the beginning he has had an obsession about that very objective. Well, Martin, no way. He never succeeded, and it constitutes a reassuring fact about our errant fellow Jews in that, fortunately, they can tell the difference between intellectual ramblings, no matter how virulent and moving, and actually taking up arms against their brothers even though they may disapprove of their actions."

"You mentioned four names. What are the other three?"

"Number Two is Ulrika Raad. She's Austrian. Twenty-eight years old. In the hierarchy, she fulfills both the roles of 'revolutionary mother figure' and resident piece. Her sexual role is purely mechanical, however. These men view their sexual appetites as something to be satiated and then forgotten. But her functions do not stop there. It seems that she's also thought of as a very level-headed advisor, as paradoxical as that adjective may seem when applied to the activities of this bunch. According to our information, she really does have a lot of common sense. She overrules quite a few of Schrantz's wilder, unworkable schemes. Our Japanese prisoner described her as being lusty, tall, with brown hair, dusty blue eyes and a deep tan. He said that in the improbable event that one of the Lod commandos had returned, he would have been promoted several ranks and admitted to the brain trust, wherein he would have enjoyed all of the girl's contributions as well."

Hamlekh paused, then continued. "Cozy arrangement, isn't it? Fuck Ulrika and the world too."

"You're not really being serious about this girl, are you?"

"Yes, I am. That's all straight from the Lod prisoner's mouth. You know, he was terribly obstinate at first, but we finally gave him a little pharmaceutical encouragement."

"Pentathol?"

"We're beyond that, Martin. Our laboratories now have a formula that's so precise we can tell how many words a minute we're going to get by the strength of the dosage. The base is amphetamines, but we add tranquilizers to loosen them up and destroy their willpower and they sing beautifully. No, my friend, it's no longer a problem getting people to talk."

Martin checked his notes. "The other names?" he asked.

"Karl Volker and Ernest Schaffner. Along with Schrantz and Ulrika, they make up the nucleus, but I can assure you that none of them ever uses his real name. They have as many perfectly forged passports as they need. The Japanese didn't give us these names because he didn't know them. We were able to come up with them after comparing some earlier intelligence we'd gathered with certain sections of the Japanese boy's confession."

"Do you have any starting points on hand?"

"One. Frankfurt, Schiffer Strasse Nine. Do you know Frankfurt?"

"Quite well."

"Schiffer Strasse is a small street perpendicular to the quay on the left bank of the River Main. It starts right opposite the front of the Handicrafts Museum. Can you picture the area?"

"I don't know the street, but I know where the museum is."

"Well, at any rate, at that address there's an artist's studio that serves as the central offices of a perfectly legitimate and legal corporation called the Franco-Belgian Society for Graphic Arts."

"That's very quaint. What do they do?"

"Get ready for this: they produce comic books for children between the ages of seven and thirteen living in Arab countries."

Hamlekh reached inside his attaché case once again and

produced another manila folder. This one contained three color comic books captioned in Arabic. "These are Algerian versions," he said. "They use the same drawings in all of them, but they change the text, name and nationality of the hero into Egyptian, Syrian or Lebanese, depending on where they're going to be sold. The Algerian superman here is called Meddy Brahim. He's kind of a combination of Tarzan, James Bond, Mandrake the Magician and Zorro."

"Creating national heroes for children is not their invention. We've done the same thing in France with Astérix, who often spouts more Gaullisms than old Charles ever did."

"Yes, but these comics have a much more sinister effect. The cartoonists spice all their drawings with the most insidious little insignificant details that cumulatively leave their mark on the minds of the children who read them. Look at this one here. It's about an Algerian supersonic fighter. Look at the face of Moshe Dayan here when he learns that Meddy Brahim has one of these planes. And look at the terrified faces of the Israeli pilots who're refusing to take off."

Martin burst out laughing. "My God, Hamlekh, these little books really annoy you, don't they?"

"It's not funny, Martin. Don't forget that mass manipulation is a Jewish creation. Even though they want to see the state of Israel go up in flames, in an indirect way they're paying us a big compliment by employing our methods. The thing is, many adult Arabs read these little masterpieces too. After a while, they can't help but believe them. As a matter of fact, Boumédiene reads them himself every week before authorizing their distribution. I'm sure the day's not far off when he'll start believing them as well."

Martin handed the comics back to the Israeli. "Let's get back to Frankfurt."

"Frankfurt. We know that's where they do the drawings,

conceive the ideas and write the texts in French. They have three employees there: a French draftsman named Bernard Lemoine who does the drawings and layout, his assistant, a Belgian girl by the name of Carola Hotten, and an Algerian writer, Isar Khader. Those are all their real names.

"The printing is done in Lebanon in the Haour Tala region, nearly on the Syrian border, south of Baalbek. We haven't been able to fix the location precisely because the area is so mountainous and all approaches are guarded. It's particularly maddening because we think Schrantz's headquarters is located there too."

"Do you think the girls could be there as well?"

"It sure as hell would seem to make a lot of sense."

"How much do the three people in Frankfurt know?"

"It's difficult to say with any degree of certainty. They obviously must know something, but probably not enough to jeopardize Schrantz's operations."

"Do you have anything else on this bunch in the mountains?"

"No. Now you know just as much as I do. I hope you can put it to use."

"I'm sure we'll be able to make something out of it. Don't worry."

"Well, then I'll leave you now and retire humbly back to the tourist compartment where I belong."

"Thank you, Hamlekh. I'm glad you know your place. Be discreet when you get to New York. I'll see you at the UN."

When Hamlekh left, the plane was still four hours out of New York. Laurent took advantage of the time by moving across the aisle and forward two rows to where Helène was napping peacefully. Martin gently roused her and asked a few rather indiscreet questions. In the course of their conversation, though with great reticence, she informed him of the existence of Sabine Fargeau's lover, Patrice Thibaud, and went on to explain the circumstances behind his brief voyage on the *Rosebud* just prior to the girls' abduction.

The agent was not pleased with this new information, presenting him as it did with some very somber new perspectives on the case.

The Japan Air Lines flight landed on time at Kennedy International. Since the early hours of the morning, almost every major airline terminal at the airport had been besieged by the press. The wire services had placed lookouts on the observation bridge above the International Arrivals Building and the television networks had crews roaming everywhere.

A young vice-consul, in collaboration with the New York police, was in charge of transferring the couple from the airport to Manhattan. In order to insure secrecy, the limousine detoured through the streets of Richmond Hill instead of taking the Van Wyck Expressway north. The police had set up a roadblock on Woodhaven Boulevard at the entrance to Forest Park. As soon as the consulate's car had passed, they stopped all traffic behind it for three minutes. The car entered Manhattan through the Midtown Tunnel and then headed west toward Central Park.

Martin was taken to an apartment on the fourth floor of one of the plush, high-security buildings on Fifth Avenue overlooking the park. It had been placed at the disposition of the French consulate by one of Senator Donovan's personal friends.

It was 4:15, New York time, when they arrived. Inside the apartment, Laurent discovered a pushbutton phone in one corner of the huge living room and immediately placed an overseas call to the S.D.E.C.E. on the Boulevard Mortier. Before long, Colonel de Savigny was on the other end of the line.

"How was the flight, Martin?"

"Interesting. Did you know Sabine Fargeau had a lover?"

"First time I've heard anything about it."

"Well, then the police are trying to put something over on us for sure. The Fargeau girl has had this little affair going since 1968. His name is Thibaud, first name Patrice. He's an assistant professor of philosophy on the faculty at Aix-en-Provence. Leftist. Home address is 11, Rue Frédéric-Mistral. He was on board the *Rosebud* between Cannes and Saint-Tropez the morning before the kidnapping and spent all afternoon with the girls. It's impossible that scores of people haven't reported seeing them together. If I were you, I'd contact Commissioner Le Breton. I'm damned near positive he's already arrested him. Young leftists are always Le Breton's idea of perfect suspects."

"I'll contact the minister then," de Savigny said. "If this starts out badly, we'll never get off the ground with it."

"Do you have my address here?"

"Affirmative. The embassy transmitted it to me this afternoon right after you left."

"All right. Our conference at the UN starts in less than two hours. The press created a small holocaust at the airport, but I think they'll have things a little more tightly controlled there. Oh, do you have any information on the English, American and German representatives?"

"Yes. Sir Edmund Wycherly will be representing the British, Richard Sanders, the United States and the B.N.D. delegate from Germany is your old friend Schloss. The Englishman and the German traveled together from London. They arrived in New York an hour and a half ahead of you on a BOAC flight. We haven't been able to get any information on the Israeli observer."

"That's all right, I've already spoken with him."

"Well, who the hell is he?"

"Hamlekh."

"Where did you see him?"

"He was on our flight."

"Goddamned Shin-Beth."

"Yes. They're good, aren't they. I'll file you a report. *Au revoir*."

17

Shortly before Helène Nikolaos' liberation, Patrice Thibaud was arrested at his home in Aix-en-Provence at six o'clock in the morning. At 6:30, a black police Peugeot 404 turned onto Route A-7 heading north toward Paris. It stopped only once, for gas, in a little town between Lyon and Mâcon.

At the beginning of the investigation, Police Commissioner Le Breton had received the first reports and briefings concerning the crew members of the *Rosebud*. In Toulon, Brian Joshman's wife had repeated to a National Police Inspector all the details of the last conversation she'd had with her husband the night he was murdered. She was able to remember Patrice's last name, first name and profession—professor of philosophy, but she could not recall where he lived or at which university he taught. Nevertheless, it did not take Le Breton long to find Thibaud.

For several years, now, the young professor had been highly visible as a leader of several extreme left movements. His police record was sufficiently stuffed with enough provocative details about his activities to allow the old commissioner's mind to run wild with speculations. As far as he was concerned, he had all the evidence he needed in order to arrest the young man.

Thibaud himself was not the least bit surprised when the police raided his home that morning. He had been expecting them for days. Like most young French leftists, he had nothing but contempt for the brutal, fascist methods of law enforcement employed by the French National Police. Consequently, he had decided to let them come to him. Anyway, in his heart he sided with the Arabs even though one of their splinter groups was now responsible for the abduction of Sabine. There was nothing he could tell the police to further their investigation anyway.

When they arrived at his door, though, he decided he would not go with them easily. His resistance cost him a broken nose and two deep cuts over both eyes.

Unfortunately for Commissioner Le Breton, Thibaud's classes had attracted a large following among the leftist students in Aix-en-Provence. When the facts of his relationship with Sabine were released to the press by one of his friends, as well as a statement on his pro-Arab stance, there was a demonstration within twenty-four hours on the Cours Mirabeau, the main street in Aix, calling for his release. Le Breton, convinced of Thibaud's innocence after two days of interrogation, unwittingly let him go. The press was waiting for him when he stepped through the heavy twin doors of the prefecture on the Quai des Orfèvres. When he appeared with his nose pushed all over his face and his eyes swollen purple and cut, the television crews had a field day. By the end of the week, he'd become something of an international pro-Arab martyr to the International Progressive Students Union that rallied behind him. Not long afterward, he obtained silent financial backing for the I.P.S.U. from Charles-André Fargeau.

In New York, the meeting of the intelligence agents at the UN had resulted in nothing more than six and a half hours of carefully guarded rhetoric. Laurent informed the delegates that the French were going to go ahead and comply with the latest set of terrorist demands and Hamlekh argued unsuccessfully for forty-five minutes trying to get the other nations to take a firmer stance. Everyone seemed to have a different theory on how to keep the situation in control until the whereabouts of the girls had been discovered. In the end, they were all disgusted with each other and parted on worse terms than any of them could ever remember.

Laurent and Helène returned to Paris two days later and the girl moved back home. The film she had brought with her from Corsica was scheduled to be broadcast that night on the 7:45 national news. It was to be followed immediately by Charles-André Fargeau's public confession. The public, however, was still not aware of the French government's unconditional capitulation to the Fedayeen's demands. Fueled now by the rising tide of the student movement behind Thibaud, they were starting to voice their dissatisfactions openly.

Everywhere, it seemed, demonstrations organized by student groups were starting to fill the streets. Their slogans, passed by word of mouth and splashed over placards and banners, differed in various countries only in the language they were spoken and printed in. "Broadcast the Film!" "The Public Must Be Informed!" "Silence Is Murder! . . ."

But the real measure of the danger involved became apparent to the governments when they realized just how much popular support the youth movements were receiving.

For the first time in contemporary history, sympathizers came forward from all classes of society, regardless of age, to join the ranks of the demonstrators. Workers, students and settled members of the middle class marched through the principal cities of France, Germany, Great Britain and the United States, linked arm in arm in a dangerously cohesive human tide of indignation. Those who pulled the strings of the Palestinian operation had proved to be subtle prophets—the population was reacting like spectators at a tragically suspenseful play; a captivating and intoxicating drama, one which could end badly at any moment. Nevertheless, public opinion was demanding that the show go on, and their arguments were irrefutably humanitarian. The Palestinians had gained a great victory. The whole world was now talking of nothing else but their Operation Rosebud and worrying about the lives of the four exquisite young girls involved.

So it was in a feverish atmosphere that night that the Fedayeen's film and the confession of Charles-André Fargeau were broadcast simultaneously throughout the Western world.

The first mass reactions to the Palestinians' new demands were mixed—surprise, curiosity, but also frustration and deception. It was ignoble, but human. Everyone was expecting something sensational and they were disappointed when they were given little more than a modest ultimatum. Nobody had ever heard of Rachid Ben Aloush. As far as world opinion was concerned, the fact that Fargeau had sold arms to Jordan was little more than inconsequential detail. Wasn't it normal for a millionaire arms industrialist to try and sell his wares to anyone who would buy them? And these Jordanians and their little king, weren't they Arabs and consequently enemies of Israel?

Except for the intellectual minority, who was fully informed about the problem, the greater part of the public had swallowed the press's lengthy commentaries on the real objectives of the terrorists. The irony of it all was that the terrorists had obtained their objectives precisely through the same commentaries.

The true significance of the name Black September, which for three years had been used all over the world to describe a certain wing of militant Palestinian refugees, came as a surprise to many. Up until then, in the minds of most people, the label chosen by the terrorist organization had been incorrectly identified with an anti-Arab action by the Israelis. Few people realized exactly what role Jordan was playing in the continuing tensions of the Middle East, and the massacres of September, 1970, were not really put before the world until Fargeau's confession.

The governments, though, made no mistake about the Palestinians' objectives. Fargeau's confession had turned a spotlight on the real nature of the Palestinians' problems, and now that it was on them, they would make every attempt to keep it there as long as possible.

On the other hand, the heads of state of the Western governments, like individual members of a symphonic orchestra, had all banded together to deceive themselves concerning the true identity of Rachid Ben Aloush. The world of politicians was nowhere near guessing the real facts about the man. It wasn't illogical. To understand, one would have had to credit the Fedayeen with being extremely subtle. Up to now, Black Septemberists had been considered little more than just a bunch of dangerous fanatics who regularly and energetically threw themselves blindly into actions that were invariably ruthless and bloody, but which, nevertheless, were not capable of shaking the foundations of the Western world. To think that these men could lay a trap as Machiavellian as the one the politicians were falling into now was something they were incapable of grasping.

With all the political foresight of Richard Nixon marching into the Watergate affair, they assumed that Rachid Ben Aloush was just another special agent whom the Palestinians wanted back.

The truth though, was very simple, and as old as the game of revolution. It sprang from the classical tactics of amplifying the "internal contradictions" of the society one wishes to overthrow.

And the French judicial apparatus was doing just that, by making a public demonstration of the paradoxes inherent in a democracy. As a defenseless Arab worker, Ben Aloush had been punished with exemplary severity for an insignificant offense. Now that he was a secret Palestinian agent, however, even if he'd been facing murder charges, he would have been released. Not only was justice not being applied equally to everybody, but the Garde des Sceaux had the power to annul a sentence that had already been passed. But could this power to reverse Ben Aloush's sentence even be considered a true power, seeing that it was exercised under the threat of blackmail?

As for Rachid Ben Aloush, he had no idea of what was happening to him and could do nothing but allow himself to be carried along in a daze. Almost beatifically, he submitted to three days of intensive grilling at the hands of the French Territorial Security Forces on the Rue des Saussaies. A dozen of the best counterespionage agents France could muster together worked on him in four six-hour shifts, twenty-four hours a day, trying to root something out of this Muslim exhibitionist that would give them a clue to his true purpose and identity.

Speaking in his best, onomatopoeic pidgin French, he answered all their questions evasively. In the end, he gave it up and let the agents put forth every argument, question, theory and angle they could think of. As far as Ben Aloush was concerned, they might as well have been speaking Chinese.

His attitude only reinforced their preconceptions about this unskilled laborer that he was indeed a superagent who was quite brilliantly playing the part of a happy imbecile leading them through a dance.

The summit of these absurdities was arrived at when Ben Aloush was finally released. Two hours after the TV broadcast of the Palestinians' latest demands, a chartered Caravelle flew the Arab to Algiers, where he was given a hero's welcome on the order of Colonel Boumédiene, the Algerian chief of state.

The French, having capitulated, left the whole world waiting feverishly for the liberation of the next hostage.

PART III

18

Laurent Martin left Paris a few hours after the liberation of Ben Aloush.

Provided with a passport and papers under the name of Lucien Moliguer, an antique dealer on the Rue de l'Université, he crossed the German border at Morsbach, driving a rented Renault 16.

He arrived in Frankfurt at four in the morning. Driving through the old town, now deserted, he found the Hotel Swille on the Grosse Bockenheimer Strasse, where Hans Schloss had taken a room. He was not surprised to find a message waiting for him. The B.N.D. agent asked Martin to wake him no matter how early he arrived.

At 4:25, Schloss, dressed in a motley bathrobe and still half-asleep, carried a jar of Nescafé into Martin's room. He made himself a strong cup of coffee in a water glass with hot water from the tap and then stirred it with his finger to dissolve the coffee crystals.

Laurent Martin gave the German agent all the information he had obtained from Hamlekh on the pro-Arab comic-strip factory.

"It's absolutely necessary that we get a bug on their phone," Martin concluded. "And you must get me an apartment or even just a room from which I can watch every one of their movements."

"Don't worry about any of that, Martin. The police chief here is a personal friend of mine. His services are particularly efficient when it comes to this kind of thing, and what's more, you can count on his discretion. They'll do as we ask without any questions."

At nine o'clock that morning, Martin and Schloss took the elevator to the second floor of the central police headquarters. There they were immediately ushered into the office of Polizeichef Hersfeld. The police chief's dry manner betrayed his history as a former German officer. Martin judged him to be just about sixty years old. Schloss explained their requirements without connecting them in any way to the *Rosebud* affair. But in light of the way the B.N.D. agent insisted on the importance of this mission, the absolute silence and discretion that was to surround it, as well as the high caliber of men asked for, it was quite clear that Hersfeld knew what was happening. As a professional law-enforcement officer, he nevertheless showed no outward signs of his understanding. He simply unfolded a huge map of the city and noted Schloss's instructions on it with a red grease pencil.

"By noon tomorrow, not even a mouse could get in or out of your apartment on the Schiffer Strasse without our knowing about it," he said. "Until I receive further instructions, every visitor to Franco-Belgian will be thoroughly identified without him or her having the least suspicion or knowledge of it. Whatever the number or frequency of the visits might be, I will send you a daily summary compiled by our central services on each individual who has entered this building or who might have contacted the occupants by phone."

Less than an hour after this interview, a small Audi NSU van, supposedly a service vehicle owned by the Thorens-Hafrabba Elevator Company, pulled up in front of 9 Schiffer Strasse. Two repairmen wearing green uniforms entered the six-story building carrying their toolboxes. There was only one office on each landing. The offices of the Franco-Belgian Society were on the second floor. On the door, there was a small Formica sign with the company's name and the daily business hours engraved on it. At the bottom it said, "Visitors may enter without knocking."

After hanging a sign on the elevator doors on the ground floor reading *"Ausser Betrieb,"* the repairmen made their way to the third floor and started to unpack their equipment.

If, at that instant, a curious or suspicious tenant had phoned the Thorens-Hafrabba Elevator Company, he would have been told that two electronic technicians were indeed checking the wiring on the elevator at 9 Schiffer Strasse. Hersfeld never left anything to chance.

While pretending to test the elevator's call-button system on the third floor, the two policemen were in fact carefully staking out the floor below them.

After twenty minutes, an unidentified visitor entered the Society's offices. When the door was opened, it set off a buzzer inside that did not go off until the door was closed again. It was more than the repairmen ever could have hoped for. It took them seven minutes to finish their work on the third floor. They then went down to the second floor and removed the metal plate on the elevator call-button panel. This time, the Thorens-Hafrabba plate they replaced contained a miniature radio transmitter and receiver. Its sensitivity was such that even if there hadn't been a buzzer in the office, it would have been able to react only to the sound of the door opening and closing, and transmit a signal out of the building within a radius of a mile and a half.

The repairmen left the building without having been noticed by anybody.

Meanwhile, an inspector and two technicians had themselves introduced to the curator of the Handicrafts Museum on the left bank of the River Main opposite the end of Schiffer Strasse.

The curator had just been notified of their impending visit by Hersfeld. Without losing any time, he led the policemen into the dusty storage room on the fourth floor reserved for the eighteenth-century porcelain.

There were only three low windows on the front wall of the room. The policemen had noticed them just before entering the museum and had decided that the one on the right would give them the best angle of observation. The technicians installed their equipment. The windows were covered on the inside by black cotton curtains to protect the colors of the porcelain from the fading effects of the sunlight.

The curtain on the right-hand window was drawn back no more than two inches in such a way that it could not be noticed from the outside. The men very carefully cleaned a small circle two inches in diameter on the window and then mounted a television camera on a tripod directly in front of it. Looking through the viewfinder, they adjusted the camera angle until the screen was focused directly on the entrance to No. 9 Schiffer Strasse. Unfortunately, the curtains on the windows of the Franco-Belgian Society's offices kept them from seeing anything but shadows moving around inside, but that would not defeat their purpose. They locked the camera into position.

The stakeout squad returned to the curator's private office and called Polizeichef Hersfeld, who then gave them the information they were waiting for. A third crew had installed themselves in another apartment, which would serve as central communications. This third flat was estimated to be 1,400 yards from Schiffer Strasse. It suited them perfectly. The building stood at the corner of Mainzer Strasse and the quay of the River Main, almost directly opposite the museum on the other side of the river. The technicians took down the phone number and then fed their television transmission lines directly into the phone system.

The location on Mainzer Strasse was an unassuming three-room apartment owned by a widowed police officer who had recently retired. Less than an hour after Martin and Schloss spoke with Hersfeld, his services selected eleven apartments, with telephones, belonging to civil servants, retired or otherwise, which were within a one-mile radius of Schiffer Strasse. When they finally selected the location on Mainzer Strasse, they discovered that the owner was on a three-week vacation at Mummelsee, a little village located high in the Black Forest. They had contacted him through the police in Baden-Baden, eighteen miles away. He immediately gave them his permission over the phone. His door was opened by the department locksmith.

As Hersfeld had assured Martin and Schloss, at 11:25, half an hour ahead of time, his entire stakeout squad was in place and operating.

The television camera was monitored by two men located in the apartment on Mainzer Strasse. Each time someone entered the building, they usually had to wait no more than forty seconds to find out whether or not that person had entered the offices on the second floor. The transmitter was working perfectly.

Ten plainclothesmen on foot and twenty unmarked patrol cars had been placed strategically around the area. Each of the patrolmen was equipped with a walkie-talkie, the receivers of which were no larger than hearing aids. The transmitters worked off the outside of their larynx and were hidden under their shirt collars. Central communications simply broadcast the physical descriptions of the subjects to be followed, and the tailing system worked flawlessly.

During the next two days, Laurent and Schloss compiled complete dossiers on each and every one of nineteen people who visited the Franco-Belgian offices and twenty-four who had communicated with them by phone. The information they received from the police revealed one thing for certain, and that was that the Franco-Belgian Society of Graphic Arts did conduct a large quantity of legitimate business other than just the creation of comics for the Arab countries.

This fact only reassured Martin that he'd chosen to attack the network from the right angle. The three artists were obviously lesser allies within Schrantz's structure, but nevertheless the comics were printed each week in Lebanon. Therefore there had to be at least one, if not a series of contacts made each week in order to relay the drawings. This initial contact was the lead the French agent was putting all his money on. Now all he had to do was find it.

Laurent and Schloss hardly ever left the Hotel Swille. They were waiting for one of the suspects tailed from Schiffer Strasse to lead his trackers to an unusual location.

After thirty-one hours of vigilance, their patience paid off. The police chief called in person. Twenty-four minutes before his call, an unidentified visitor had entered the Franco-Belgian offices, stayed for less than a minute and then walked down to the quay along the River Main. There he picked up a Mercedes 220D taxi that apparently had been waiting for him. The taxi was registered to the Western Company.

According to Hersfeld's men, the taxi was at present crossing the magnificent Stadtwald Woods on the highway heading southwest out of the city toward the Flughafen-Rhein-Main, Frankfurt's civilian airport.

"Specifically," Hersfeld said, "this man seems to be about forty years old. Five feet eight at the most. Wearing narrow-brimmed hat, steel-framed glasses, faded dark-blue serge suit, green-and-black striped tie, dirty beige nylon shirt, old suede loafers and carrying a medium-sized case that looks like it could contain camera equipment.

"I thought," Hersfeld concluded, "that you might be interested in tailing him if he were going to leave Frankfurt by plane. There should be an unmarked Deutsche-Fiat waiting for you outside your door right now. If you step on it, you can join your man at the airport less than ten minutes after he gets there."

They did step on it. As soon as the door of the German Fiat was shut, they established radio communications with Hersfeld. The traffic was moving easily. It was 7 P.M. The driver handled the little car beautifully, taking the maximum amount of risks and allowing himself the minimum amount of room to spare in passing. Just before the zoo, he took a hard right onto the last city bridge crossing the Main and then sped out of town through the Stadtwald.

Hersfeld's voice erupted over the radio.

"Affirmative on the airport. Right now he's paying his taxi in front of the British European Airways offices. Would you like us to book you two seats on the flight he'll be taking?"

The two agents exchanged a look of instant agreement.

"Affirmative. Whatever the destination may be," Schloss said.

"Roger. Where are you now?"

"We're crossing the Stadtwald, approximately three miles from the airport."

"Slow down and wait for my instructions."

The driver seemed disappointed, but he slowed the car down to thirty miles an hour. After three minutes the radio fired up again.

"The suspect has booked a tourist-class seat on BEA flight four one two to Berlin under the name of Thorwald Klaus. We managed to get a first-class seat under the name of Moliguer and a tourist-class seat for Schloss. I'll advise Berlin to have a team there to pick up the surveillance. Don't worry about your man, the Berlin police won't lose him. The English plane takes off at eight-oh-five. You've got plenty of time. In Berlin, contact my counterpart, Arno von Kleist, he's the Polizeichef there. I'm sure at this very moment he's receiving orders from the Regierender-Burgermeister. I just spoke with him on the phone. Happy hunting. Over and out."

The BEA Trident landed at Tempelhof at 9 o'clock. Laurent and Schloss hadn't had any trouble spotting the man who was traveling under the name of Thorwald Klaus. In the vast terminal, Laurent and Schloss let their prey slip away and then met up again outside. There they hailed a taxi and told the driver to take them to the Ambassador Hotel on Bayreuther Strasse.

They checked into two rooms on the fourth floor and called central police headquarters.

Arno von Kleist told them their man had already taken a room in a cheap hotel on the Mexikoplatz—the Zehlendorf, No. 57 Beeren Strasse. He had registered under the name of Klaus.

Their man did not leave his room at all that night, and the tail on him didn't start up again until the next morning at 8:40.

At 9:45, Laurent and Schloss were informed by one of Kleist's subordinates that Klaus, after having cleared his hotel bill, had gone to a color photo lab on Kobis Strasse that handled the work of most of Berlin's professional photographers. He had stayed in the shop for four minutes and then hailed a taxi. He was now heading for the airport. Shortly after getting the cab, however, he had stopped at the post office at 135 Mockern Strasse. There he climbed out briefly and dropped one envelope into the mailbox near the front door.

The policeman who was briefing them asked them to wait a minute and then continued. "I've just been told that Klaus is indeed at Tempelhof airport and has just produced both a ticket and an embarkation card for the Lufthansa flight to Frankfurt."

Schloss hung up. "I'm going to get back in touch with

Hersfeld," he said to Martin. "He's going to have to put his circus back in place."

"All we need is to figure out where this guy fits in," Martin said rather abstractedly. "But I think I've got it."

Schloss looked at the Frenchman inquisitively.

"Either you're more intelligent than I am, or you've got more background information."

"Think about it. Let's just assume that the original drawings are photographed sheet by sheet in Frankfurt, say with a twenty-four by thirty-six Leica. Klaus's mission is to pick up the films, fly to Berlin and have them developed in an enormous professional laboratory. And what does he obtain? A numbered receipt with which anyone can go and pick up the developed slides. On his way out, Klaus hails a taxi. In his pocket, he has a stamped envelope, addressed to an accomplice whom he most likely has never met. He slips the receipt into the envelope, seals it and then drops it into the nearest mailbox. He returns to Frankfurt and the chain is broken."

"That could hold water," Schloss admitted. "But you haven't explained one thing. The post office at One Thirty-five Mockern Strasse is not the 'nearest mailbox.' He could easily have mailed the letter at the airport."

Laurent lit a cigarette, pondered Schloss's question for a moment and then jumped up.

"My God! It's obvious. It's only a question of time. He mails the letter in the central post office, knowing that it will be possible for the addressee to pick it up within a specific period of time. Schloss, if Arno von Kleist isn't too fastidious about principles, we can relink the chain. All we have to do is find the letter before the addressee picks it up."

"Do you mean you want to open the mail? Don't count on that, Martin. Chancellor Brandt himself couldn't get it done."

"Well, then all we have left is the laboratory. So let's go."

They were received by the directress of the Grosse Kobis

Pictorial Organization. She was a young girl with blond hair pulled back tight. She seemed rather hard. "Lesbian," Martin thought when he first caught sight of her.

She absolutely refused to assist them: to betray a client, even for state security reasons, was impossible. She punctuated her refusal with bombastic little asides on the needs for professional secrecy. She would intervene only on a written requisition from the justice department.

"How long?" Martin asked once they stepped outside.

"A minimum of twenty-four hours, and it could also leak out quite easily," the German answered.

"Well, we're going to have to see von Kleist," Martin said disappointedly.

They took a taxi to central police headquarters on the corner of Columbiadamm and Fricesen Strasse.

Arno von Kleist switched on one of the four intercoms in his office and demanded the records division immediately.

"Get me the file on Mauren Schueller, directress of Kobis Pictorial."

A few minutes later he was scanning through her dossier. He appeared to be very happy with its contents.

"It's beautiful," he said. "Frau Schueller sleeps with her secretary, who just so happens to be underage. Seventeen, to be precise. She's the daughter of an ex-noncommissioned officer employed by the railways."

Her face flushed and her lips tightened. The directress gave in. The films were being mounted in separate little cardboard frames. Schloss and Martin viewed them without much surprise. As expected, they were shots of the complete series of drawings needed to print one comic book. The man in the lab told them he processed them every week. The firm's files said they were picked up by a young girl named Elsa Wintherhalter. She would be there that evening between 6:15 and 6:30 if she followed her normal routine of coming every Tuesday.

By five o'clock, a new mousetrap had been set at Kobis Pictorial even though they already knew by then who this girl was. Elsa Wintherhalter had a police record. The information in her file was excellent. The only reason the police were interested in her was because she was one of the thousand young girls who lived in East Berlin but held permanent jobs in the western sector of the city. Every morning she passed through the Brandenburg Gate checkpoint, and each evening she returned the same way.

So Martin's chain was once again broken. The B.N.D. did, of course, have numerous clandestine networks established in East Berlin, but none of them could come close to carrying on the type of surveillance on the girl that Martin needed.

The chief B.N.D. agent currently working in East Berlin was nevertheless asked to try and relink the chain. Now there was nothing to do but wait for his report.

19

Laurent had just asked the clerk at the desk of the Hotel Ambassador to book him a seat on the first flight out of Berlin to Paris. He had forty-five minutes to kill.

He stretched out on his bed, lit a cigarette and let his thoughts run with the music on the radio in his room. A quarter of an hour later, the telephone interrupted his drowsy napping. It was Hersfeld calling from Frankfurt.

"Marian Carter, the English girl, was found this morning at dawn in the south of Corsica near Sartène," he said.

"At seven P.M., that's in seven minutes, Channel One will be broadcasting a full report."

Laurent hung up just as Schloss rapped on his door and entered the room. The B.N.D. had also just been informed by Frankfurt. Without a word to Martin, he dashed over toward the television set and flipped it on.

The two men remained seated on the edge of the bed silently, impatiently, waiting for the variety program to end.

At seven on the dot, a news flash was indeed broadcast by the A.R.D. Though the announcer had no details, he did give a broad outline of the latest developments of the *Rosebud* affair. The English girl had been found at dawn under conditions similar to Helène's liberation. The only change had been in the location where she had been left blindfolded and bound.

The announcer went on to say that the young girl had not been maltreated physically in any way, but that her ordeal had left her emotionally frazzled. She had been discovered by a group of Scandinavian campers, and the police in Sartène had immediately driven her to the airport in Ajaccio where Lord Carter, her father, along with several agents of the Special Intelligence Service, had flown in to meet her. She carried a new sixteen-millimeter sound film.

Marian Carter's interrogation had taken place on the plane between Ajaccio and London. At Heathrow, Lord Carter and two of the special agents disembarked briefly to turn over the film to the authorities, and then, along with Lady Carter, the private jet took off again, heading for Glasgow. As the announcer spoke, Marian was recuperating near Dufftown in northern Scotland. She was supposed to spend at least a week there in the family's Victorian castle.

It is traditional in Great Britain for the press never to reveal the slightest bit of information about the secret service. Laurent and Schloss knew, however, that the screening would take place either in the offices at 21 Queen Anne's Gate or, more probably, on Curzon Street, on the second floor of the Curzon House Club, seat of the British Joint Intelligence Committee.

Laurent snapped up the phone, canceled his reservation to Paris and requested two seats on the next flight to London.

Five minutes later, the desk called back to tell them the next flight for London left at 11:15 P.M.

"Do you have any flight schedules down there?" the French agent asked.

"Yes, we do."

"I'll be right down."

Twenty minutes later the two agents were on their way

to Tempelhof to catch an SAS DC-8 to Copenhagen, where they would make an immediate connection on a Finnair flight coming from Helsinki and Stockholm to London.

It wasn't yet ten o'clock when Laurent and Schloss, firmly ensconced in the rear of a little old English Morris taxi, wheeled around Piccadilly Circus and headed on down the avenue that led to Pall Mall.

From the outside, the Curzon House Club had the ordinary, traditional appearance of most private British clubs. A short flight of five granite stairs flanked by wrought-iron banisters led to two massive wooden doors. A uniformed guard stood on the top step. His costume was just a little less formal than a coronation robe and his posture was ramrod straight. Since the age of twenty, he had been studying the art of speaking while moving only his lower lip.

"May I be of some assistance to you, gentlemen?" he recited at the approach of the two agents.

"Sir Edmund Wycherly is waiting for us," Laurent prevaricated.

A few minutes later, Laurent and Schloss made their way up the thickly red-carpeted staircase to the screening room, where sixteen members of the secret services and Parliament were waiting to see the film.

When the two agents entered, the men were gathered into several small groups speaking in grave, hushed whispers. Laurent thought they all looked like cardinals attending an ecumenical council. Sir Edmund Wycherly came over to greet them, followed like a shadow by Yefet Hamlekh. The Shin-Beth, obviously, had also reacted promptly.

"Have you seen the film?" Laurent asked Hamlekh immediately.

"Of course. We'll talk about it after the next screening, and unfortunately, I'm sure you'll agree with me. When we first saw it, we had the impression that it was a grim sick joke. But if you look a little deeper . . . well, you'll see. Let's find some seats, the second projection should start soon."

Laurent, anxious and excited, seated himself between Wycherly and Hamlekh. Schloss sat down in the first row of seats and slipped on his thick, horn-rimmed glasses. After having glanced around the room, Sir Edmund signaled to have the doors closed and the lights turned off.

Almost immediately, the first images appeared on the screen. Sabine Fargeau was now playing the part of the narrator.

Laurent was immediately struck by the sadness that distorted her expressions. One would have thought ten years separated this film from the first one shot on the fantail of the *Rosebud,* where the girl then looked superb and arrogant in spite of her nudity. Yet only two weeks had passed since the release of the first hostage. Today, her complexion was pale and waxen, deep lines furrowed the skin below her eyes, her gaze was empty and flat and her eyes gazed fixedly on some infinite point in space. She was a perfect picture of despair. Her shirt was soiled and wrinkled and there were dark circles of perspiration under her arms.

Her voice came on in a flat monotone.

"We have just learned that Marian will be freed tomorrow. There will be only three of us left here, and I know that I will be the last to be released. We have neither the courage nor the strength any longer to be happy for Marian. We have become indifferent about everything and know even less about our future fate than you do. We live in a state of perpetual anguish and we know that, for me at least, this agony will last for many more weeks, maybe months.

"These are the conditions laid down by Black September for the release of the next one of us. The Palestine Liberation Organization requests that you, the public, come up with propositions. After this film has been broadcast, the entire world must now take it upon themselves to produce constructive suggestions. Each day, these suggestions are to be broadcast and published by the television stations and the press, who will be entrusted with choosing alternatives that the governments could accept and then enact within twenty-four hours.

"When the Palestine Liberation Organization considers one of these ideas acceptable, it will indicate its approval through a series of open letters to the press. At that time, the suggestion must be put into effect and it will only be after that has been done that the next one of us will be released.

"In addition, Black September demands that a minimum of two suggestions be broadcast and published in each country every day. In order to insure that all the people have an equal voice in the submission of these suggestions, they also require that an international competition be established. This will cost my grandfather five million dollars and he can, if he so desires, request assistance from the other families involved.

"This money is to be used for ten different prizes. As soon as Black September considers one of the propositions to be acceptable, they will designate the winner's name in an open letter. The first prize will be one million dollars. What's more, in descending order, they will release the names of nine other winners. At the same time they will indicate how the remaining four million dollars' prize money is to be divided.

"Our abductors have asked me to add that though this procedure may seem to be nothing more than a cruel and childish game, in fact, it constitutes an enormous step toward their only true goal—to enlighten the people of the world on the fate of a martyrized nation. In order to take part in this competition with any hope of success, the candidates must obviously have a thorough understanding of the suffering the Palestinian people have endured since the creation of the fascist state of Israel. Anyone conducting this kind of an investigation will soon realize to what extent this information has been kept from the eyes of the public.

"Well, that's all. Black September is now waiting to see whether the world, the people, the masses will make them play the role of executioner or that of liberator. They hope to set us free."

The light was turned on, but the room remained silent. For more than a minute, no one moved. Then one by one, the gentlemen rose and left the room quietly, each of them deep in thought.

Richard Sanders, the American agent, had arrived just after the projection had started. While Sir Edmund was giving him a copy of Sabine Fargeau's text, the last of the Members of Parliament left. With a show of typically British stoicism, they had all refrained from launching into any conversation on the matter. The five delegates of the special services were once again by themselves. Sir Edmund bade them follow him up to the conference room on the next floor.

The Joint Committee's briefing room was vast and lofty. On one wall, three windows curtained in dark, heavy velvet looked down onto Curzon Street. In spite of the size of the room, it retained the air of a warm, well-protected retreat. The Victorian furniture, along with a massive portrait by Johann Zoffany and two smaller pieces by Sir William Beechey, contributed to the charmingly antiquated yet austere atmosphere.

Richard Sanders immediately scrutinized each and every piece of furniture in the room in the hope that one of them might contain a bar. Sir Edmund, two mental jumps ahead of him, moved straight to an armoire in the corner of the room, opened it and poured drinks for everyone. After inviting them to sit down, he started speaking in hesitant, abrupt phrases.

"I'm afraid that since our last conversation in New York

we really haven't been able to make much progress in this whole matter in any area. This evening, we're confronted with the same painful alternative—either we cede to them or we affront public opinion which, at this stage, certainly will not fail to force our governments to take the blame and the responsibility for the execution of one of their hostages. Don't you all agree?"

"We agree, but you're wasting your time," the Israeli interjected. "We know all that. What you are not considering, perhaps what you even refused to admit, is that the situation is worse today than it was yesterday. And I can promise you, Sir Edmund, that it will be worse tomorrow than it is today. You're letting yourself be strapped to a runaway machine and you don't even seem to be able to begin to comprehend the fact that the more fuel you give it, the faster it will go."

"I don't think that's the way Lord and Lady Carter feel today," Wycherly said.

"Enough hypocrisy, Wycherly!" Sanders snapped. "Our little conversation, to my knowledge, is not being televised."

"Let's get back to the facts," Laurent suggested. "First. It's certain that, as usual, their text and their demands will reach the press within forty-eight hours, and whatever we may attempt to do to stop it, the papers will print it. Invariably, they'll justify themselves by saying they didn't want to get 'scooped' on it. In France, for example, why would we bother to muzzle *France-Soir* or *Le Monde* when there's no way in hell of stopping *Le Canard enchaîné* or *Minute* from publishing it? I won't even bother to mention the papers on the extreme left. I would think that the same thing holds true for your countries as well."

They all agreed except for Hamlekh.

"Fine," Martin continued. "First point settled. We must let the television networks broadcast the film. Any attempt to censor them would be clumsy and childish. So, the public is informed, we will assume.

"Second point: Since the beginning of this affair the public has been following the whole mess breathlessly. The huge number of people represented by our four nations has been reacting in complete concord. Today, the Palestinians are offering them the chance to make a fortune by participating actively, and what's more, they've provided the participants with a perfect humanitarian alibi. So if the film's broadcast—have no doubts about it—there'll be hordes of people offering their silly little suggestions to anyone who'll print or publicize them."

"In other words," Sanders sneered, "you don't see any other way out than to go ahead and just blindly give in! I really wonder why we even bother to get together. Why don't we just admit once and for all that we're going to give in to their future demands and get the atomic bomb ready that they're probably going to ask us to dump on the state of Israel in order to comply with their last 'request.' "

"No, Sanders," Laurent replied. "Unfortunately they wouldn't be so stupid. They're out to undermine the very foundations of Western civilization, and they're not going to do it by even pretending or threatening to play with large numbers of human lives. The most important problem in front of us right now is to stop the sympathetic demonstrations and stifle the proclamations of those who support the Palestinians. That will necessitate violence, and since we cannot wage war on two fronts, we must yield to everything else."

"Do you have any idea of the consequences of this suggestion competition?" Schloss said.

"Schloss, *mon ami*, to ask me whether or not I've thought of the consequences is a gross understatement. I foresee 'suggestion competitions,' thousands of them. Every newspaper, from the most serious to the most absurd, will be holding its own little competition with its own little prizes according to the tastes of its clientele. And all the contests will be distressing, comical and sad. But, once again, you can count on every damn one of these editors to label us as murderers if we make any attempt whatsoever to censor them. Rest assured that *France-Dimanche* will publish, before the week's out, its first batch of suggestions from its readers, and its circulation will double."

At six o'clock the next morning, Laurent Martin telephoned Charles-André Fargeau from Orly, where Martin's plane had just landed.

"You can come straight over to my suite here at the Raphael if you want," the old millionaire said. "I hardly sleep at all anymore."

Laurent was accompanied up to the old man's apartment by the night desk man. Fargeau was freshly shaven and fully dressed, though his drawn features and badly bloodshot eyes spoke plainly of his anguish and sleepless nights. Although he would not admit it, Fargeau had suffered deeply from the wounds to his own prestige. There was no serious financial burden imposed. It was the threat of losing Sabine, however, that troubled him most.

"Anything new, Martin?" he asked in a wavering voice that only now had finally caught up with his age.

"Nothing much you don't already know, monsieur," Martin replied. "In fact, I've come to ask you a few questions."

"I don't understand what you're getting at."

"Patrice Thibaud, monsieur," Martin said curtly. "You've met your future 'son-in-law,' haven't you?"

"Don't be too abrupt with me, Martin. You know I'd do anything to save the life of my granddaughter."

"Then explain yourself. You've seen the last film. We don't have time to screw around any longer, Fargeau!"

The old millionaire dropped back into an armchair and closed his eyes. All the blood had drained from his face. Suddenly Laurent felt sorry for him. There was no longer anything in common between this broken old man now slumped in his chair and the cold-blooded industrial magnate on television who so efficiently and brilliantly had explained the reasons behind his sale of arms to the Jordanians. "Diversification of investments . . . multinational capital spread . . . repercussions from political crises on the long-term economic policy of a financial group . . ." His statement had been close to Churchillian, though in no way had it been softened by emotion, and even less by regret. Had Fargeau been so foolish as to entertain the dream that his confession might bring about the release of his granddaughter? Was he blaming himself for not having been able to find the phrases that might have moved Sabine's abductors to the point of releasing her? Laurent thought this old man's grief must now be almost immeasurable. Until his granddaughter had been kidnapped, his intelligence had been enough not only to carry him through every obstacle he had ever encountered but to insure him success as well. Today, his head was still above water, but he was caught in a current he could not control. The millionaire reopened his eyes.

"All right, Martin, what do you want to know?"

Deliberately, the French agent remained severe and hostile. "The . . . I.P.U.S."

"The I.P.S.U., the International Progressive Students Union," Fargeau corrected him.

"Forget the labels. I don't give a damn what this umpteenth red-fascist movement calls itself—where did all its sudden wealth come from?"

"From me, Martin. I've given them practically unlimited funds. Even if this leads me to the apex of absurdity, I'm going to do everything I can to increase the amount of public pressure on the government."

Laurent restrained himself. He understood the old nabob. If he'd been in his place, he most likely would have reacted the same way.

"I must meet this boy, monsieur."

"Martin, are you on my side or the government's? Or

are you trying to arrange the survival of both the girls and the government?"

"I've told you before, monsieur, as I told the highest members in the administration when I accepted this mission: The lives of the girls are my first and foremost concern."

"I have to believe you, I have no other choice. Thibaud and his brain trust have installed themselves on the two top floors of a building on the Rue Turbigo, practically right on the corner of the Rue Étienne-Marcel. My secretary will give you the exact address. However, if you want to meet him, get in touch with the little Nikolaos girl. She's working with them."

20

Laurent didn't even bother to phone. In spite of the early hour, he insistently rang the bell outside the door of the Nikolaos apartment on the Rue Guynemer. Helène's mother finally came to open the door. Fredericque had nothing on but one of her husband's sport shirts. Even though she'd been so rudely awakened and was not exactly fully clothed she carried her forty years splendidly. Her deep green eyes were sparkling with an almost malicious air of inquisitiveness.

"My name's Martin, Laurent Martin," the agent said, crossing the threshold of the doorway.

"Ah, yes! Helène's spy! Are you suffering from insomnia?"

"I would like to see your daughter. I might remind you that the lives of her three friends are still in danger."

"I haven't forgotten that. I was joking out of reflex."

"It doesn't bother me as long as you go and wake up your foolish little daughter."

Fredericque Nikolaos was a bit taken aback but nevertheless remained cordial.

"Please come in—pardon the mess. I'll make some coffee. . . . You don't agree with Helène's new political activities, I take it?"

Laurent followed her into a large room overlooking the Luxembourg Gardens. It was still cluttered with the remnants of the lively intellectual discussion that had filled it the night before. Fredericque intercepted Martin's scornful gaze.

"My daughter, my husband and our friends rebuild the world here every night between eleven P.M. and five in the morning," she said cheerfully.

"Was Thibaud here last night?"

"Of course! He's here every night. We enjoy the privilege of being the last stop on his nightly rounds. Every evening he makes a grand tour around the quarters to exhibit his wounds while extolling the virtues of the imminent revolution, which will enable the oppressed to throw off their yokes."

"I know the music."

"Yes, well, sit down, please. I'll tell Helène you're here. Would you like milk in your coffee?"

"No, black, please."

"I'm sorry we don't have any made, but it won't be long."

Ten minutes later, Fredericque reappeared pushing a small serving cart. The strong, fresh smell of the newly brewed coffee cut through the odor of cold tobacco and alcohol that permeated the room. A door slammed down the hall and Helène came shuffling barefoot into the room. She had quickly slipped on a pair of faded blue-jeans and a wrinkled cacharel shirt. The top two buttons on her jeans were unfastened. She was playing at being much more half-asleep than she really was.

"How's it going, Laurent?" she mumbled.

Before getting an answer, she turned away and pretended to be more attracted by the coffee her mother had made than she was by the agent. She quickly swallowed two large gulps, grimaced at the heat of the liquid and then started looking around the room for her cigarettes with all the concern of an addict looking for a syringe. She finally found a pack shoved down between two cushions on the sofa. She lit one, took a deep drag, then exhaled luxuriously.

"Well, Martin, it's very kind, this visit of yours," she said. "Unexpected, but very pleasant."

"I must see Patrice Thibaud," Laurent said simply. "I've been told that you two are inseparable. So I'm counting on you."

"I had a feeling this wasn't just a social visit, but I think an appointment can be arranged. Patrice is in great demand, as I'm sure you've surmised."

"Listen, Helène. I want to meet him quickly and discreetly, otherwise I wouldn't have bothered you."

"You two most certainly will not get along together at all."

"Phone him up. Tell him to be at his party offices at nine o'clock and wait for me there."

"He's sleeping. He left here at five this morning."

"Wake him. I haven't been in bed yet myself."

"Have you seen the film that Marian brought back?"

"Yes, and that's the first question you should have asked."

The young girl blushed slightly. She was about to say something, probably to apologize, but Laurent cut her short.

"It's not important," he said. "But we're giving in once again. The film will be broadcast at one o'clock and again at eight tonight."

Laurent had just made a quick stop at his apartment on the Quai Voltaire to shave, take a shower and change his clothes. At 9:05 on the dot, preceded by Helène, he climbed the staircase to the young professor's offices on the Rue Turbigo.

Patrice Thibaud was waiting for them surrounded by a dozen young men and women moving aimlessly through the rooms. They all wore serious and somber expressions which clashed with their youthful faces. The high walls of the big room in which Thibaud had set up his central office were papered with brightly colored posters covered with crudely painted demands and slogans. The only furniture was a table constructed out of two large planks set on sawhorses and six unpainted wooden chairs. Three telephones were scattered around the floor.

Thibaud was on the offensive right from the start. "I want you to know that the only reason you're here is because of Helène. No matter what your rank may be in the police hierarchy, to me you're just a cop, and I don't collaborate with cops. That said, go ahead and say what you came here to say."

"I want to talk to you alone."

"Nothing that you have to say to me needs to be concealed. You can speak to me in front of my friends or get the hell out."

Laurent had a hard time containing himself, but he answered calmly.

"No. You can always tell your friends what we spoke about if you think it's necessary once we're finished, but right now, it's imperative that our conversation take place without witnesses. Let me remind you that it's about the life of your fiancée."

Thibaud relented. Helène and the young militants left the room.

"I have good reasons to believe," Martin continued, "that I might be able to make contact with the instigators of this whole affair. Unfortunately, your collaboration is mandatory."

The eyes of the young philosopher brightened with a sudden interest. "Explain."

"It's out of the question. I won't tell you another word about it. I'm giving you five minutes, with me standing here, to leave instructions with your little friends. Then we're leaving together and will remain together until your services are no longer needed."

Thibaud sniggered. "You've got to be kidding. You couldn't possibly be so naive as to—"

"That's enough," Laurent interrupted. "I haven't got time to waste. I'll dot the *i*'s right now: you're in a position of strength, or so you think, because three kids are still being held with knives at their throats. This situation, no matter what the issues may be, will not last forever. I've come here today to propose a collaboration that could be dangerous. Nevertheless, I'm prepared to share this risk with you. It won't be easy for either one of us.

"If your answer is no, you can be sure that one day or another, I will make it public knowledge that you refused to offer your assistance to three young girls whose lives you might have saved. And on that day, Thibaud, I will handle it myself and arrange a version of the facts in such a way that you will never recover from it. Count on it. Do you read me?"

"Bastard."

"Fine. You're a fast learner, that's essential. You can call your children back into the playroom now."

Laurent and Patrice left Paris by car at eleven that morning. This time Martin was traveling under his own name at the wheel of his 911-S Porsche. Convinced that the Thibaud affair concerned only France, West Germany hadn't broadcast the films taken of Patrice's release. Only two weekly papers with a small circulation had published a picture of the young philosopher. Martin had decided not to leave from a French airport because Thibaud would surely have been spotted. They were bound for Berlin.

It took them less than six hours to reach Düsseldorf, where they caught a Lufthansa flight to Berlin. At seven o'clock, a taxi dropped them off at 72 Wund Strasse, in front of a quiet little hotel near the Funkturm fairgrounds. Hans Schloss was there waiting for them. Throughout the trip Thibaud had tried in vain to draw Martin into a dialogue. Laurent had done no more than answer with indifferent monosyllables.

The three men went directly to the room Schloss had reserved for them. The German agent had prepared all the equipment Martin had asked for: a typewriter, a Leica camera with a set of Macro lenses and two floodlamps.

"I now have to tell you more about what's going on," Martin said to Thibaud. "Do you speak German?"

"I understand it."

"Good. I'm going to type a letter and you're going to sign it."

Puzzled, Thibaud leaned over Martin's shoulder to read the words of the letter he was typing as they appeared.

"Schrantz,

"I'm typing this letter from Berlin, where I have just arrived in the company of a representative of the French government, Laurent Martin. He and I will be in Beirut at the Hotel St. George just about the time you receive this letter, that is to say, in about 48 hours from now. It was of course M. Martin who discovered your identity and the thread of communications which will allow us to reach you. And yet he has assured me, and I believe him, that no other governmental agencies or authorities have been told anything about this matter. He suggests that you contact us in Beirut and promises to abide by any security measures you may deem necessary to transport us to your location.

"You must be familiar with my active political position in the *Rosebud* affair. I decided to endorse this request because I am convinced that, in light of the present state of affairs, a meeting between the two of us and this man Martin can only prove to be beneficial for the pursuit of our mutual aims."

Laurent removed the paper from the carriage of the typewriter.

"Do you understand it?" he ask Thibaud.

"I think so, but translate it to me anyway."

Laurent complied.

"And Schrantz?" Thibaud asked.

"There'll be plenty of time to explain it to you. Sign it." Thibaud hesitated.

"Sign it. You don't have any choice." Although Martin didn't totally mistrust Patrice, he knew he would continue their relationship from a distance. A signature, a departure and uncomplicated moves were all that Martin hoped for.

Schloss picked up the letter and pinned it on the wall. Then he set up the floodlamps in crossbeams against the wall and checked the illumination with a light meter. That done, he mounted the Leica on a tripod, popped on a fifty-five-millimeter lens and took eighteen shots of the message.

By telephone, they ordered a taxi to take them to central police headquarters. Arno von Kleist immediately ushered them into the photo lab. Half an hour later, a single slide had been mounted in a cardboard frame identical to those used by Kobis Pictorial.

On Monday, the miniature photocopy of the letter was slipped into the box of slides that, the next day, as on all Tuesdays, would then be dispatched to Lebanon and the headquarters of Schrantz.

The Lufthansa 727 landed at Athens the next morning at 9:45. Laurent had slept throughout the flight. Thibaud had devoured all the daily German newspapers on board. Most of them said they were prepared to begin publishing the suggestions of their readers immediately. The Berlin *Morgen Post* and the *Bild Zeitung* were starting a long series of in-depth articles on the Israeli-Palestinian problem. It was a brilliant demonstration of the perfection of the Palestinians' blackmail. The rightists conceded, powerless to lead, the intellectual left engaged in pumping out misleading editorials. But the strangest phenomenon was that for a while, everyone continued to minimize the responsibilities of the organizers of the plot.

In the transit lounge, Thibaud instinctively glanced at the closed-circuit television screen listing the day's departures. Puzzled, he turned to Laurent. "I don't see any flight to Beirut."

"I know. We're flying El Al Flight One Twenty-one to Tel Aviv."

"What?"

"We've got forty-eight hours ahead of us and I have a few things to take care of in Israel. It has nothing to do with you. You're just coming along, that's all."

"It's a trap. I'm not going."

"Don't be so stupid. You don't represent a thing to the Israelis, plus we're only staying twenty-four hours in Tel Aviv. Then we'll fly back here and catch the first plane to Beirut. I'll repeat it for the last time. I don't give a damn about you, my only aim is to save Sabine."

They landed at Lod around midday. Yefet Hamlekh was waiting for them there. He made sure their passports weren't stamped in order to assure them free access into Lebanon the following day.

The Israeli agent had reserved them a room at the Tel Aviv Sheraton. They stayed there just long enough to drop off their luggage and then went to Zukermann's, a vegetarian restaurant, on Yehuda Street. Hamlekh liked Zukermann's for the simple reason that they served their food quickly and it was within walking distance of the Shin-Beth headquarters. At 2:15 the three men climbed the stairs leading to Hamlekh's office.

While Hamlekh and Martin went up to the next floor to have a private conversation, another Israeli agent was called in to keep Thibaud company. The philosopher, much to his delight, had finally found an apparently attentive ear for his political harangues, which Martin had thoroughly ignored. The Shin-Beth, never one to miss a chance, took mug shots of him from every angle, recorded his voice for speech patterns and lifted fingerprints from the edge of the table where he was sitting. The young man never had the slightest suspicion of what was going on.

In the Shin-Beth's briefing room, Hamlekh and Martin settled down in two deep armchairs. From his chair, the Israeli could control a small carousel slide projector. Martin pulled out his metal box of cigarettes and offered one to Hamlekh.

"I think this is going to work," Yefet said. "Bringing Thibaud along was an excellent idea. Schrantz won't be able to resist the idea of meeting an accomplice who's provided him with such excellent though unasked-for support. Besides that, he's probably dying to know how you were able to track him down. Let's accept the idea then that you're going to be meeting him soon. Who knows what could come of it? The only thing we know for sure is that you will undoubtedly be taken to the place where they do the printing. Hopefully, from that, we'll be able to pinpoint his headquarters."

"Even that could be a long shot, Hamlekh. I think it's quite unlikely that Schrantz will let us see anything. He's no fool. God knows he's shown us that."

"He doesn't know what we know. That's our only trump card. I'm going to show you twenty-one aerial photos of Palestinian commando camps in Lebanon. They were taken by one of our reconnaissance planes from an altitude of thirty-six thousand feet. On each one of them, you'll notice a small building. You'll certainly be taken to one of these twenty-one shanties, Martin. After each photo, a rough schematic plan of the layout of the buildings will appear on the screen. All of them are rectangular and their orientation to each other is different enough so that if you can determine the angle of a single wall where you're taken, we can figure out which house it is."

"What do you have in mind? A wristwatch with a camouflaged compass?"

"No, they're too bright to let a gadget like that slip by them. To try it would only be an unnecessary risk. But you do have this: the sun's position at any given time of day and the corresponding shadows it will cast, or the stars at night. This is all providing of course that you'll be allowed to see either of them. I'm only giving us one chance in a hundred, but we've got to take it."

"Even if I'm taken to this place, we still don't know for sure if the girls are there."

"Look, we don't know anything for sure. We don't even know if they'll come and get you. But we have to try everything and hope that Schrantz isn't infallible."

"He's not, Hamlekh. None of us are. Start the photos."

21

Thibaud and Laurent landed at Khalde airport the next evening. As usual, Laurent had napped during the flights from Tel Aviv to Athens and then from Athens to Beirut.

In front of the airport, they caught an old Chevrolet taxi, climbed in and rolled down the back windows to get some air. As they were heading into town, the sun sank slowly into the placid Mediterranean off to the left of the car. Even with the breeze created by the speed of the taxi, the air remained sultry until they turned onto the Rue Souleiman. The chauffeur headed up toward the Pigeon Grottos just before they reached the UNESCO Building and from there took the road leading to the little port of Minel el Hosn near the palatial Hotel Saint George, which had been built at the turn of the century.

Before being conducted to the room Schloss had reserved for them, Laurent had a long conversation with M. Tair Ben Djebaa, the old chief concierge who, after more than forty years in his position, knew a great deal more of the activities of his guests than he let on. Tair, the man with the keys to everything at the Saint George, was a member of that vanishing elite of hotel employees who truly understand what service in the grand style entails. Laurent had known him for a long time. The excellence and affability of their relationship was based on the discreet generosity the French agent habitually showed the old man.

M. Tair had just welcomed the two "tourists" with the respectful enthusiasm of a chamberlain welcoming his sovereign. After checking in and depositing his passport at the desk, Laurent motioned the old man aside with a nudge on the arm. As the agent started speaking, the concierge's face darkened as if he were a fellow conspirator in a melodramatic mime.

"M. Tair," Laurent whispered, "we're expecting some friends to contact us here at the hotel, but we don't know them. Tell your key employees that they're to get in touch with us whenever our friends may call. I don't care what time it is or whether it's day or night. Whenever we leave the hotel, we'll advise them of our itinerary, how long we'll be there and how they can reach us. That way, they'll be able to notify us within a maximum of ten minutes."

"It shall be done, M. Martin."

During the delivery of these instructions, a one-hundred-pound Lebanese note had changed hands. Any observers, even if they'd been standing close by, wouldn't have been able to detect the exchange.

They left for dinner at nine o'clock, strolled up to the Pigeon Grottos and took seats on the terrace of the Ghalaili Restaurant. On Martin's suggestion, Thibaud decided to share a *koubbé*, the national dish of Lebanon prepared with ground lamb, cracked wheat, onions and spices, baked in a pie shell and covered with *lebené*, a white cheese made from sheep's milk.

With skillful and inexorable determination, Martin repulsed each of Thibaud's attempts to draw him into a political dialogue. In fact, they ended up talking about nothing more volatile than the geography of the Near East. Even though they had not gone so far as to be deferentially courteous to each other, their relationship had become more human. A truce.

It wasn't yet eleven when the two of them, still on foot, returned to the Saint George. After quick cold showers they went to bed and were both asleep by midnight.

Laurent was yanked out of his sleep by the harsh, persistent ring of his bedside phone. It was still dark outside. He fumbled around half-asleep for a moment trying to find the switch to the reading lamp. He checked his watch. It was 2:05 in the morning. When he picked up the receiver, the voice of the night man on the desk blurted into his ear in a confused babble of bad French.

"Excuse you, M'siou Martin, I think I do good. M'siou Tair he told me I ring if friends he come. So I no know."

"You've done the right thing," Laurent cut in. "Is somebody down there asking for me?"

"I no know," the night man continued. "Yes, but it not your friends, right? It's the old Abou, the taxi of the Zahour Company. *Alors,* I no know if should ring your phone because me, I know the old Abou, he uncle of my wife, he stubborn like mule, he no say to me nothing, only that I must ring phone, that he must drive you place. *Alors,* I no know, M'siou Martin. I wouldn't want tomorrow, M'siou Tair he give me trouble, you know? So you want talk to the old Abou? He's an old mule, but he speak French like in the radio."

"Yes, that's right, get him on quickly," Laurent replied. He had trouble trying to hide his exasperation.

The old man did indeed speak perfect French. "Is this M. Martin? Listen, I've been assured that you and another man would be willing to come with me. I prefer to make things clear now: I don't like this kind of job much, but I was paid generously and my boss doesn't like me to refuse such lucrative errands."

"We'll be down immediately. Wait for us," Laurent answered hurriedly. He hung up and turned to Thibaud. "They haven't wasted any time."

Awake since the moment the phone rang, Patrice Thibaud had been anxiously studying Laurent's reactions to the call. The two men were up and dressed within a minute and a half.

The taxi was a diesel Peugeot 403. Laurent sat in the front seat next to the cabbie and Thibaud dove into the back. The old man threw the car into gear and hung a U-turn on the spot. He wasted no time in getting through the ancient part of the city. On the long, straight, deserted Rue Madame Curie he shifted into fourth gear.

"Where are we going?" Laurent inquired.

"Listen, I was paid, and paid handsomely, by some guy I've never met to drive you to a stretch of deserted road running between here and Abadiyé. As I've already said, if you don't want to go along with this, I'll take you back to the hotel."

"Did he say anything else to you?"

Without taking his eyes off the road, the old cabbie opened the glove compartment, pulled out a hastily wrapped packet and handed it to Laurent. "He only told me to drive you there and leave you there. He said you must open this. That's all. He told me that you'd agree. Otherwise, I wouldn't have accepted."

"We agree."

"*Alors,* then everything's all right."

The 403, without slowing down, veered onto the Avenue Fouad. The little car continued speeding along next to the racetrack and then made a hard right onto the Rue de Damas in front of the museum. As soon as they were outside the city limits, Abou branched off the road to Saida onto the highway leading to Baalbek by way of Zahle. Four miles later, he left the highway and turned onto the Abadiyé county road. After no more than nine hundred yards, the old Abou started down-shifting as they passed a power relay station by the side of the road. In first gear, he pulled the taxi onto a mule track and headed off into the desert. The only way he could back out was in reverse, and he knew it. The taxi jolted laboriously over sixty yards of the road and then stopped in front of an abandoned water tower.

"Here we are," he said. "This is where you get out. But, as I've said before, if you don't like it—"

"It's fine," Martin said, slipping him fifty Lebanese pounds. "Now disappear. Everything's okay."

"I told you I've been well paid."

"I know. Keep it anyway."

The old man shrugged his shoulders and put the taxi into reverse as soon as the two Frenchmen had closed the doors.

Laurent watched the movements of the headlights of the receding car. When the vehicle had reached the paved surface, he opened the little packet. Using his Dunhill for light, he examined the contents without surprise—two hoods made of black cotton and a piece of paper on which a laconic message had been written in French: "Put on the hoods. Sit down under the water tower. Wait."

Thibaud read the message over Martin's shoulder. They exchanged brief looks in the glow from the lighter, and then complied with the instructions. Laurent noted with satisfaction that the hoods had breathing holes cut over the nostrils and the mouths and took advantage of the convenience by lighting a cigarette. Very soon, however, he realized that he took no pleasure in smoking blindfolded. He stamped out his cigarette after leaning down and placing it carefully beneath his shoe.

They had waited scarcely five minutes before they were able to make out the sound of an approaching car. Laurent's trained ear told him that the engine was larger than normal and that the vehicle was coming down the mule track in reverse gear. Almost simultaneously, he heard two car doors closing softly in the distance. The precise resonance of these sounds convinced him that the car must be a large Mercedes. More by instinct than by sound, he sensed that someone was approaching on foot. The total blackness before his eyes glowed strangely and he realized that someone was shining a strong flashlight on his hood. In French, a sharp order barked into the night.

"Strip, both of you. Quickly."

They undressed, Martin completely and without surprise. Thibaud kept his underwear on.

"I said strip!" the voice repeated.

Thibaud complied.

Laurent felt a firm hand remove his wristwatch. Then two hands began to move over and into every bump and orifice on his head. From there, they moved roughly, unabashedly, down his body, under his arms, over and around his genitals, up his rectum and on down his thighs to his toes. Finally, he was handed a pair of pants and a jacket cut from coarse cloth. The two strong arms then helped him dress.

Laurent couldn't help but admire this flawless display of caution Schrantz's man had just put on.

He counted thirty-two steps to the car, and as he entered noted to his satisfaction that his judgment had been correct: the vehicle had indeed been backed down the road. Inside, it still had the odor of a practically new car. The two of them were shoved into the back seat. Laurent casually ran his hand over the central arm rest until his fingers found the ashtray: it was a Mercedes, as he had guessed. He put his left hand on the door and his right hand on the arm rest in order to get a rough estimate of how much the car would be turning in either direction.

Once the Mercedes had reached the paved road, he knew immediately that it had turned to the left, that is, it was heading back in the same direction from which they had come in the taxi. When they reached the intersection of the highway running between Beirut and Baalbek, however, they turned in the direction leading away from the capital.

For an hour they drove at a speed that was frightening even for Martin. He thought they must be doing well over a hundred. Finally, the car slowed down and then plunged onto an old road heading up into the mountains. The hairpin turns came one after another. From the sound of the tires, Martin thought the asphalt must be in very bad condition. After approximately half an hour they took a sharp turn to the right onto a totally unpaved road. Laurent concluded that the information gathered by the Shin-Beth had been correct. Most probably, they were driving through the rocky foothills between Bika and the mountain range of Anti-Lebanon.

Several times, the two Frenchmen had tried to start up a conversation, but they had been silenced by authoritative commands from the front seat.

The Mercedes finally came to a stop. Laurent estimated they had been driving for three hours. It was then close to six o'clock in the morning.

As soon as they stepped out of the car they were revitalized by the cold, sharp air. Undeniably they were in the high mountains. There was still no sunlight where they were standing. Martin thought it must have been cut off by a peak or ridge somewhere close by to the east.

They were led inside a building. A door closed behind them. Their hoods were torn off.

They were not dazzled by the sudden reappearance of some light around them. The room contained only two low-voltage bulbs that threw off an insipid yellow glow.

The walls had been crudely whitewashed. The room, vast and rectangular, looked like a college dining hall with one immense table bordered by two makeshift wooden benches. There were six windows, all of which had been completely covered with blankets nailed in place. Two stern-faced Arabs and two smiling Europeans were standing in front of them.

"Which one of you is Martin and which one is Thibaud?" one of the Europeans asked in German. "Ah yes, of course. Thibaud is the younger one with the puffy face. Do both of you understand German?"

"I do perfectly but not Thibaud," Martin replied. "I can translate if you wish."

"Do you speak English?"

"Yes, both of us," Thibaud replied.

"Then we're in good shape. We'll speak English. They'll be bringing us some coffee soon. Have a seat."

"Is one of you Wilhelm Schrantz?" Laurent asked as he sat down.

"Our chief, whom you refer to as Schrantz, will be joining us in a minute."

"Then you're Karl Volker and Ernest Schaffner."

"Those persons are dead, but it's true that we did use their names."

An Arab in a black caftan with a cartridge belt tied around his waist entered through one of the interior doors carrying a tray with eight bowls, a large Turkish coffee pot and a dish of *fattouch,* a salad made with cucumbers, mint and watercress. There was also a bottle of sumac liquor and . . . a red carton of metal-boxed cigarettes, filterless.

"Congratulations," Martin said with a smile. "But I had four boxes in my pockets. You shouldn't have gone to the trouble—"

"All of your belongings are now in your hotel room at the Saint George. You'll find them when you return," one of the Germans proudly declared. "Your four boxes of cigarettes will be there as well. It is just a matter of precaution, Martin. It's not that we don't trust you, it's just that the 'James Bondies' our fascist Israeli friends have such a sweet tooth for can be a pain in the ass sometimes. On the other hand, we have no reason to prevent you from smoking."

The door opened. Schrantz entered the room, followed by Ulrika Raad. He was tall and thin almost to the point of emaciation. He had a face like a desert vulture and the few remaining wisps of blond hair around his ears did little to cover his bald pate. His eyes were amazing. The whites were pale and faintly bluish, the retinas yellow like a goat's.

Ulrika Raad, the woman, moved with the grace of a large cat. She had thick blond hair and broad Valkyrie's shoulders. She was obviously naked under her light caftan, and one could easily make out the line of her high, pear-shaped breasts. She had a fine and sultry face and the combined effect of the two created a look that was both magnetic and mad.

She sat down opposite the two Frenchmen. Schrantz greeted them with a gesture that was more of a twitch than a sign of politeness. He never stopped moving, even while he was speaking. His lungs could not suck in enough air to push out all the words of his endless sentences. His speech came in short, halting gasps interrupted by deep inhalations that never seemed to provide him with enough oxygen.

"So, Martin," he said, "you've worked your way up the river to its source and now I'm standing here before you. Do you think that's going to get you anywhere? Well, my handsome agent, it won't! Our organization is indestructible now. And if you take any more of your little steps forward, you will find you will go no further. In a few hours, you'll be driven back to Beirut. That's how much I fear you and your whole apparatus. You can even release my name to the press. I'd be delighted."

"Listen, Schrantz," Martin said. "I haven't come here to do combat with you, but to try to convince you. Release the girls and stop this tragic blackmail. The world would only admire you more for it."

"The world will forget us within a week, you know that quite well. My actions have a timetable that covers years. My plans are final. Nothing will stop them from being put into effect. Each representative of your press and information establishments will, from now on, perform his duties with a dagger at his throat. But when you get back, tell the others what I've said. One false move, one hesitation, and I'll toss them the corpse of one of these kids with her throat slit like a sow at slaughter."

"It's most likely that we'll yield until the last one of the girls is freed," Martin conceded, "because I'm sure you're shrewd enough to have assessed just what demands you can force upon us and which ones you cannot."

"Don't you worry about that."

"Before leaving, could we see the girls?"

"You couldn't be stupid enough to think they've been kept here! As I've said, Martin, you have met me, but it's only a theoretical step forward that will bear no fruit. We have nothing left to say to each other. I would send you back immediately if I didn't have to wait for nightfall to cross the country."

"I suppose from what you've just told me that after you liberate the last girl you're going to start to put your next coup into motion?"

"Obviously. But don't waste your time trying to divine what it will entail. The originality and effectiveness of our future actions will surprise you every time."

"You're a dreamer, Schrantz. If you think this planet can or will support more of your demented little games in the future, you're further out of your mind than I ever imagined you to be."

"Perhaps that is the case. At any rate, this meeting is finished, Martin. I've assigned two men to guard you until dusk. Then you'll both be driven back to Beirut. Thibaud, your work has been appreciated. Thank you."

Then abruptly, he turned on his heel and was gone.

Laurent and Thibaud remained behind with the two Arabs. Martin broke open the carton of cigarettes and took out one of the metal boxes. He was bitter and disappointed.

Thibaud felt totally disillusioned. He had expected a hero's welcome.

Martin realized now that any attempt to pinpoint the location of the building would be futile. He had no hope of getting out of the room and he was now certain that in addition to the blankets covering the windows, the panes themselves were painted black. Not even the slightest bit of light penetrated into the room from the outside. If he'd had even so much as one thin beam, he might have been able to determine the sun's movements.

Martin estimated that it was around noon when a man entered the room with a plate of unleavened bread and sheep's cheese. The two guards responded to none of his questions and said nothing to each other. One or the other of them always had a Czechoslovakian machine pistol pointed at his head. Thibaud, they ignored.

22

For a long time after the meal, Laurent did little more than pace around the table. His guards didn't try to stop him, but they never took their eyes off him and the barrels of their pistols followed his course like divining rods. Patrice had fallen asleep in the corner.

He finally sat down on one of the benches with his back to the table, propped his elbows on the edge behind him and lit his fifth cigarette. Without the slightest idea of what to do, without the slightest hope, he started scrutinizing each square inch of the floor. There seemed to be nothing else to do. The floor itself was packed earth with a deep ocher color. It was quite flat and appeared to have been leveled out with an air hammer. Laurent started to follow the random buzzings of a fly. The insect approached a faint line traced in the earthen floor, turned away from it before crossing it and then started flying back toward it again. Out of boredom, Laurent bet himself that next time, the fly would cross the line. The fly did not cross it, but turned away again and flew toward the other side of the room. Laurent's gaze followed it until he could no longer see it and then he lit another cigarette with the butt of the first one. He was furious with the fly for botching up his imbecilic little game. He could hear it buzzing up near the whitewashed ceiling now, but he could not see it. Something was troubling him, but he could not figure out what it was—an idea forming somewhere he could not pin down. He abandoned his silly game with the fly to concentrate. Very soon, he figured out what had been working on his subconscious.

Maintaining an outwardly nonchalant composure, he let his gaze slowly wander back to the ground. The line he had used to play his game with the fly was unusual. It had been cut into the packed floor with either a knife or a razor, starting from the wall and extending out into the room four feet. But what intrigued Laurent was that whoever had drawn the line had obviously used a straight edge of some kind to guide his blade. This meant that this thin furrow had been traced out with particular care and, therefore, for a definite purpose. What that purpose was, Laurent could not figure out. In fact, he hadn't the slightest inkling. Geometrically, it made no sense. The line left the wall at an acute angle, ran four feet out into the room and stopped without any logical explanation. And yet, there must have been some reason for it.

Martin racked his brain on the line for more than an hour. Twice he gave up out of frustration, but impulsively he came back to the puzzle. Then a wild idea crossed his mind. He dismissed it several times. It would be too good to be true. After another hour had passed, though, he still could not come up with another explanation.

Finally, he decided to act as if this wild idea did indeed have some merit. If he played it carefully, he had nothing to lose. He started fiddling with his box of cigarettes. Rather adroitly, he slipped the little printed insertion out of the box. That done, he pretended to concentrate on the printing on the paper advertising the qualities of the tobacco used in the preparation of the cigarettes. All of his movements seemed casual almost to the point of indifference. For a good half hour he kept the piece of paper moving between his fingers, passing it from one hand to the other. The guards paid no attention to his fidgeting, thinking that it was only nervousness brought on by the long wait. Laurent stood up indolently and sauntered up and down the room. Then, quite naturally, he plopped down on the floor two inches away from the line and leaned back up against the wall.

After a while, he started nodding his head sleepily and then slowly slid down off the wall until he was lying flat on the floor. Soon, he appeared to have fallen into a deep sleep. He decided to count to a thousand at a pace of about one beat per second.

When he reached a thousand, he rolled over on his side as if he were seeking a more comfortable position in his sleep. His back was now turned to the guards. He opened his eyes. His left hand, in which he still held the piece of paper, lay just at the crux of the angle where the mysterious furrow met the wall.

Keeping his body perfectly still, he managed to fold the piece of paper with the fingers of his left hand in such a way that it perfectly duplicated the angle that the line drawn on the floor made with the wall. With his thumbnail, he accentuated the crease on the paper and then unfolded it and smoothed it out. The line of the fold was still visible.

A few moments later, he stretched languorously, stood up as if still half-asleep, strolled over to the table and fished another cigarette out of his pocket.

He needed both hands to strike a match for the cigarette, and so to slip the piece of paper inside his jacket pocket seemed like a reflex action.

The hours dragged on interminably. Nothing disrupted the enervating monotony. The frozen, stoic patience of the guards never faltered; they even refused to tell him what time it was. The silence they maintained between each other seemed almost mystical.

Laurent was now only trying to keep track of the hours.

Suddenly, everything broke. Within a few seconds he knew he had succeeded in his mission beyond all his expectations.

The silence, which for hours had drawn on and on without respite, was now shattered by a distant nasally whining cry. Laurent recognized the mourning sound as the chant of the *salat*. Without much difficulty, he could imagine the minaret outside, from the top of which the muezzin was calling the faithful to prayer. He knew the litany by heart: "There is no God but the one God and Mohammed is His prophet. . . ."

While one of the guards kept an eye (and a pistol) on Martin, the other one moved over to where the agent had sprawled on the floor. The brief, furtive glance the Fedayin shot at the line did not escape Martin's attention. The Muslim knelt down in the direction of the line and started praying in the ritual fashion. He described a quarter-circle in the air with his arms outstretched, bent forward and placed his palms flat on the floor in supplication. In a high-pitched moan, he proclaimed his faith in the supremacy of Allah and the irreproachable probity of his messenger Mohammed.

Laurent's heart was pounding madly. His wild hypothesis had proved true. The line ran straight in the direction of Mecca, and in his pocket he had the exact angle at which it joined the exterior wall. With these figures, a ninth-grade child could calculate the exact directional orientation of the rectangular building in less than three minutes.

Laurent knew he'd been inside almost all day and felt sure that this *salat* was either the evening prayer or the one that occurred one hour after sunset. He could not figure out why he hadn't heard the other three or four during the day, but it didn't matter. He knew his waiting period was almost over, and he had the information he wanted.

Indeed, just after the second guard had finished his prayers, the hood was replaced over the French agent's head. After a three-hour drive, he and Thibaud were let out behind the El Khoder mosque, still blindfolded. When they removed their hoods, they found they were in Beirut's slaughterhouse district. The area was deserted.

Ten minutes later, they hailed a cab and returned to the Saint George.

The clothes they had stripped off when they were first picked up were carefully folded on the beds.

Martin took a shower, then phoned the desk and left instructions to have someone wake them at 5 A.M. The daily Alitalia flight to Rome via Cairo and Athens took off from Khalde at 6:30.

Laurent fell asleep contemplating the sweet axiom that there wasn't a man on earth who could foresee everything, Schrantz included.

23

Laurent had the radio engineer on the Italian plane to Athens measure the angle he had copied from the paper onto a piece of cardboard. It was exactly 28.3 degrees. At 9:45 he caught an El Al flight to Israel. He was in Tel Aviv for only three hours. In the Shin-Beth's screening room, it took Hamlekh's specialists no longer than eleven minutes to pinpoint Schrantz's hideout from their aerial photos.

It was a long, rectangular building wedged into a little mountain clearing four thousand feet above sea level. As the crow flies, the refuge was twenty-five miles from Baalbek and approximately the same distance from the Syrian border.

It was out of the question that the girls were being kept there. Both Helène and Marian had been positive about the amount of time they spent on the road before they were put into the light plane that brought them to Corsica—one hour. It didn't jibe. Hamlekh's men calculated that it would take a minimum of two hours' driving to reach level ground from Schrantz's, and Laurent estimated that he'd spent at least that much time in the mountains when he was driven both ways.

Martin and Colonel Fulham, without much enthusiasm,

suggested that perhaps the Lebanese authorities ought to be informed. Hamlekh settled that point quickly.

"Absurd. Even if we assume that they'd go along with us, the news would surely reach Schrantz before our forces did."

"I don't think an Israeli commando action would be too desirable," Laurent said. "Schrantz must have made provisions for such an eventuality. The Fedayeen holding the girls could easily execute one in reprisal. If word of your raid ever leaked out, we'd be in fine shape."

"Nevertheless, we will make contingency plans for a commando attack," Hamlekh replied. "I give you my word, though, that it will only be put into action with your approval."

"I'll remember that, Hamlekh. The only reason I believe you is because our interests are so closely intertwined."

"It's the best guarantee of mutual confidence, *mon ami*."

Hamlekh drove Martin back to Lod shortly after two. He had just enough time to catch BOAC's daily flight to Zurich. From there he could get a quick hop to Paris.

Over the Adriatic, the weather conditions deteriorated. The English Trident bounced like a ball in a washing machine. There was one storm after another from there to Zurich.

Above Zurich, the visibility was nil. The plane went into a holding pattern while they waited for a landing clearance from the Zurich tower.

Finally the cloud cover broke. The tower estimated the clearing would last no more than four minutes, and the pilot put the plane into a steep descent.

In the cabin, the passengers exchanged troubled looks. The sudden change in altitude and cabin pressure brought on severe earaches for almost everyone, Laurent included. He forced himself to swallow several times. As the plane was touching down in a pouring rain, his ears finally cleared. Almost simultaneously, he had an idea. He just remembered a remark Helène had made that he had not previously paid any attention to, even though now, in retrospect, it seemed blatantly illogical.

In the Zurich transit lounge, Laurent bought all the European papers. He skimmed through them during the flight to Paris. It was incredible. The most preposterous suggestions were spread all over the front pages. Each one gave the name and address of the author.

The first to try to cash in on the deal were the sharks who are always looking for easy money. An important real estate corporation proposed to build a chain of modern apartment houses on the east bank of the Jordan River over a period of several years, to be occupied solely by Palestinian refugees. The president of the corporation had specified that all the capital needed to finance this gigantic enterprise would naturally be deposited in various banks in Lebanon, Syria or Jordan before the hostages were liberated. Thus the Fedayeen would be insured against a double cross.

But the most shameless aspect of the whole project was the possible variations put forth by the authors. In an addendum to their proposal, they made the development sound like a vacation community. Why not simply build on the banks of the Sea of Galilee? This would offer the uprooted Palestinians not only decent living accommodations but a return to "the Art of Living." It was all written in the seductive jargon of a real estate promotional prospectus. The copywriters hadn't even had the grace to exclude standard phrases like "elegant but functional" and "every apartment with a view." As a final, magnanimous gesture, the promoters promised that if they were to receive the $1,000,000 first prize, they would immediately turn it over to be used as additional capital for financing the project.

The film sharks were also trying their luck. One of the largest international production companies had offered to start shooting an epic on the Palestinians, with an unlimited budget. They then listed a number of script writers for the screenplay who, because of their open political positions, could not refuse the offer. The names of several actors, actresses and directors who never missed a chance to remind the public of their leftist sympathies were also included. In conclusion, the producers said they hoped the film would more than counterbalance the Preminger production of *Exodus.*

It was the same song and dance in each of the other daily and weekly papers. Opportunists from all political parties, professional avengers, the uninformed, fanatics from the extreme left, former Fascists on the extreme right nostalgic for the days of Nazi anti-Semitism, all offered up their own little "original ideas." The Fedayeen had again achieved their aim without tarnishing their image: the "affluent" society was disintegrating from within and yet no one could talk about anything but the Palestinians.

Charlie-Hebdo, the caustically sarcastic French leftist weekly, ran a cover illustrating a reader's suggestion that Golda Meir put on a color-televised striptease to the revolutionary anthem of the Palestine Liberation Organization. Laurent thought the stance of *Charlie-Hebdo,* all things considered, to be the least debasing suggestion of the lot.

PART IV

24

As soon as he landed at Orly, Laurent Martin phoned Colonel de Savigny from a booth at the airport. When he dropped into the back of a taxi a few minutes later, his ears were still ringing from the string of invectives the colonel had launched into. After the first forty-five seconds of the one-way conversation, the agent had simply set the receiver down quietly and walked out of the booth.

When Laurent entered de Savigny's office in the old station on the Boulevard Mortier, de Savigny seemed relatively calm. He recited his complaints in a subdued voice, but nevertheless they rang false.

"The world is breaking apart in a crisis of collective delirium. We're being overrun on all sides, betrayed by the press, stepped on by the government, which then turns around and places all of its responsibilities and failings on our shoulders, and you disappear for four days without a word."

"I needed a vacation—"

"You can take mine, Martin. But I really would have preferred it if you had run off somewhere to get a suntan. I never thought for an instant that you had set this affair aside, knowing as I do how bloody tenacious you are. But the same knowledge obliges me to suspect that there are certain elements in this case that you have extracted from the mud and are keeping from me. This, I cannot allow."

"Even if I assure you that this silence is necessary if my investigation is to continue?"

"Do you distrust me?"

With a smile, Laurent lit a cigarette before responding. "Don't you trust me? It's nothing against your integrity personally, Colonel, but what if the Minister of the Interior should call tomorrow and ask you the same rhetorical question? And what if the President should call him the day after that, and say the same thing? I'm in no way suggesting that you may share my confidences with your friends over whiskey, but, believe me, if you force me to file a brief on this for you, I'll drop the whole thing completely, and I'm not joking. Though you will then have all the information I've gathered at your disposal, I will pack my bags and leave for the country, there to install myself in front of a television to follow the results of your investigation."

De Savigny had restrained himself too long. He exploded. "All right, go ahead and blackmail me. It seems to be the tactic in vogue these days. It's almost become an institution, a doctrine as highly regarded as democracy. Soon, the most insignificant requests will be systematically rejected if they're not submitted along with a threat."

"I had demanded carte blanche freedom at the beginning of this and I received it," Martin cut in. "Today, all I ask you to do is stand by your word. I'm fully aware of the fact that you've got politicians to deal with, and I know it's not pleasant playing the role of a shock absorber, but there's nothing I can do about that. I'd like to go now, I've got things to do."

"Then get the fuck out of here, Martin! I've been summoned to the ministry of the interior and I have nothing more to tell them than what's currently being broadcast on television. So thanks for the help."

Martin was just walking out the door when the colonel called him back.

"Laurent!"

"Yes, Colonel?"

"Pardon me."

"Forget it."

Martin took two steps back into the office and stopped directly in front of the colonel's desk.

"I'm going to be leaving again soon," he said, "maybe for several weeks. Any one of your first-year men could follow me without much difficulty. I could lose him eventually if I wanted to take the trouble, but it would force me to waste precious time. I want your word, Savigny, don't play against me."

"All right!" the S.D.E.C.E. officer bellowed. "Now get out of here."

Twenty minutes later, Laurent was ushered into Charles-André Fargeau's suite at the Hotel Raphael. Senator Erskine Donovan and Gunther Fryer, the fathers of Joyce and Gertrud, were there. The faces of the three men were deeply lined from exhaustion and despair. The tall old man looked like an automaton. His eyes, now lifeless, met Laurent's in silent inquiry.

"I'm sorry, sir," Martin said. "I have nothing to say that could ease your grief or anxiety. I've only come here to ask you to intervene on my behalf with Lord and Lady Carter. I must have Marian with me for a few days, but I can't tell her parents any more than I can tell you what the reasons behind my request are. I would like to take Marian and Helène Nikolaos down to the Maritime Alps. I haven't yet chosen the spot, but it would be secluded and they wouldn't be bothered. I'll try to make it as close as possible to Cannes."

"I beg of you," Donovan interrupted. "You must be

acting on some kind of solid clue to be doing this, and your duty is to tell us."

"Let me assure you, Senator, that my duty is to remain silent. Don't think I'm suffering from a conspiracy psychosis. My only aim is to recover your girls safe and sound. Don't make my task any more difficult than it already is."

Fargeau picked up the phone and gave the operator the number of the Carter residence near Dufftown, Scotland. Their call lasted twenty minutes. Fargeau felt sure Lady Carter was listening to the conversation on another phone and objecting to his request. Finally, the old millionaire passed the receiver to Laurent. The three men listened in amazement to the French agent's demands.

"I want," he began, "to meet your daughter as soon as possible at the London airport, where I will be waiting for her along with Helène Nikolaos. By then I will have rented a light plane to fly the three of us from London to Nice."

"I can put my personal plane at your disposal," Carter answered.

"It's essential that the plane be a particular type. Please don't ask for explanations. I can assure you that your daughter won't be running any risks whatsoever."

The distress of Fargeau, Donovan and Fryer finally convinced the Carters to go along with Martin's request. It was decided that Martin would phone back in an hour to fix the exact time for their rendezvous in London.

On the Rue Guynemer, the Nikolaoses asked no questions. Helène obediently started to pack for the trip.

Helène and Laurent landed in London at 1:30 in the morning. Twenty-five minutes later, Carter's private jet touched down.

At three, Laurent, Marian and Helène were fastening their seat belts in a Beechcraft Twin Bonanza rented from a company in Weymouth. Normally, the plane was used as an air taxi between the British mainland and the Channel Islands.

The pilot was a stocky Royal Air Force veteran in his early fifties. He'd been given specific instructions not to mention the details of this flight to anyone. He'd also been told to follow Martin's instructions without question, otherwise he might be endangering the lives of the two young passengers.

The interior of the Beechcraft was as well outfitted as a Lincoln. Martin took the copilot's seat while the two girls seated themselves in the rear.

As soon as the little plane had started rolling down the runway, Laurent turned around to face the girls. During the entire takeoff he watched the girls attentively. He didn't face forward again until the Beechcraft had reached its cruising altitude and speed. He remained impassive and mute until they passed over Newhaven. He then turned to the pilot. "What's our altitude?"

The pilot pointed toward the altimeter. "Nine thousand five hundred feet."

"Could you descend as slowly as possible to one thousand five hundred feet?"

The pilot shrugged his shoulders indifferently, and cut back the rpm's of his engines.

"Ah no, Laurent. That's enough!" Helène protested. "My ears have been hurting for the last fifteen minutes, and they're just starting to clear now."

"That's exactly why we're here, so just sit back and shut up. And you, Marian, how're your ears?"

"They haven't bothered me much," the young English girl replied. "But you must know that almost everyone has the same reactions to variations in altitude."

"Yes, I do. But all you have to do to equalize the air pressure on both sides of your eardrums is either yawn or swallow."

"What are you getting at?" Helène asked with open irritation.

"It's simple. The first day we met at Calvi, you told me that the light plane that brought you to Corsica had flown very low. You also told me that you didn't have any earaches during the trip, and yet since then each time I've flown with you in an unpressurized plane you've complained bitterly."

"True."

"At the time, I didn't pay the slightest bit of attention to this detail, and yet it's essential. Why should the plane have flown just above the ground all the way across the Libyan desert, Tripolitania and the sea? I watched you while we were taking off, Helène. We hadn't reached an altitude of three hundred feet before you grimaced."

"But I'm sure I didn't feel any pain in my ears the day I was freed either," Marian interjected.

"That's exactly what I wanted the two of you to tell me."

They landed in Nice a few minutes before six. The strong, warm breeze outside the plane picked them up immediately. The cloudless sky had the veiled pallor of Mediterranean dawns.

A driver was waiting for them in front of the deserted terminal building. Before they had left the Hotel Raphael the evening before, Laurent had accepted Charles-André Fargeau's offer of the use of his estate on the Cap d'Antibes. Laurent, Helène and Marian said good-bye to the pilot and settled themselves in the back of a beige Rolls-Royce with Swiss plates.

Twenty minutes later, the tires of the luxurious car squealed on the packed gravel drive that ran from the gate at the edge of the estate to Fargeau's stately provincial mansion.

The main house sat on the edge of a cliff ninety feet above the sea and was constructed in the style of a country farm. It was, however, the kind of farm that no farmer could ever afford to own. Every architectural detail of the building had been designed to lend credence to the rural motif. Both inside and out, though, the effect seemed embarrassingly overdone. The girls and Laurent were led to their rooms by two silent chambermaids.

"Get a good rest," Laurent advised the girls, "but be up and dressed by nine."

"Yes, Daddy," the two girls chimed in unison.

Laurent smiled. "I'll be right next door in case you're afraid of the dark."

"I'll remember that," Helène said just before she followed Marian into their room.

Laurent slept fitfully. He was shaving when the chambermaid, after knocking on his door, came into the room and set a pot of hot coffee on his table. He took a cold shower and then swallowed three cups of black coffee in rapid succession. He slipped on a pair of light slacks, a loose-fitting Austrian knit shirt and some sandals. He lit a cigarette and noted that he still had half an hour ahead of him before he had to use the phone. He decided to take a leisurely walk through the gardens surrounding the estate.

His aimless stroll brought him to the artificial clearing where Fargeau had had a huge diamond-shaped swimming pool installed. The pool itself was lined with multicolored mosaic tiles and surrounded by six low bungalows.

Much to his surprise, he discovered Helène there, swimming evenly and gracefully from one end of the pool to the other. She was entirely naked. He decided to stop and enjoy the scene to the fullest without any restraint. When he arrived, Helène was heading toward the opposite end of the pool.

Reaching the far side, she executed a perfect competition turn off the wall. She spotted Laurent as soon as she broke the surface on her way back. She was startled momentarily, but then fell into her normal rhythm again without hesitation.

A few yards from where Laurent was standing, she stopped swimming and let her body slip into a vertical position in the water. Without any sign of emotion, she surveyed Martin from head to toe with a look that was almost impudently casual. "You can get me a bathrobe from one of the cabanas," she said with a smile. "Well, go on, don't just stand there like a fool. You look like Rachid Ben Aloush."

Laurent admitted that his gaze did justify her sarcasm. Nevertheless, he decided to take advantage of the situation.

He flung his clothes over a lounge chair and dove into the water.

Helène called out, "You dirty old man, where's my towel?" She giggled.

Laurent swam well. He wasn't half as tan as the girl, but his suppleness and strength showed. He disappeared under the calm water and sprang up beside Helène, taking hold of her ankle. She resisted and splashed water into his face, squirming like a wild brown trout who might not be set free. He took hold of her thigh and slid his palm up the side of a long leg and around the curves of her back. His movements were controlled and gentle. His hand caressed her breast.

Helène let him move down her body, down, as she released all restraint, the feel of his hand moving through the liquid pool on her flesh, made hard by the air and the water, and moving slightly to the cadence of his touch. She was floating in his arms. Her soft, dark eyes closed and her arms pulled him toward her. The lightning of their bodies touched, mouths soft and flaming, a moment, then the sound of laughter from Helène. She took control, bit his lip lightly and kicked and splashed suddenly, an escape. She swam away as fast as she could, the spray of fresh water now in Laurent's eyes. She had won her game.

Out of the water she climbed into a robe. "You're a beautiful old man, though," she shouted, and ran in to get dressed.

Back at the manor a few minutes after nine, Laurent phoned the Navimer Agency. He reached Mme. Girardin, who then passed the phone to her husband. For some years, Girardin had been the director of the luxury-yacht rental company in Cannes. In his field, he was a specialist whose prestige was well known. Laurent had met him several times, and yet he had to speak with the man both diplomatically and firmly in order to get him to leave his office immediately and come to the Fargeau estate on the Cap d'Antibes.

Girardin arrived by sea, using the time to give a client's new Riva Super-Aristo a high-speed open-water checkout. He had been to the Fargeau place several times and used the elevator cut into the cliffs in front of the house, which carried the old man's guests directly from the dock to the estate's front lawn.

He was a stocky, healthy-looking man who obviously spent a lot of time in the sun and on the sea. His prematurely white hair contrasted sharply with his deeply tanned face. He declined Hélène's offer of a drink and plopped down in an armchair, curious and attentive.

"I don't think there's any need to introduce you to the young ladies," Martin said. "However, I must warn you that whatever assistance I'm going to request from you must not go any farther than this room. If it does, it could cost the lives of the three girls who are still being held hostage. So whatever your decision, I will count on your discretion. Enough said on that."

"Yes, enough said on that," Girardin replied. "Go ahead."

"I'm sure that you, like the rest of the world, have followed the progression of events in this kidnapping rather attentively, especially those events which took place at sea."

"That's true."

"Up until now, I hadn't thought of consulting you or any other maritime specialist on a point I've considered to be of secondary importance, that is, the identification of the kind of boat on which the girls were transferred from the *Rosebud* to the coast."

"If my memory serves correctly," Girardin said, "from what I've read, the girls, all five of them, were locked in a cabin for forty-eight hours. Is that what you want me to go on?"

"Exactly." Turning to the girls, the agent continued. "I want you to try and remember everything you possibly can about that boat. Even details that may seem to be totally insignificant to you. Then try to answer M. Girardin's questions as precisely and accurately as you can."

"We'll need paper and pencils," Girardin said. "That's fine," he added when Helène returned carrying a large legal pad and a jar of pens and pencils. "Now I want you to try and give me a sketch of the interior of the cabin, including the position of each of the bunks. Don't compare notes. I want separate drawings."

The girls complied and soon handed him nearly identical drawings. The first conclusion was obvious. The cabin was in the bow of the boat.

Their recollections coincided also on another point. The bathroom was located just to the left of the cabin door if one was facing the stern of the boat. Helène described it very carefully and Marian agreed on all points. The toilet itself had another, smaller aluminum bowl inside of it that could be used as a bidet, and this was hinged at the back together with the lid.

"That's very common," Girardin said with a smile. "Many of the newer yachts, even the most luxurious, are not as spaciously equipped as the *Rosebud*. But you said the shower was to the left when you entered the bathroom. Are you sure about that?"

"Quite," Marian said.

"Did you notice how the toilet was flushed?"

"Of course," Helène answered quickly. "You had to pump it by hand."

"Are you sure it wasn't just a hand pump to be used in case the normal electrical flushing system broke down?"

"Fairly sure," Helène continued. Marian nodded in agreement. "I remember when I first used it, I instinctively looked for the pedal. All the bathrooms on the *Rosebud* were automatic."

"Well, that's something," Girardin declared. "I assume the two of you have spent a lot of time cruising on different kinds of yachts. Can you remember what the engines sounded like?"

This time Marian answered. "Twin diesels. I'm positive," she said.

"That's obvious. I meant the auxiliary motors."

"Yes, I see what you mean. Before we were transferred to shore, I remember they shut off the main engines and another, smaller one was started up."

"That's not what I'm talking about. That was probably the generator."

"It seems to me," Helène said, furrowing her brow, "yes—I'm certain that sometimes I heard the sound of an electric pump way at the back of the boat."

"Think it over carefully, mademoiselle. It's extremely important."

"Of course. . . . Now I can tell you for sure. I'd looked for the pedal to flush the toilet next to our cabin because I'd heard the sound of an electric pump in the rear. You know, in spite of the regular, continuous sound of the main engines, you can always hear the sound of those electric johns flushing, even on the *Rosebud*."

Marian, when questioned, admitted that this was a detail she had not noticed.

"I wouldn't have paid any attention to it either," Helène

said, "except that I was rather surprised not to find the pedal in our bathroom."

Girardin cut her short with a wave of his arm, and turned to Laurent. "Would you like to know what kind of a yacht it was? I think I know."

"No, don't!" Laurent said quickly. "Do you think it'd be possible to find the same model anywhere around here?"

"Certainly. There's one in the old port. I take care of it in the winter when it's not being rented."

"Were you thinking of any others before you decided it was this one?"

"Yes, there are four different makes of boats with heads located just to the left of the forward cabin."

"I'd like to have Marian and Helène board each one of these five different kinds of yachts," Martin said. "Can you arrange that quickly?"

"Between Port Canto and the old port of Cannes? Certainly. Give me an hour to get in touch with the captains or the caretakers, though."

"Could you just give them some excuse to get the keys? I don't want any other witnesses around."

Girardin thought about it for a moment. "Well, maybe. But in that case, give me two hours."

The forward cabin and the bathrooms of the five large cabin cruisers were all inspected separately by the two girls. The length of the yachts ranged from forty-two to sixty feet. Three of them were inspected at their moorings in Port Canto and the other two were boarded where they were anchored alongside the jetty in front of the main casino.

Helène and Marian were positive. Individually they picked the yacht that Girardin had had in mind. It was an Ischia Baglietto, approximately ten years old. Laurent was inwardly elated. He finally had a solid line to work on.

"What kind of mysterious procedure did you use to arrive at your conclusion?" he asked Girardin.

Girardin smiled with satisfaction. "Simple," he said, "Ischia Bagliettos are the only ones with electrically flushed toilets in the stern and manually flushed toilets in the bow."

"I see," Laurent said. "Well, thank you very much. And remember, say nothing about this to anybody." Turning to the two girls he added, "And that means you too. I don't want you mentioning a word about this, not even to your families. I'm going to phone your parents and tell them to come and get you. I want to see them personally before you leave."

"You can count on me," Marian said. "Would you let me call my father myself, though? My parents are still a little worried about me."

"Of course, but wait till we get back to the house. We're leaving right now. And Girardin, I'm going to need your help for a little longer. I hope you don't mind."

Five minutes later, the Riva Super-Aristo was blasting over the open sea between the Lerin Islands at seventy miles per hour.

25

The butler was setting out a cold buffet in a shaded corner of the front terrace when Marian appeared to say that she had reached her father. He would arrive late in the afternoon. She seemed overjoyed.

"Call your family," Laurent said curtly to Helène. "Tell your father he can catch the four fifteen Caravelle out of Le Bourget. We'll have a car meet him at Nice."

Nonchalantly, indifferently, Helène strode over to the bar on the terrace. She picked up a large crystal glass and dropped in three cubes of ice before pouring herself two fingers of vodka.

"Did you hear me?" Laurent snapped.

She didn't answer. With great affectation, she leaned up against the bar and looked out toward the sea for a minute, apparently deep in thought. Finally she opened a bottle of tonic and poured half of it into her glass.

"Let's stop this comedy, Helène," Laurent said firmly. "Put that glass down and go phone your father."

She turned around as if emerging from a dream and surveyed Martin mischievously.

"I'd like to talk to you alone," she said. "Please excuse us," she said to Marian. "Go ahead and eat, our discussion might take a long time." Without waiting for an answer from the French agent, she took him by the hand and led him down the path toward the pool.

Halfway down the path, she stopped.

"Well then," Laurent snapped. "You've got five minutes."

"I refuse to go back to my parents. I feel I can be of more use to you here."

"Out of the question. And you're out of your mind."

"Not at all. I understand everything now, and besides, I get bored in Paris."

"The purpose of my investigation is not to alleviate the boredom of a spoiled little girl."

"Spoiled little girl or not, you didn't complain this morning, did you? You snap your fingers in the middle of the night and we have to pack our bags. Now, you're through with us and you think you can just throw us away. I don't have any illusions about this, but tomorrow or the day after, you're going to need me to verify your latest theory, and then the whole finger-snapping business will start all over again. As I've said, I've guessed what your deductions are."

"That's very interesting. Would you like to tell me what I've deduced?"

"We were kept in Corsica. Sabine, Joyce and Gertrud are still there, and you and I are the only people in the world who realize it. Marian could've caught on, but she's an idiot."

"I'm glad I'm not one of your friends."

"Marian is not one of my friends."

"At any rate, no deal. Let's go back to the terrace."

Helène changed both her tone and her attitude, and started stating her case simply, solemnly. Laurent couldn't help but admire the bright but cunning way in which she displayed her natural talents as an actress. With great command, she'd slipped into the role of a level-headed collaborator who was preventing her partner from jumping to a confused and hasty decision.

"Use your head, Martin. The secrecy with which you're trying to shroud your actions is clear proof that you don't want any of this to get out. If it did, it would mean the end of my friends. You're now going to try and find the exact boat that took us off the *Rosebud*. But there's a distinct possibility that just locating and identifying the boat won't be enough to lead us to the cellars where we were kept. Any detail that may escape your notice is just one more strike against us. Whereas there are quite a few things that would jump right to my eyes, my ear, my nose or my touch. You're obviously going to go over Corsica now with a fine-tooth comb. With all the tourists there, a couple would blend right in with the crowds, but a single man could stand out like the bastard at a family reunion. I can easily change my appearance. All I have to do is dye my hair black, have it cut and put on a pair of glasses. What's more, if it'll set you at ease, I promise to disappear at the first sign of danger."

Martin put his palm on his forehead and massaged his temples. When he looked up, Helène was standing with her hands on her hips and her legs set apart. Martin shook his head and then laughed in resignation.

"All right," he said. "All right."

Lord Carter arrived at five o'clock. He left with Marian shortly after having given his word to Martin that he and his daughter would remain silent about their journey.

Laurent and Helène, after packing quickly, were driven to the airport in Nice where they thanked and dismissed Charles-André Fargeau's driver.

Laurent stepped up to the counter of the Europ-Car Rental Agency. A few minutes later, he had the keys to a practically new Renault 16 T.S. They threw their travel bags into the trunk and jumped into the front seat of the car. With a squeal of tires, Laurent whipped the little coupe around the parking lot and then plunged down the tunnel leading to the two-lane highway out of Nice.

Just before six o'clock, they left the car in a no-parking area in Cannes on the Place de l'Estaque. They were about to open the door of the Navimer Agency when Laurent checked himself. He caught Helène by the arm, turned her around and led her twenty yards back down the street. The beauty salon was just getting ready to close. Laurent, for fifty francs, convinced one of the employees to work an hour overtime.

"I don't want to recognize you," he said simply before leaving Helène.

Girardin was waiting for him alone. The director was on the phone, deeply engrossed in a conversation in Italian. With the pencil in his right hand, he motioned Laurent to a chair and then continued jotting down notes. When he hung up, he was all smiles.

"Four hundred and forty Ischia Bagliettos have been built and launched. According to your request, I asked for the names of all the original owners. They're coming over on the Telex downstairs right now."

"Thanks, Girardin. You're saving me a lot of work."

"Let's just say you're profiting from the excellent relations I enjoy with the directors of that Italian firm. They don't exist without reason. I sell a lot of their boats. What's more, when you came in, I was talking to the head of French customs. I also have friends there. They gave me the names and numbers of all the Ischias that had been imported into France until 1973."

"Do you know most of the European owners of these boats?"

"That would be somewhat of an exaggeration, but I should be able to locate the majority of them. That's my job. You can't imagine how many people walk into this office each summer with the intention of purchasing a yacht with a tag of more than two hundred thousand dollars on it, even though most of them have a hard time making the monthly payments on their second-hand Simca one thousands. That explains the financial files I'm going to show you now."

In the next office, they sat down to work using the lists supplied by the Baglietto Corporation, the French customs department and the considerable confidential files of the Navimer Agency.

Laurent had forgotten all about Helène. When she knocked on the glass front door, Girardin didn't recognize her and gestured toward the business hours posted in the window. Laurent realized who she was and stood up to unlock the door.

Helène had lost neither her grace nor her femininity. Her sultry charm, a mixture of awkward sexuality and adolescent shyness, had not been altered in the slightest. She moved across the office in her usual shuffling gait, smiling, and yet she was totally disguised. Her hair was as short as a young boy's and now almost jet black.

Playfully, she slipped on the rimless glasses Girardin had left lying on his desk. She looked like a cover girl straight off the front of the latest edition of *Mademoiselle*.

"Go and get us some sandwiches and something to drink," Martin demanded.

By three o'clock in the morning, they had seven names left on their list. They had cut it down rapidly to sixteen, but the elimination of the last nine names had been long and painstaking.

Helène was asleep in an armchair; Laurent was exhausted. Several times during the night he'd thought of taking the easy way out and phoning in his list to de Savigny. It wasn't that he doubted the discretion of his superior at the S.D.E.C.E., but he knew there was no way of preventing him from making his own inquiries into the matter. If that happened, the colonel would quickly understand what Martin was on to and then most probably launch an investigation of his own. That, Martin could not allow, because since he'd stumbled onto this one little open door to the truth, he'd been planning to follow a rather unorthodox course of action which no high official would ever approve.

But above all, he instinctively felt he had the right name now. For quite a few hours, he'd been returning to the third name on his list. This Adrien Tardets, farmer, born in Vialar in the heart of the Ouarsenis, intrigued him. He'd purchased an Ischia and kept it moored in the harbor at Bastia. These facts kept spinning through his head. Both girls had been found in Corsica. Tardets owned the only Baglietto on the island. And why should a farmer have invested more than $200,000 in such a luxurious boat? Girardin knew everyone who used his Baglietto for pleasure purposes, and he'd never heard of this man Tardets.

A quick call to the D.S.T. would have allowed Martin to verify his intuitions within a few minutes. An important former colonist from Algeria resettled in Corsica would certainly have a record. And yet he did not make the call, but chose instead a much riskier way of getting the information.

"Do you have a Var phone book, Girardin? After that, I'll let you go."

He opened the phone book to the listings for Toulon, lit a cigarette and dialed a number. The voice of the woman who answered was drowned out by the sound of a jukebox blaring in the same room. She nearly had to shout in order to be heard.

"M. Antoine? Who's calling? . . . Captain who?—" Antoine Morachini's voice erupted over the phone.

"Oh! It's you, Captain. . . . *Ayo* do you know . . . hold on . . ."

Laurent waited impatiently.

"Can't you turn down that music a little bit?"

Laurent smiled. Morachini's Corsican accent was so thick, every word he spoke sounded like a local joke. "Wait for me," Laurent said simply. "I'll be at your place in less than an hour."

The Bar des Amis was situated behind the shipyards on one of the more exotic back streets of Toulon. Helène slept during the drive. Laurent gave her a nudge as he turned onto the Boulevard de Strasbourg.

"I'm going to a whores' bar in the heart of a pretty shady district," he explained. "Do you want me to leave you at a hotel, or would you like to enjoy some of the local folklore?"

"What time is it?" she mumbled.

"Five past four."

"I'll go. I'll go with you."

The Bar des Amis was bathed in its usual reddish halflight. It was now in its most oppressive, despairing hour, that time before dawn when all the pleasure cheaters who inhabited its dim dank bowels did the last of their night's drinking as they waited for the day.

Two tired old whores were leaning up against the bar watching the usual "new girl from Brittany" working naively and in vain at a corner table trying to talk a drunken insomniac into going upstairs. The two old whores said nothing, though they knew the man had come in only to drink.

Antoine Morachini never suffered from the melancholic atmosphere of the place. He threw his arms around Laurent and kissed him three times. In his buttonhole, he was wearing the Legion of Honor he'd been awarded after losing his left leg in Algeria.

Suddenly, his welcoming smile disappeared.

"Get the hell out of here, all four of you." He bellowed at the customers. "Leave your drinks, they're on the house. Is that your wife?" he asked Laurent.

"No, she's just an acquaintance," Laurent said wryly.

Morachini insisted on taking them to his "country place," a grossly overdecorated house situated on the heights of Claret. Day had dawned when Laurent, sitting at the kitchen table, explained the purpose of his visit.

"I need some information quickly, very quickly and as complete as you can get it, on a 'Pied Noir' settled in Corsica in the Ghisonaccia area. His name is Tardets. Adrien Tardets."

"You'll know everything you need to know in a few minutes, *mon capitaine*. First, let's drink the coffee."

"Antoine, it's serious, very serious. And silence is essential."

"*Mon capitaine!* To me, you're talking about silence! I make my living by silence, it's my profession."

"It's not you I'm worried about, Antoine."

"It's the same for my friends. Otherwise, they wouldn't be my friends, they'd be dead. You know that."

After they'd finished their coffee, the veteran picked up his phone and asked the operator to get him a number in Bastia. Then he launched into a long, undecipherable conversation in the Corsican dialect. When he hung up, he was frowning.

"This man Tardets is a real bastard, believe me. I've seen the estate he bought in 1960 before the Algerian independence. That's enough to tell you how big a bastard he is. He completely rebuilt the whole joint. He's old, maybe sixty or more. He doesn't employ a single islander, nothing but Arabs. He had a high wall put around his place as if he thought everyone else on the island had the plague. He also has a big boat in Bastia. No Corsicans on that, either. Again, only Arabs. He's a real bastard, *mon capitaine*."

"Well, I think I'm going to take a little tour around Corsica then," Martin said quietly. "Yes, a little Corsican vacation."

26

Hacam quickly threw down the dregs of the *café au lait* he hadn't yet soaked up with the numerous pieces of spongy white bread he habitually dipped into his breakfast bowl.

With the point of his switchblade, he scraped up the clump of crumbs that had settled to the bottom of the bowl. His hunger satisfied, he belched, and then as if by reflex, he wiped his mouth and the six-day stubble on his chin with the back of his hand.

"Okay," he said, "let's go!"

Followed by Kirkbane, Cheikh and Kateb, he unlocked the Gothic-style door in Tardets' office and started down the stairs to the cellar.

The three girls now rarely got up off their cots. Every morning and every night they simply held out their hands for their Valium. They no longer even tried to keep clean and hardly used the soap and running water that was always at their disposal. The regular consumption of the tranquilizers had dulled their nervous systems to such a point they could barely move around. They slept constantly and had lost all track of time. More than a month in captivity had not sharpened any hidden instincts. The regular overdoses of pills had kept them in a stupor.

"Would you please come with us, Mlle. Fargeau," Hacam said.

Sabine stood up in an apathetic, submissive daze. She stared at her jailers with dull resignation, her eyes now pale, flat and lifeless. In a barely audible tone of voice that was now indifferent to everything, she mumbled, "Are you going to kill me?"

"No, no," Hacam reassured her. "We're just going to make another little film."

Everything was ready. Sabine sat down mechanically in front of a microphone installed on an old wooden table. Hacam placed several typewritten pages in front of her and the girl lowered her eyes to start reading them. Hacam slipped his finger under her chin and forced her to raise her head.

"No, not today. I don't want you to see the text until you read it on camera. You're going to learn something rather important today, and I want to film your reaction. Turn on the lights, Kirkbane. Are you ready, Cheikh? Kateb?"

The four spotlights converged on Sabine's face and torso. Kirkbane stepped in front of her with a black-and-white-striped film clapper that had "Operation Rosebud" chalked on the front of it. He held it there a moment while the camera started rolling and then pulled it away.

"Start reading," Hacam said.

Sabine picked up the papers and began.

"I am just learning the content of this text as I read it to you. Our captors refused to let me look at it beforehand as they usually do. I, Sabine Fargeau, am only discovering now that even if their ultimate demand, which I will be delivering soon, is scrupulously accepted and satisfied, I, Sabine Fargeau, will not be liberated until a year from today."

She raised her head and stared at Hacam, who knowingly had positioned himself close to the camera. Her blue-green

eyes seemed insensitive to the harsh glare from the spotlights, but her dry lips opened slowly in silent disbelief.

Three times she shook her head softly, childishly refusing
to accept the cruel truth of the statement she'd just been
forced to announce. Unconsciously, she realized that since
the beginning of the drama, the only thing that had carried
her through the ordeal had been a hope—a hope that had
just now been shattered by a few words. Because for her, at
that moment, a year seemed as long as forever.

Her lips still open, she tried in vain to speak. But she
couldn't find the words, and even if she had, she didn't
have the breath to expel them. Without knowing it, she
would alternately shake her head and then suddenly stop to
stare blankly at the lights. Neither was she conscious of the
tears now streaming down her cheeks. Her facial muscles
were frozen in an impassive mask that contrasted sadly with
the disarray, the anguish and the pitiful, pleading look in her
eyes. Somehow, from somewhere deep inside, she gathered
up enough strength to mutter a few intelligible syllables,
although her lips barely moved. "Oh God . . . no—help
me . . ."

She faltered for a moment and then spoke up a little more
clearly. "Grandfather, tell them to kill me! I can't stand it
any longer. . . . Please . . . get them to kill me."

Hacam was expecting her to break down entirely at any
moment. Logically, he thought she would collapse in spas-
modic sobs on the table in front of her. He had planned
to film a nervous breakdown, but Sabine's reaction after
her desperate appeals was unforeseen. She froze completely,
as if she'd gone into a cataleptic fit. The camera was still
rolling. Sabine was staring straight at it, motionless, her
tears now running in a solid stream down her face.

Sliding over her chin now, the stream of her tears had
reached the base of her neck.

"Cut," Hacam shouted.

Kirkbane looked up disdainfully at his chief and then

spat at his feet. Hacam hit him with the back of his hand before he'd even had a chance to look up. He poured some plum alcohol into a shot glass and then downed it. Kirkbane was on his knees on the floor staring at the blood running out of his nose onto his hands. Hacam poured another shot of the alcohol and ordered Sabine to drink it. She managed to get it down after three tries. The sudden extinguishing of the spotlights snapped her out of her stupor.

"You have five minutes to pull yourself together," Hacam barked. "Now read the rest of the text. I want you to be able to speak clearly when we start again."

They waited a quarter of an hour before turning on the spotlights again. Sabine, in a voice that was now calm but hollow, began reading.

"I'm speaking for the Palestine Liberation Organization. The suggestions offered during our attempt to reach the people have proven to be shameful, grotesque, naive, disgusting or insulting. This leads us to think that there isn't a single soul in the entire Western world who might understand us. More pitiful and revolting still in our eyes are those who, instead of inquiring into the tragic and unjust fate of our people, chose to try and make a personal profit out of the sincere and honest invitation we extended.

"This fiasco has forced the organization to take the matter of its demands into its own hands once again. This message, and the ultimatum that follows, will be our last. The liberation of the three young girls we still hold hinges solely on the satisfaction of this last demand. Unfortunately, many months will be necessary to allow us to decide whether or not the Palestinians' conditions have been respected.

"If we are satisfied with your reactions, four months from the date this film is broadcast, Gertrud Fryer will be released, safe and sound; four months after that, Joyce Donovan; and finally, at the end of twelve months, I, Sabine Fargeau, will be set free.

"We're quite sure that now there are millions of people

watching my image on television screens all over the Western world, curious and fascinated. You will be even more so when you hear what I'm about to say, because our last demand will certainly seem to be both equitable and absurd to you. In fact, we're simply going to ask you to respect one of your own laws. This law has been in effect for years, but for almost as long, it's been ignored, toyed with or voluntarily dismissed. All the Western nations have ratified it, and all of them are guilty of violating it.

"We are asking you to put a total boycott into effect on all exports from Israel. Because every product grown on Palestinian soil, every product fabricated over Palestinian soil, is nothing more than booty from one of the greatest armed thefts in history: the theft of a fatherland, of a nation torn from the hands of three million martyrs.

"We are convinced that thousands of you have only been acquainted with these irrefutable facts today, and it is to these people in particular that we are addressing our message. Let us remind you of one of the most common laws of all societies: he who consumes, enjoys, or profits from stolen goods is himself as guilty as the thief. For centuries, Western civilization's most highly regarded jurists have considered the recipients of stolen goods more at fault than the thieves themselves. By law, they're subject to the same penalties.

"From today on, whenever you eat an orange imported from Israel, you can consider yourself an accomplice to the most odious, infamous crime in contemporary history.

"We realize that this point of our exposé seems quite paradoxical. Because Israel violates another one of your laws, and that is that everything produced by a nation for export must bear the mark of the country that produced it. Israel, along with the countries that serve as middlemen for its goods, has been breaking this law for years. So how can one know? We're going to tell you. We're only sorry we can't suggest a more tactful way of determining the 'country of origin,' but we have no other choice. Today, all of you who understand us must not hesitate to denounce the wretched profiteers who are allowing this to go on.

"Each year Israel exports more than eighty thousand tons of bananas, thirty million crates of oranges and grapefruit, hundreds of millions of tons of eggs, sugarbeets and vegetable oil, millions of flowers, billions of dollars' worth of various merchandise—industrial diamonds, textiles, fashions, rubber, beverages, steel, chemicals, nonferrous metals, wood, paper and soon petroleum, automobiles, plastics and computers.

"We're not trying to say the Jews don't work. They're simply in the position of a murderer who's killed off a whole family for no other reason than to get his hands on a huge diamond. Granted, he's had to work on this gem, maybe quite hard, for a long time, in order to cut it properly, polish it and show it in order to increase its value prior to selling it. Nevertheless, no matter how hard this work has been, it does not excuse the original crime.

"Now we are addressing ourselves to you, Charles-André Fargeau. Put the power of your fortune in the service of the truth. Publish the names of those organizations that do business with the Israelis, all of them, from the largest to the smallest. Print and distribute stickers to put on products from Israel, so that those who are with us won't hesitate to mark the store-front windows of collaborating shopkeepers.

"This is our last communiqué. From here on, we shall be only spectators. Those of you who understand us, we implore you: do all you can to explain our motives for having to resort to such heinous methods as kidnapping and blackmail. We're as disgusted with and grieved by these methods as any of you, if not more. Our people are desperate, and we have been left with nothing but desperate forms of action to call your attention to our plight. We hope you have heard our appeal."

Hacam motioned to the other men. The four Fedayeen

moved up to stand behind Sabine Fargeau. The camera and the tape recorder were still turning. Hacam grabbed the microphone, brought it up to his lips and stared arrogantly straight into the camera lens.

"My name is Abdel Mejid Hacam. My companions, Kirkbane, Cheikh and Kateb, no longer have any reason to remain hidden from you. If ever you should find any of us, we will make no attempt to escape our due punishment. But let me make one point clear—we still have three girls here as hostages. If our demands are not respected, one of us will execute one of the girls and then commit suicide. Each time, you will discover two bodies, the martyr's and the executioner's. I shall remain alive until the end. If this should happen, when all is done you have my word that I shall then also take my life, because our actions would lose all meaning if we were to attach more importance to our lives than to those of these unfortunate girls."

Cheikh walked around from behind the table and switched off the camera and the spotlights. The last image recorded on the film was one of Sabine, stunned and alone, surrounded by the three Fedayeen proudly staring straight ahead at the camera.

27

At first light, Martin woke with the sun now coming through the window of their hotel room. Helène was asleep with her head on his chest. Gently, he ran his hand over her hair, across her shoulder and down onto her breast. She stirred but did not open her eyes. Martin caressed her nipple and then reached over to the bedstand for a cigarette. She sighed and slowly cuddled closer to him. With the cigarette in the corner of his mouth, he picked up the phone and waited for the desk to answer. When they responded, he ordered a pot of black coffee, asked them to place a call to Paris for him and hung up. Three minutes later, the phone rang. Colonel de Savigny was on the other end of the line.

"Ah, Martin is it! Martin at six o'clock in the morning no less. How lovely of you to finally show me the courtesy of contacting me. Where in the hell are you?"

"In Porto-Vecchio, Corsica."

"Well, get your ass back here. The O.R.T.F. received another film from the Fedayeen last night. We're having a screening at eight P.M. for Hamlekh, Wycherly, Schloss, Sanders and the fathers of the girls."

"I'll be there this afternoon."

"You're goddam right you will be. There's rather a strong feeling against you here that's growing stronger by the hour and I've been officially asked to get a few explanations. The Élysée is considering dismissing you from the case if you don't comply."

"Perfect, Colonel. Just send their little summons to my home address. I won't be at the screening this evening."

"Don't be ridiculous, Martin. I'm covering you. I just wanted you to know what the temperature was around here before you met with the government representatives and the families tonight."

"All right. I'll come straight to your office as soon as I get back."

He hung up. Hélène turned her face up toward his and opened her eyes.

"Are you leaving?"

"Just for a night. I'll be back tomorrow morning."

"And you're going to leave me here all alone?"

"Sorry about that, but you're a big girl now."

She buried her head in his chest again, pouting. Martin bent down and kissed her behind the ear, slowly.

"And what's to keep me from forgetting you?" she murmured.

Martin was not listening. He had kissed her ears, her neck, her shoulders and her breasts by now and besides, he reasoned, the plane doesn't leave till midmorning.

The lights were switched back on in the S.D.E.C.E. screening room on the Boulevard Mortier. The surprise created by the announcement of the Fedayeen's final demand hadn't dispelled the vivid emotion caused by Sabine's appearance on the screen. During the last moments of the film, a strange feeling of uneasiness had spread through the audience, as if the representatives were embarrassed by the Palestinians' grandiloquent demonstrations of self-denial.

In heavy silence, the officials rose from their seats and

left the room. Almost as if by tacit agreement among themselves, they pretended not to notice the shattered figure of Charles-André Fargeau still slumped in his chair. The old man had broken down during the screening and was now crying, his face hidden behind his fine hands. At random intervals, his whole body shook convulsively.

Several delegates from the ministries of the interior, foreign affairs, and justice, along with observers from foreign countries, had attended the screening. They were now going to hold a meeting in a nearby conference room.

Savigny had not been exaggerating when he had told Martin he was no longer trusted. Senator Donovan was the first to lay into the colonel.

"I think I can speak for all the families still involved in this affair," he said. "We consulted one another before joining you and we've decided to summon M. Martin to give us a full account of his investigations. At present, his attitude indicates that he is either hiding certain elements from us, or he's leading us on a wild-goose chase."

"As I've told you before," de Savigny interrupted, "I don't know any more about M. Martin's investigations than you do, but I nevertheless still have complete confidence in him."

"We have more reason to worry than you do, Savigny," Fryer interjected.

That was an argument that could not be refuted.

"They're right, Martin. So tell us, now. That's an order!"

Charles-André Fargeau had just entered the room. His face was completely drained of color. The effort he was obviously making to hold his head high and muster up some of his former authority was both childish and moving.

"No sir, I'm sorry, but I have to refuse. Your grief is taking complete control of you—all three of you. I've notified the President. If I'm forced to hand in my conclusions, they'll be accompanied by my resignation. Don't think I'm being either headstrong or a coward, but right now I must maintain total autonomy over the leads I'm on to. I will repeat, and for the last time, my one and only concern is the safe return of your daughters."

Donovan leaned forward angrily. "So now you're trying to blackmail us too, huh?" he snarled. "All right, Martin. We'll go along with you, but I swear that if you blow this, I'll make sure you pay for it."

"If, unfortunately, I should not succeed, I'm sure you'll forgive me when you know my reasons. However, just by being here I'm wasting precious time, so I'll leave you gentlemen to decide among yourselves just when you're going to broadcast this last film. I must insist that it be broadcast. It's essential if I'm to pursue my investigation any further."

Hamlekh hadn't failed to catch the quick glance Martin had shot in his direction; he understood. Martin wanted a word with him.

The two men left the building on the Boulevard Mortier separately and met later, apparently by coincidence, at the Porte des Lilas taxi stand.

"Could you drop me off at my hotel, Martin?"

"With pleasure."

The taxi deposited both of them in front of Martin's apartment on the Quai Voltaire. They hadn't exchanged a word during the drive and remained silent until they were both comfortably settled in Martin's library.

"Our comrade Schrantz must be exterminated," Hamlekh began. "He's laid out his hand now and he's holding some pretty dangerous cards. Because you can be sure this boycott against Israel is going to set off a wave of anti-Semitism the likes of which we haven't seen since the thirties. Jews all over the world are going to consider themselves gravely insulted, and out of their naive pride, they're going to reject both this ultimatum and this embargo, thinking that by doing so they're supporting Zionism and the state of Israel. Overall, their reaction will probably be aggressive. And if it is, they'll be playing right into Schrantz's hands and we'll have no way to stop them. I can already see the broken shop windows, vigilante gangs, threats against Jewish industrialists, burning synagogues, in a word, the slow and tragic evolution of a movement that inevitably ends in pogroms."

"You're exaggerating, Hamlekh!"

"No, that's Schrantz's aim, his only aim. He has allies all over the Western world, don't forget that. Every nation enjoys the sad privilege of harboring fanatical young utopists like Patrice Thibaud who know how to convince and encourage the masses with their delirious, paranoid rantings. Schrantz controls enough of these maniacs to realize his goal. Don't forget Chamfort's maxim: 'One ignores those who start the fire, but prosecutes those who sound the alarm.'

"Don't think I'm not aware of the thesis of anti-Zionists like Schrantz, Martin. The strength of the Jewish people lies in the fact that they're dispersed throughout the world and persecuted. That's not entirely incorrect. Israel was built on the martyrs of Nazism. . . ."

Hamlekh rambled on for hours. Laurent listened attentively in spite of his sleepiness and his own train of thoughts. He finally decided he had to interrupt the Shin-Beth agent. He had made up his mind to take him into his confidence. A few minutes later, Hamlekh knew everything about Martin's investigation.

The two men spent the major portion of the night planning a counterattack. Hamlekh was in contact with Tel Aviv on seven different occasions. Laurent had phoned Morachini, in Toulon. They slept for only an hour, but when they arrived at Orly the next morning, every last detail of their plan had been taken care of.

While the 6:40 flight to Bastia was preparing for takeoff, Laurent let himself slip into the torpor that precedes sleep.

With half-closed eyes, he watched the Israeli agent in the seat beside him. Hamlekh was deep in thought, but smiling beatifically.

"What's brought on this euphoric reaction?" Laurent inquired.

"Something stupid. I had been thinking that this bastard Schrantz truly had the most Satanic, scheming mind of any man I'd ever run up against. Thanks to him, I thought I had a clear idea of the essence of Machiavellianism. But that was last night, Martin. Since then I've discovered how your mind works. . . ."

28

On their arrival in Bastia the two men rented another Renault 16 and headed south on the main highway. In the glove compartment Laurent found a map of Corsica, which he handed to Hamlekh.

"Check Morachini's directions. The village is called Libbia di Pietra Bianca: the only way to get there is on a small dirt road that runs between Guardia Pass and Paraxa Pass."

"I've got it," Hamlekh responded shortly. "It won't be any problem. I'll tell you where to turn off."

Laurent checked his watch without taking his hand off the wheel. It was 9:25. They'd be there on time.

"Do you know this Colonel Santi well?" Hamlekh asked.

"I don't know him personally, but I've heard a great deal about him. He's one of the big contemporary personalities in the Foreign Legion: a born fighter and a born leader whose spectacular operations during the Indochina War have already become a part of history. As far as we're concerned, we couldn't have a better man to work with. He's retired to his native village with all his laurels. From everything I've heard about his guerrilla activities, I'm sure he'll keep his mouth shut."

After leaving the highway, they bumped along over a

bad mountain road for six or seven miles. Coming around one of the last corners, they caught sight of the little village of Libbia di Pietra Bianca clinging like a spider to the rocky mountain walls.

Though each year the island of Corsica literally swarmed with tourists, few if any of them ever ventured as far as this little town. The way of life there consequently had not changed in a hundred years.

Laurent parked the car in front of a tiny church.

The first Renault 16 was already at the square. Laurent had phoned Helène from Bastia to ask her to join him. She had just arrived. He signaled her to wait in the car. Three men were sitting at a table in front of the post office which, in an unofficial capacity, also served as the local tavern. They had several shotguns propped up against the wall of the building. Their hunting dogs growled at the approach of the two men.

"Could you tell me where Colonel Santi lives?" Laurent asked.

The question prompted a brief conversation in the Corsican dialect among the hunters. Finally, one of them spoke up. "We don't know him."

"But he's expecting me at eleven thirty," Laurent insisted.

"That's none of our business."

"Captain Martin?"

They turned around. Santi, built like a small buffalo and standing with his feet apart, was staring at them with the eyes of a hawk. "Come with me."

They followed him through all the winding streets and stairways of the little town until they finally entered a house which, like the rest of the homes in the village, seemed to be a part of the mountain itself. Santi asked them to sit down in a room that looked like a large kitchen. A very old woman entered and set a platter of sliced meats and a pitcher of Corsican wine on the main table.

Laurent spoke for half an hour without being interrupted.

When he'd finished, Santi filled their glasses for the third time. They drank to one another's health before the ex-Legionnaire responded.

"I'll make sure you have everything you need," he said. "Let's meet tomorrow at noon in front of the church in the village of Cagnallela. I'll show you where it is on the map. The mayor, François Locci, is a friend of mine. He farms land that couldn't be more than eight miles from the Tardets estate. I can assure you that Locci will be able to quarter the twelve men you've got coming. However, it'd be still better if they waited until dark to join us. The equipment you've just mentioned could arouse some unwanted curiosity."

"Don't worry about that," Hamlekh interrupted. "My men'll look like tourists. They'll be traveling in three Volkswagen buses they've rented in Milan. They're on their way to Genoa now. There, they'll catch a plane to bring everything over tomorrow evening."

"Are you sure you can get the three buses on the Genoa-Bastia ferry without a reservation?"

"It was difficult, but it's been taken care of."

"Okay, then let's do it that way. Tomorrow afternoon you can study the master plans and surveys of the water systems and the forest."

The next evening after dinner they all moved out to the terrace of the mayor's home in Cagnallela. The sound of the crickets had grown progressively louder now that the sun had gone down. Helène was stretched out in a hammock, daydreaming as she rocked herself back and forth by pushing against the ground with her finger

François Locci, settled comfortably in a wicker chair, was smoking a stubby pipe. In two matching armchairs, Santi and Martin were enjoying the warm, scented tranquillity of the Corsican countryside.

Hamlekh had left during the afternoon to meet his men. The mayor's wife and daughter-in-law were moving about as indecisively as the insects in the night air. Helène's offer to help them with dinner dishes had been firmly refused. Santi had explained their rejection laconically. "Don't insult them."

In the distance, they heard the droning of the cars' engines way before they saw the shafts of the headlights. They all rose once the third van had pulled up and stopped.

Hamlekh introduced the twelve men, who were visibly embarrassed by their Boy Scoutish attire. While Locci escorted them to the barn he'd outfitted as a dormitory during the afternoon, Laurent pretended not to notice the pouting air Helène had assumed. She'd been told to go back to her room as soon as the Shin-Beth technicians had arrived.

The crew reassembled in the silo next to the barn. The sixteen men sat down in a circle on the earthen floor. By the light of three butane lamps, Colonel Santi unfolded the survey plans and maps he'd acquired the day before.

Saul Yaari, the head of the team, was about thirty years old. He was thin and bony, with rimless glasses that pinched the sharp bridge of his narrow nose. After having received his engineering degree from the University of New Mexico for studies that concentrated on oil-field exploration, he had spent three years with Royal Dutch Shell in Venezuela. Then he had returned to Israel, where he was with one of the first groups to discover the Helets oil fields in the Ashkelon region.

That night, all eyes were turned on him. After more than an hour's discussion and study of the project at hand, he lifted his head and lit a small cigar.

"I think it can be done, here, at this exact spot."

A unanimous sigh of relief went up in the room.

"It's ideal," François Locci added, "because you'll be able to start on it at dawn. You'll be completely hidden by the Solena ridge. On top of that, you'll be a good two miles from the Tardets property, so there's no chance of your motors being heard."

"The sound of the motors will be insignificant. They'll

only be started once we're down inside the ditches we have to dig."

"There's still one problem," Locci said, pointing to a military topographical map. "You can get your cars here to the edge of the forest quite easily, but no farther. After that, you've got a good two-mile walk. How heavy is your equipment?"

"It's been disassembled and packed into crates. The heaviest one weighs one hundred twenty pounds."

"How many do you have?"

"Six."

"Okay. At dawn I'll have six donkeys and a wagon for you. By oh-seven-hundred hours, you should be there."

They reached their destination only fifteen minutes later than the mayor had predicted. The clearing where they stopped seemed like an ideal spot for the work they had in front of them. They were in the middle of a dense and deserted forest where nothing less than a miracle could have given their presence away.

Hélène had been given permission to accompany them. Sitting between Laurent and Hamlekh some distance away, she admired the competence and silent efficiency of the Israeli technicians. The first team had scientifically pinpointed the exact spot where they were to drill. Then the second team dug a small hole in the ground after having removed a young cedar tree. While all of this was going on, the third group had opened the crates and reassembled the equipment.

At nine o'clock, six men started digging a four-yard by two-yard ditch. At 10:30, all twelve men assumed the role of ditch diggers. Laurent, Hamlekh, Colonel Santi and François Locci also took turns. At one o'clock, Hélène set out a picnic lunch that was quickly consumed. Then, in spite of the sun, which was now directly over their heads, they returned to their painstaking task like moles digging burrows in spring.

Near the end of the afternoon, they finally reached the

water mains they'd been digging for some fifteen feet below ground, though it still took them a long time to expose the pipes completely. They then started the delicate operation that oil-pipeline specialists call "hot tapping."

A five-horsepower diesel generator was first carefully lowered into the ditch. It was to be used to power a circular saw and a high-speed drill. With a dexterity and speed that elicited open admiration from the laymen, they cut a section out of the pipe and replaced it with a meter, which measured the amount of water consumed by the Tardets estate, and with two valves. All they had to do then was prepare the rest of their equipment and wait for nightfall.

When they'd finished, they stretched out to rest on the ground. Hamlekh, who up until then had always been ready to rush into action, was seized with uncertainties about their plan.

"What if it's just a series of coincidences, Martin?" He wiped his forehead with a rag the technicians had used. "Do you realize what a mess we'd be in?"

"Of course. But if we don't act on the leads we have, we might just as well turn it all over to the regular services. I mean, do you really want to wait until the police can obtain a search warrant so they can march up here with their loudspeakers and lay lawful siege to the place? Between the risk of losing the lives of those young girls and the risk of losing my career, I'll choose my career—" he added with a smile—"at least that's what I plan on telling the judges at my trial if I've made a mistake. But I'm quite sure our assumptions are well founded."

"God, I hope so."

Saul, the engineer, was still sitting at the bottom of the trench with his eyes riveted on the water meter. At seven o'clock, the water flow increased. Then at 8:30, it jumped considerably for twenty minutes.

"Probably doing the dishes," Saul announced.

At nine o'clock, the water stopped flowing altogether.

They all gathered along the rim of the trench. At irregular intervals, Saul flashed his pocket light on for short, lightninglike instants: The needle remained motionless. At midnight, it still hadn't budged.

"Let's go!" Laurent decided. "You've got three hours."

Immediately, Saul shut off the water supply going into the main leading to the Tardets estate. A six-foot section of the pipe below the valve was then removed. Even though the house was at a higher altitude than the section that was cut out, the water retained in the two miles of pipe between them did not flow out because there was no air coming into the system at the other end; all the household taps were shut. Then they started a "gas lift" operation which required them to inject air into the full pipe by means of a small, flexible tube that had to be inserted almost all the way up to the house.

Quickly, they moved the drum of tubing they'd brought in by donkey into place in front of the open pipeline. The tubing itself—which had the diameter of an infant's little finger—was lined with a Teflon fabric to keep it rigid enough to prevent it from collapsing as it was fed up the main line but nevertheless was sufficiently flexible to allow it to snake around all the curves of the water system.

It took them two hours to slide the little tube all the way to the end of the line. When they encountered their first resistance, they had fed 3,374 yards of tubing into the system. Saul concluded that if the maps and surveys were absolutely accurate, which would be logical, it was likely that the end of the tube was now caught in one of the joints in the interior plumbing of the house. That was neither good nor bad.

They cut the tubing at their end and then Saul asked Martin what time it was. He held his little pocket light on the agent's wrist.

"Go ahead," Martin said after glancing at his watch.

The end of the conduit was connected to a compressor,

which started forcing air up into the Tardets household plumbing system. Almost immediately, water started flowing out of the pipeline into the trench which soon took on the appearance of a small swamp. After a while, the engineer had the compressor shut off.

"Okay, here's the situation," Saul explained. "We've got enough water out of the pipe now to start injecting the corrosive gas."

"Are you sure it'll reach every valve and faucet inside the house? It's absolutely essential," Laurent said.

"Listen, monsieur," Saul explained stoically. "At this end, we're going to reseal the main line and then attach a gas canister, with a meter on it, to the tubing. The corrosive gas we're injecting now will fill the entire system in the house as long as the circuit remains closed. The gas only has to come into contact with the water still standing in the pipes in order to start attacking the joints. I can assure you that they'll disintegrate within a few minutes, and, anyway, the meter will let us know as soon as the pressure drops in the system."

The rubber washers did indeed give in, one after the other. The meter measuring the escape of the corrosive gas attested to it.

They removed the canister of corrosive gas from the end of the tubing and attached a second tank of liquefied gas to it. This was the part of the plan that troubled Laurent the most.

"Are you quite sure?" he asked. "You have to stop immediately if you have the slightest doubt—"

Saul interrupted him bluntly.

"I've told you a hundred times, the gas is not dangerous. Vitamin C has the same properties. The human organism will eliminate all it can't absorb. This isn't an experiment. We know. We can make an individual sleep as long as we want, just by keeping him in a room filled with this gas. This artificial sleep can go on indefinitely if the subject is fed intravenously. Don't worry. In fifteen minutes, every breathing creature in that house will be in a deep, peaceful sleep. And believe me, they won't be in the slightest bit of danger. All right?"

"Okay."

"Okay, send it in!"

For a few minutes his eyes fixed on the meter measuring the flow of narcotic gas.

"The soporific gas is starting to reach the house through at least fourteen different openings," he concluded. "In that it's odorless and escaping without any noise, by now you could walk into the place singing at the top of your lungs."

"In that case, let's go," Martin decided. "M. Locci, we'll follow you. Hamlekh, be sure your men have their weapons."

Without a sound, they set off through the woods that separated them from the Tardets estate. Locci knew every square inch of the terrain. He'd been hunting wild boar there since he was a child.

29

It was dawn when François Locci gathered his little group together on the back side of a rocky knoll overlooking the Tardets estate. The mayor crawled forward on his hands and knees a few yards and examined the house with a small pair of Leitz field glasses. After a while, he stood up and continued surveying the house boldly. He called Martin out loud and handed him the glasses when he appeared at his elbow.

"Take a look! There're two dogs fast asleep out on the lawn. The gas must've poured outside through the open windows."

In his turn, Laurent scrutinized every square foot of the property before responding.

"There're also a few blackbirds sprawled out there. The gas must've come up through the sprinkler system as well. I'll go have a look. Don't move under any circumstances until I signal."

By walkie-talkie, Saul contacted the technician who had stayed back at the camp and told him to shut off the narcotic gas.

Laurent slipped on a rucksack and then slung a small Thompson submachine gun over his left shoulder and thirty feet of climbing rope over his right. The rope was equipped with a grappling hook. Finally, he fitted a gas mask over his face and had Hamlekh check to be sure it was airtight.

"Do you really insist on going down there alone?" he asked.

Laurent nodded and started down the hill toward the wall.

On the second try, the grappling hook caught hold on the other side. Nimbly, with the aid of the rope, he scrambled up the ten-foot face. The mortar on top of the wall was embedded with broken bottles. To protect himself, he wrapped the rope around his left wrist and then smashed the glass with the butt of his Thompson. But as he clambered over the top, he ended up cutting his knee anyway. Ignoring the pain, he examined the ground beneath him and then jumped down inside the private compound.

Everything seemed calm, but Martin nevertheless checked the chamber of his submachine gun before cautiously starting off in the direction of the house.

The kitchen window was ajar. He pushed it open slightly, glanced inside and then out of reflex flattened himself back up against the wall.

The scene he'd taken in, in that flash of a second, had left him a little startled.

Six feet from the sink, a man was lying face down on the floor with a submachine gun still clenched in his right hand. It was obvious that the weapon had fired off a short burst before the man had lost consciousness. The direction of the barrel, the pieces of broken pots and glasses and the traces of his brains on the wall all testified that the man had collapsed with his finger on the trigger.

Laurent felt a slight prickling sensation under his mask. A few seconds later, a large drop of perspiration rolled down off his forehead into his eyes. It unnerved him. He continued standing with his back up against the wall, listening for something out of the ordinary, but the place was completely silent. When another drop of sweat rolled down into his eyes, he took a deep breath, whipped off the mask and wiped his forehead on the sleeve of his shirt. Replacing the mask, he peeked back inside the kitchen window. There was still nothing moving, and so he climbed in.

He rolled the small man on the floor over with his foot. The Fedayin's eyes were glazed and open, even though the back of his skull was missing. Without much surprise, Laurent recognized the little Kirkbane.

He moved into the hall. Hacam was lying there, wearing only a pair of shorts. He had a Parabellum pistol in his fist. It was clear he had fallen hard in midstride.

Laurent could feel the warm perspiration pooling up on his eyebrows. Looking at Hacam, he realized that the plan had not come off as smoothly as expected. Thirty seconds more, and the game would have been lost. The man standing watch, probably Kirkbane in the kitchen, had somehow managed to sound the alarm. If the gas had taken just a few more minutes to work, all the French agent's worst fears could have proved true.

Very carefully, Laurent removed the Parabellum from the man's grasp. He shoved the gun into his pack and then removed a pair of handcuffs. He flipped the Arab over on his stomach and then locked his wrists together behind his back.

The door to Tardets' office was open. Laurent found the two other Fedayeen there, frozen in sleep at the foot of their cots. Two new pairs of handcuffs clicked into place. Quickly, he inspected the other rooms. Tardets was sleeping peacefully on his bed. There was a washbasin in one corner of his room. The scene was the same in the other bedroom, where Tardets' wife had also been knocked out.

He now had to find the door to the cellars. He fumbled around for a few minutes before he realized that the staircase to the basement could only be behind the Gothic-style door in the old man's office.

He searched the pockets of all the sleeping men and took advantage of the frisking to collect all their weapons. The keys were in one of Hacam's pants pockets. Two minutes later, Laurent switched on the lights in the cellar and discovered the three girls sleeping soundly on their cots.

He rushed up to them to reassure himself that their pulses were still strong and even. Satisfied, he bolted back up the winding staircase out of the cellars.

In the office, he slipped off his rucksack and removed a walkie-talkie. He extended the incorporated antenna and pressed the transmission button.

"Hamlekh, do you read me?"

Instantly, the answer came back. "Roger."

"We have optimum results. You can move on up now. I'll be covering you from the east in case we have any unexpected guests. There's no problem if the Nikolaos girl wants to follow you. Tell the camp to start pumping in the oxygen. Everyone inside is out of harm's way."

"Roger your last and bravo. We're on our way."

Laurent stiffened suddenly: A loud hissing sound had just broken the silence. Then he realized it was just the oxygen streaming out of the taps. He made another tour through the house and opened all the windows and the faucets. He checked his watch. In ten minutes he could remove his mask.

The agent took advantage of the time to carry the three girls up into the hall and drag the bodies of the Fedayeen into Tardets' office. Only then did he move to the kitchen to stand watch in the window.

Hamlekh decided that it was not necessary for his men to wear their masks. Without trepidation, they all entered the house.

The Muslim servants arrived at eight o'clock. The terrified couple were taken into the kitchen. Their interrogation
confirmed the information provided by François Locci.
They were the only two people allowed inside the grounds.
Their countrymen who worked on Tardets' land were only
innocent laborers who never came into contact with the
owner. That seemed logical. It was highly unlikely that
either Hacam or Tardets would have allowed any of their
accomplices to come and go freely if they knew anything
about the girls in the cellar.

"It's okay. Send all your men back now," Martin said to
Hamlekh. "Colonel Santi and the mayor will stay here with
me."

"And you," he added, turning to the servants. "One of
you will go back to your village tonight. Tell your neighbors
that you'll both be staying here in the house for a few days:
Mme. Tardets is sick."

"What's going on, Laurent?" Helène asked in astonish-
ment. "Everything's settled, isn't it? My friends will soon
be awake and then we'll contact their families. . . ."

"No, *ma chère,* I'm afraid this case isn't over yet."

The sun had already disappeared behind the mountains
when the first of the Fedayeen emerged from his slumber.
It was Kateb.

He groaned sluggishly, bothered by the handcuffs without realizing it. By chance, Laurent had discovered a large
stock of mineral water in the pantry. He poured one of the
bottles on the face of the groggy Palestinian. Instinctively,
the man closed his eyes tightly and then blinked several
times. He stared up blankly at Laurent. A sudden flash
crossed his eyes and he tried to move. The handcuffs bit
quickly into his wrists and he understood everything.

"It's finished, my friend. All done," Laurent said simply.

Arching his back, the Fedayin sat up and glanced around
at his handcuffed companions.

"Allah has so decided," he snarled through his teeth.

"I gave him a little help," Laurent said angrily.

Half an hour later, the other two had come around as well. While Laurent propped them up against the walls of the room to keep them separate, Helène waited anxiously for the first sign of consciousness from her friends. Hamlekh had explained that the amount of tranquilizers they had received during their incarceration would prolong the effect of the gas.

Tardets and his wife came to, one after the other. Laurent and Hamlekh had decided not to handcuff the old woman. Adrien Tardets, however, was thrown into the office with the others. The old colonist was also stoically resigned to the situation. Only his pallor revealed his fears.

"When will the police be here to take us?" he asked.

"I've decided to prolong your vacation for a few more days," Laurent replied. "There's no rush."

"Are you going to execute us here and now?"

"No, but I can assure you I wouldn't have any qualms about it. Now shut up. I have nothing else to say to you."

The three girls had been carried into a room with two large beds. Gertrud and Joyce were asleep on one of them. Helène had remained near Sabine throughout the entire afternoon, watching and waiting impatiently.

For a quarter of an hour, Sabine had been stirring sluggishly. Several times, she had whined uneasily. All afternoon Helène had gone from one of her friends to the other. Now, she moistened Sabine's lips with a small spoonful of mineral water. This time, the sleeping girl reacted differently. Her parched lips opened slightly and she swallowed the spoonful of water. Holding her head up now, Helène offered her a glass to drink from. Sabine managed to take two small sips of the liquid before coughing it back up.

The young girl opened her eyes. For a moment, she seemed to be perfectly awake, but then her eyelids fluttered and she fell back asleep. She didn't come around again until close to ten o'clock that night, and even then she was only half-awake. Haggard and dazed, she stared stupidly at Helène, who was smiling down at her and crying.

Sabine's eyes widened and wandered slowly about the strange room.

"I'm still dreaming," she muttered, "still dreaming . . ."

"Wake up, Sabine," Helène whispered, kissing her friend and tenderly stroking her hair. "Wake up, you're not dreaming. . . . It's all over, wake up. . . ."

Sabine unconsciously took hold of Helène's arm and squeezed it tightly. She was now fully awake, but still refused to believe she wasn't dreaming.

"Is she coming around?"

Laurent, followed by Hamlekh, had just entered the room. He emptied the rest of a bottle of water on a face cloth and handed it to Helène. She touched it lightly to Sabine's forehead. The girl moaned pleasurably and then took the cloth and pressed it firmly against her brow. Finally, she saw Joyce and Gertrud on the other bed.

"It's finished, Sabine, you're free. . . . You're completely out of danger now. These people are our friends. The kidnappers have been locked up."

"Where are we?" Sabine asked softly. "How did you get here?"

"We're in Corsica, *ma chérie*. We never were in the Middle East."

"No! This is another nightmare. . . . It's not possible. Why did you come back?"

"I'll tell you later. Just lie here, Joyce is waking up now."

By midnight, they were all sitting around the big table in the kitchen. The girls were still a little dazed, but they no longer thought they were dreaming. However, they couldn't understand why Martin had forbidden them to contact their families.

"The men we've locked in the cellar where you were kept are not the leaders behind this," he explained. "If we broadcast anything about your rescue, the real organizers, the real brains, would have time to disappear. That's why I'm keeping you here. It's unpleasant for you, and cruel to your parents, I know. But it has to be that way for a while."

"Why not phone my grandfather?" Sabine stammered. "He'd understand and he wouldn't say a word."

Pale and thin, she mustered up all the strength she could to sit up straight on the wooden bench that ran around the table, but her body would no longer obey her and she reeled slightly.

"There's a ninety percent chance that that's true," Martin said. "But to play with the remaining ten percent is a risk I can't afford to take. The suffering and anxiety of your families is such that it would be impossible to predict their reactions to the news of your freedom. So I must ask you to have confidence in me."

"I suppose we don't have any choice," Sabine said indignantly, making an effort to lift her head and look Martin straight in the eye.

"No, that's true, but I'd like you to see it from my point of view. We've run some tremendous risks to reach you and used methods which no official agency would ever have approved of."

"I'm sorry. We'll do as you say," Sabine conceded.

Laurent nodded to Hamlekh. The Israeli stood up and crossed the kitchen in the direction of the office. He picked up a phone on the desk and asked for a number in Tel Aviv.

As soon as he had David Fulham on the phone, he said simply: "You've got a green light, David. Go ahead."

30

Colonel David Fulham unleashed Operation Renegades at two in the morning.

Eighteen McDonnell F4C Phantoms took off simultaneously in formations of six from bases in the Sinai and Galilee.

Over Lebanon, the supersonic fighters peeled off separately. A quarter of an hour later, they started their erratic charades. Diving at twice the speed of sound, the Phantoms plummeted toward the ground only to pull out at the last moment, roll over on their backs and climb away. As soon as they had regained altitude, they plunged back down toward the ground once again.

The air raid and scramble sirens sounded simultaneously at every air base in Lebanon. The MIGs were quickly airborne, but even the best flight controllers weren't able to decipher the myriad blips appearing on their radar screens. The confusion was total. At this very instant, two C-130's lumbered off the runway from the Israeli air base at Haifa to turn immediately toward the Sea of Galilee and the heart of the chaos.

Flying just above the deck, they headed north along the Syrian-Lebanese border. Skimming close to each of the major peaks, they followed the long Syrian mountain range of Jebel Ech Cheikh Mandour before crossing the frontier again east of Kefer Zabad.

The squat bellies of the planes each carried forty impassive men hunched silently in their canvas sling chairs. Their chins were furrowed by double straps; their weapons, securely fastened to their flanks, glistened cold in the violet half-light; their boots were tightly buckled at the ankles. The paratroopers sat waiting, their nerves edged with ice, for the little red light by the open doors to turn green. Now, all eyes were turned to the rear of the planes, where soon they would drop in tight little clumps into the cold black emptiness of the night sky outside.

Sitting closest to the door, Lieutenant Samuel Sharef took one last drag of his cigarette and then crushed it out on the aluminum sheeting of the floor with a twist of his boot. He glanced briefly at his chronometer and reverted his gaze to the little plastic light on the opposite wall.

The red light turned green. Forty men stood up simultaneously, mechanically. Forty cartridges snapped metallically into their chambers, sending a single strong vibration down the twin steel static lines that ran the length of the cabin. Forty seconds later the two planes had expelled their cargoes out into the night.

Three of the paratroopers were slightly injured when they hit the rough terrain. One of them dislocated his shoulder and the other sprained his ankle. Unfortunately, the third man had shattered his leg. The broken bones had torn through his flesh and the platoons could not stop. As they headed on up into the hills, they heard a single muffled shot behind them.

They reached the Fedayeen's hideout at dawn. Their march through the mountainous forest had been uneventful. One single sleepy sentry was standing guard. Schrantz and his accomplices had never dreamed that their eagle's nest could be attacked.

Against all military tactics, the lieutenant himself crawled up behind the guard's back. He was squatting near a doorway, half-asleep, with his gun pointing down between his feet.

Inch by inch, the Israeli officer slipped progressively closer to his prey. He wasn't more than six feet away from the man when his fingers touched upon a large, heavy rock. Silently, he closed his left hand around it and then brought his legs up slowly under his torso. He sprang forward, and in one move brought the rock down on top of the sentry's skull with all his might. It cracked open like a green nut. In an unnecessarily hateful gesture, he simultaneously plunged his field dagger deep into the Muslim's back.

The Israelis silently filed inside the building. Making their way through the rooms, they quickly came across the Europeans. The three Germans and the girl were all sleeping on a straw pallet spread out on the floor. Ten men fell on them in perfect unison and they were handcuffed before they had time to realize what was happening.

Then Lieutenant Sharef gave a simple signal with a flick of his hand and all hell broke loose. Twelve Palestinian guerrillas were blown to pieces in a matter of seconds by a flurry of short bursts from the Israeli guns. Only four of them even managed to take so much as one step before being cut down.

Samuel Sharef checked his watch and noted with satisfaction that they were eleven minutes ahead of schedule.

"You murderers!" Schrantz screamed.

He was standing with his hands trapped behind his back and his feet spread to keep his balance. He glared at the Israeli officer with open hate and scorn. Sharef stepped closer to him and then suddenly brought his boot up into the German's testicles, hard, as hard as if he were kicking a soccer ball. Schrantz crumpled to his knees momentarily before collapsing completely on the floor.

The flat slapping sound of the evacuation helicopters blanketed the barren compound briefly before the billows of red dust they raised obscured everything entirely.

Two minutes later, the area was silent, lifeless and empty.

In the detection and alert command post at the aerial defense operations center a few miles from Zahle in the heart of Lebanon, General Abdou Saouane realized that he'd been had during the night. He voiced his rage at everyone who came near him as if he weren't the man ultimately responsible.

"We must look elsewhere! The fighters were just a diversion."

It was exactly nine minutes too late. The four Super-Frelons S.A. 312 helicopters had just flown over Tabigha.

Leaning out of the forward gunner's door, Lieutenant Samuel Sharef was quietly contemplating the flat shadows of the choppers speeding now over the white waters of the Sea of Galilee.

EPILOGUE

31

The sunlight that now filled the offices of the Shin-Beth glistened in reflections on the thin sheets of plexiglass pinned over the topographical chart on the wall.

With a pointer in his hand, Colonel David Fulham was standing in front of the map debriefing the commandos who had participated in Operation Renegades. Slumped back in two armchairs, sipping beer, Laurent Martin and Yefet Hamlekh were not paying very close attention. A stifling heat rose from the bustling streets of Tel Aviv outside the window.

Twenty-four hours had passed since the raid on the Tardets estate and Schrantz's capture. Laurent and Hamlekh had left Corsica the night before. Helène, Sabine and their two friends had been entrusted to Colonel Santi for safe-keeping.

Now, in Hamlekh's old office, the curtain was about to rise on the last act of Operation Rosebud.

Colonel Fulham opened the door and bellowed an order. Two armed paratroopers threw Schrantz into the room. They then entered to lean, impassive and indifferent, against two opposite walls with their pistols drawn to follow the prisoner's every move.

Since he'd been captured, Schrantz had been kept on ice. Nobody had questioned him, nobody had even so much as uttered a word in his direction. He had simply been locked in a small, windowless cell in which a bare bulb was kept burning twenty-four hours a day. A wire-bound bale of hay had been thrown into one corner of the room and a lavatory hole had been dug in the floor. Together, the two luxuries occupied almost all the available floor space. The door had been opened twice by his jailers, who had brought him water and food in plastic containers.

Schrantz staggered a few steps in the sunlit room. He seemed even more awkward and gangly than when Laurent had met him. His enormous pale eyes blinked without looking at anyone and his emaciated, handcuffed hands trembled with hopeless rage. He had obviously spent all his time in the cell preparing a harangue for his captors.

"You fools," he shouted in his high-strung voice. "You don't know a goddamned thing. By using your own weapons, your own rotten, spineless papers, your brainless television networks, I've started a process that nothing will ever stop! How could you be so stupid as to think that I haven't foreseen every possible way you could escape?"

He took a deep breath and launched into a new round of invectives.

"The cleverest thing you could think of to do was let your paratrooper dogs loose! You're nothing but killers, killers of the worst kind. Professional butchers have more brains than all of you put together! Any moment now the men holding the girls will be informed of my arrest. The next demand broadcast will be for my liberation. The millions of fools out there that've been trembling with morbid curiosity over each little morsel I've tossed them will force you down on your knees in front of me!"

"Calm down, child, calm down," Martin said easily. "Calm down and come over here. We've got something to show you."

Schrantz stood frozen where he was.

Martin shrugged his shoulders and then casually tapped his cigarette.

"Okay," he said. "Stay there, but have a look at these."

He picked up a small stack of photos on the desk and flicked them, one by one, at Schrantz's feet. They were pictures of the girls sitting in Tardets' kitchen and others of Hacam, Kateb and Cheikh, handcuffed, lying on the floor of the office.

Without warning, Schrantz flung himself headfirst toward Martin. The agent quickly spun around in his chair and lashed out with his foot. It caught Schrantz flat on the face and fractured his nose. He fell to the floor. Martin bent down to help him up, and Schrantz spat a bloody wad at him like a cornered cat.

"You poor cop," he hissed. "You really think that once you've arrested the criminals everything'll return to normal! You can't arrest ideas, cop! You can't destroy them, torture them, or lock them up behind walls. I know your laws, and I know how terrified you are of public opinion. Even if you kill me off, you'll be forced to try the Fedayeen who served under me. They were arrested in France. You won't be able to put them to sleep like dogs."

"He's not wrong on that point," Martin said, turning to Hamlekh. "His bullshit's as tiring as ever, but we do have to admit that fundamentally his analysis is correct. He has really predicted everything, the little bastard."

Schrantz gave the French agent a scathing look. In spite of the stifling heat, he started pacing around the room in a circle, paying no attention to the pistols that followed him like magnets.

"What counts is what the masses believe, and they've swallowed my bait whole. You can try whatever you want, my accomplices—as you call them—will nevertheless remain martyrs to a noble cause in the eyes of the public. Shoot them if you've got the balls. They'll face your firing squads proudly, will refuse your blindfolds with contempt and accept your bullets shouting, *'Vive la Liberté,' 'Vive la Palestine!'* And then you'll give in once more. Legally and officially, you'll have to put their bodies on a plane at Le Bourget in coffins draped with the Palestinian flag. The television crews of the world will give live coverage to the state funerals that will be held in Cairo, Beirut or Tripoli where the coffins of the martyrs will be passed from hand to hand above the heads of thousands of raving fanatics in the streets."

Schrantz had stopped to stand in the middle of the room. His huge pale yellow eyes had grown even larger, and were now fixed on some mystical, distant point in space. With intense jubilation, he nervously rubbed the palms of his bony hands together. For a moment, the sound of his handcuffs clinking against each other filled the room. The blood was still oozing out of his nose. At one and the same time, he was both beautiful and pitiful, pathetic and grotesque.

"There won't be any trial," Martin said. "Right now, your four puppets—Kirkbane is dead—but Hacam and old Tardets, Cheikh and Katek are on an Israeli PT boat heading toward Haifa."

It took Schrantz a few seconds to realize the meaning of Martin's last words.

"So . . ." he eventually said. "So you finally dared . . . And how are you going to explain this abduction to the public? How many times do I have to tell you I've attacked the very roots of your system! After Rosebud, nothing will ever be the same. The whole world will be wanting, demanding to know what's happened to Hacam, Kirkbane and the others. They've proven their courage and devotion to the world."

Hamlekh, who up until then had followed him in silence, rose heavily from his chair.

"You're dead wrong, Schrantz," he said. "Your accomplices aren't really the kind of human beings you seem to think they are, sublime combinations of Trotsky and Robin Hood. They're just four two-bit crooks who've now engaged in shameless negotiations to save their own necks. We've offered them money, and they've bought it."

"You're lying!" Schrantz screamed. "I chose those men myself and they're prepared to die for what they believe in! You're lying!" he screamed. "You're lying!!"

The clock on the wall behind Hamlekh's desk marked out the seconds as the thin red hand swung past one P.M. The Israeli agent reached the table in two long strides. Rather precariously, he set a Sony color television on top of a pile of dossiers, and then switched it on.

"Since you're so fond of TV, Schrantz, take a look at this."

As the small dot in the center expanded, Sabine Fargeau's face filled the screen. She was still as pathetic-looking as she had been the last time she appeared on television. She seemed a little rested, but it was plain from the puffiness of her eyes that she had been crying.

She started speaking in a monotone. A simultaneous translation in Hebrew appeared at the bottom of the screen.

"New developments which we know little about have forced our abductors to retract their last demands. However, if their new ultimatums are satisfied, the Fedayeen have given their word to release us as soon as possible."

Strangely, tears started rolling down her cheeks as she continued.

"A separate letter has been sent to my grandfather. It specifies the exact amount of money the Fedayeen want him to deposit in a numbered Swiss bank account. Our kidnappers have requested that this money be transferred to Switzerland as quickly as possible. They are also demanding that their agents be allowed to retrieve this money without any interference whatsoever on the part of the Swiss government.

"Our abductors have had to formulate these new demands because traitors have been discovered at the head of their organization. They nevertheless hope that one day they will be able to resume their just struggle for the liberation of the martyred people of Palestine."

Sabine Fargeau's face faded out and was replaced by the oval countenance of an old woman, who smiled and trailed on in a deep throaty voice.

"And that's that," Hamlekh said, switching off the television. "End of Operation Rosebud."

Martin suddenly felt a pang of sadness well up in his throat. Schrantz had lurched off toward an armchair in a corner of the room. His face was pale and streaked with dried blood. The flame that had lit the very depths of his eyes was dead and gone.

It was dark when Laurent landed at Orly. As he came through the international arrival gates, he turned right, stopped in front of the newsstand and asked the man for all that day's editions of *France-Soir*.

The last one had a five-column headline: *"Les Trois Jeunes Filles Retrouvées au Cap Corse."* (The three young girls are found on the Cape of Corsica.)

The first edition, which had come out just after Sabine's appearance on worldwide television, carried the banner: *"L'Opération Rosebud se Termine en Crime de Droit-Commun."* (Operation Rosebud ends up a common extortion plot.)

With a vague smile, Laurent scanned the first lines of the editorial, which had remained the same from one edition to another. "Probably because they have now been backed up against the wall, the Palestinian kidnappers have ended up by acting like common bandits. . . ."

Fernand Dobert had written the text. The role the old journalist had played in the screening of the first film had, for a while, made him once again one of the star reporters in Paris. Sitting in his little office with a view of the city room, he was just putting the final touches on the proof sheets of the last of a series of articles scheduled to be published the following morning. When he had finished, he rose and switched off the transistor blaring out the final developments in *"L'Affaire Rosebud,"* and started down the hall. Even though it was late, the elevator was occupied. With the heavy steps of a tired old man, he made his way to the central staircase and, clinging tightly to the wrought-iron banister, trudged down the steps. Outside, the Rue Reaumur was waking up for the night.

The kiosks were surrounded by curious crowds, and Dobert soon disappeared among them. They seemed both disappointed and satisfied. The consumer society, now glutted with excitement, was preparing once more to digest the nightmarish dramas that periodically threatened its very foundations.